Ralph Heathcote

Sylva or the Wood

Being a Collection of Anecdotes, Dissertations, Characters, Apophthegms...

Ralph Heathcote

Sylva or the Wood

Being a Collection of Anecdotes, Dissertations, Characters, Apophthegms...

ISBN/EAN: 9783337109707

Printed in Europe, USA, Canada, Australia, Japan

Cover: Foto ©Andreas Hilbeck / pixelio.de

More available books at **www.hansebooks.com**

S Y L V A;

OR, THE

W O O D:

BEING A COLLECTION OF

ANECDOTES, DISSERTATIONS, CHARACTERS, APOPHTHEGMS, ORIGINAL LETTERS, BONS MOTS, AND OTHER LITTLE THINGS.

Rerum et Sententiarum quasi ὕλη dicta est, a multiplici materia et varietate in iis contenta. Quemadmodum enim vulgò solemus infinitam **arborum** nascentium indiscriminatim multitudinem sylvam dicere; ita etiam libros suos, in quibus variæ et diversæ materiæ opuscula temerè congesta sunt, *Sylvas* appellabant Antiqui. *Bacon.*

BY A SOCIETY OF THE LEARNED.

L O N D O N:

PRINTED FOR T. PAYNE, AND SON, AT THE MEWS-GATE.

M.DCC.LXXXVI.

ADVERTISEMENT.

SOLOMON has said, that *of making many books there is no end*; but, as Grotius afks, " what would Solomon fay now, " were he to vifit our libraries[1]?"—Seneca complained, that, " as the Romans " had more than enough of all other " things, fo they had alfo of books and " authorfhip[2]:" and what Seneca faid of declining Rome, may ferve equally well for declining Britain. Look into all the departments of authorfhip, and you will find them crowded; into all our collections of books, and you will find them overloaded. And, where is the matter of wonder? it having long been the fafhion to write

---

[1] *Quid nunc diceret, fi noftras viferet bibliothecas ?* in Ecclef. xii. 12.

[2] *Sicut omnium* rerum *intemperantiâ,* ita *literarum* quoque, *laboramus.*

down

down all we think, and to print and publifh all we write. ·Nor for this is genius,
learning, tafte required : paper, pens, and
ink, with (as Fielding expreffes it) the
manual capacity of ufing them, moft abundantly fuffice. " The art of writing,"
fays Voltaire, " is become in many coun-
" tries an infamous trade ; where illite-
" rate bookfellers pay fo much a fheet for
" lyes and impertinence to mercenary fcrib-
" blers, who have made of letters the
" meaneft of profeffions[2]." So that, as
it fhould feem, the bookfellers in reality
are the capital authors of the times.

Solomon adds, that *much ftudy*, or "reading," *is a wearinefs of the flefh*. And whatever hurt it may caufe to the body, it muft
certainly caufe no lefs to the mind ; by
overloading the memory, and ftifling all
that reflection, which is neceffary to make
reading of any kind ufeful. We have in-

---

[2] *L'art d'ecrire eft devenu en plufieurs pays un vil
métier, dans lequel des libraires qui ne favent pas lire
paient des menfonges & des futilités à tant la feuille, à
des écrivains mercenaires qui ont fait de la literature la
plus lâche des profeffions.* Siecle de Louis, in Cat.
SAURIN.

deed

deed great and reverend authority in be-
half of this *copia librorum :* for Chryfoftom hath fomewhere faid, that, " he, who
" writeth good books, fpreadeth nets for
" falvation ;" and Cornelius a Lapide rec-
koneth them among the works which con-
duce to the glory of God, *ad Dei mag-
nificentiam* [4]. Neverthelefs, what was faid
upon the fubject by a great wit in his day,
will ever be found true : *dum plus hauri-
unt quam digerunt, ut ftomachis, fic etiam ingeniis, naufea fæpiùs nocuit quam fames* [5].

And now, after fuch an exordium, many
will be curious and eager to afk, what gentlemen, who thus complain of a redundancy of
books, can poffibly mean by adding to the
number ?—Perhaps it might fuffice to fay,
perituræ parcere chartæ quid prodeft ? but
we add, that we would not have ours confidered as a book : we would rather call it
(if we durft) the *Beauties of books.* There
are the *Beauties of Shakfpeare,* where a fe-

---

[4] This writer muft, in his own eftimation, have
greatly contributed *to the glory of God:* for there are
commentaries of his upon the Bible to the amount of
ten large folios.

[5] Petrarch. *in Dialog.*

lection

lection is made of his moſt brilliant paſſages, by *Doctor Dodd*[6]. There are, if we
miſtake not, the *Beauties of Muſic and Po-
etry:* and there are the *Beauties of Fox,
North, and Burke,* which contain (we ſuppoſe) the *beauties* of politics. We would
make ours, if we could, the *Beauties of
Knowledge, Wit, and Wiſdom*; ſelected from
all indiſcriminately who can furniſh them,
and brought more cloſely and compendi-
ouſly together. For the great object of
our work is to make men wiſer, without
obliging them to turn over folios and
quartos[7]; to furniſh matter for thinking,
inſtead of reading.

And

---

[6] This was no new idea. The *Beauties* of *Plato*
were publiſhed, under the title of *Gemmæ Platonis*,
at Paris, 1554, 24to.

[7] *La multiplicité des faits,* &c. " the multiplicity
" of facts and writings," ſays Voltaire, " is become
" ſo great, that every thing muſt ſoon be reduced
" to extracts and dictionaries." *in Cat.* HENAUT.
Inſtead of this, we are got altogether into the other
extreme : far from contracting and abridging, we en-
large and expatiate beyond all bounds ; as if quantity, not quality, were the point to be attained. Let
the ſubject be Politics, Belles Lettres, Taſte, Morals,

And many have been perſuaded, that knowledge, delivered in this our ſhort and miſcellaneous way, will **ſtrike** more forcibly; yea, will make clearer as well as ſtronger impreſſions, than in a tedious, formal, didactic ſtile and manner. "Concife ſentences, like darts, fly abroad, and make impreſſion; while long diſcourſes are flat things, and not regarded." So ſays Bacon, in **one** of his *Eſſays*; and another writer of deep and ſtrong ſenſe, who is alſo laid aſide for the traſh of the day, hath delivered himſelf on this wiſe. "As St. Auſtin ſaith of ſhort and holy ejaculations, that they pierce heaven as ſoon, if not quicker, than **more** tedious prayers; ſo I have reaped greater benefit from *concife* and *caſual* meditations on *ſeveral* topics, than from long and voluminous **treatiſes,** relating merely to one and the ſame thing[*]."

or what you **will—have** we not quarto piled upon quarto, till the heap grows **as** huge as Pelion upon Oſſa?

[*] The works of *Francis Oſborn, Eſq.* p. 454. 1701, 8vo.

Com-

Complaints will doubtlefs be preferred againſt us for the numerous quotations we have made, thoſe eſpecially from learned or foreign languages : but it muſt be noted, that quotations are eſſential to our plan, which is to inſtruct and amuſe by ſtory and anecdote, not by deduction or chains of argument ; by example chiefly, not by reaſoning. We have, however, generally given the ſubſtance, and often a tranſlation, of the paſſages we quote.—— Mean while, it need not be diſſembled, that this work is not ſo much intended for the mere illiterate Engliſh reader, as for men who have been liberally trained, and are not unacquainted with languages ; men, who may wiſh to have ſome *pabulum mentis*, or mental fodder, always at hand, but whoſe profeſſions and ſituations in life do not permit leiſure to turn over volumes.

As for thoſe, whoſe literary nouriſhment is chiefly drawn from the daily prints and periodical publications—to whom, as one writes, " reading is nothing better " than a dozing kind of idlenefs, and the " book a mere opiate, that makes them
" ſleep

" sleep with their eyes open²," — for such, (and various are the forts of them) there are works better fuited to their capacities and tafte. Thofe of a graver and more fedate caft will find much felf-complacency and comfort in hiftories of England, biographical dictionaries, bodies of divinity, and the like. For thofe of univerfal knowledge, (and fuch we meet with, out of coffee-houfes as well as in them) there are Magazines of various kinds, which will fupply *verbiage*, or matter of talk and harangue, *de omni fcibili et non fcibili*. For the more gay and lively, novels and romances ; and, laftly, for the critical or rather hypercritical tribe, who are ambitious to figure with airs of higher importance, there are *journals* and *reviews*, which will furnifh the titles of all publications, with obfervations and ftrictures to defcant upon them. Such afpirants will hence be enabled to pronounce upon all fubjects and all authors, without having

---

² *Effays* of *Pope, Blount :* a writer of great good fenfe and wit, *laid afide for the trafh of the day*, and now become obfolete and almoft forgotten.

read

read or examined any [10]; to appear learned, without being fo; in fhort, to be admired as critics and fcholars, by thofe who are not critics and fcholars: for this, furely, is as much as **can** in reafon be defired.

But we need not detain our reader here; **thefe** and other fimilar **points** being occafionally touched **in the** courfe of our work.

---

[10] Lord Bacon fpeaks of certain perfons, who thought it no mean thing, if, by compendious extracts from other men's wits, they could figure and parade with fome fhew of learning: *magnum certè quiddam præftare videntur, fi delibantes aliorum ingenia, ex compendio fapiant, aut in cortice doctrinæ aliquatenùs hæreant.* De Augm. Scient. l. 1.

C O N-

CONTENTS.

CONTENTS.

XXXVII. Of

2 LXVII. *Of*

CONTENTS.

SYLVA,

SYLVA,

OR THE

WOOD.

I.

OF APOPHTHEGMS, ANECDOTES, MAXIMS, BONS MOTS, &c [1].

FOOLS by profession, or (as they have sometimes been called) jesters, were formerly of great account. Cardinal Wolsey, in 1529, presented his to Henry VIII. as a token of grateful and affectionate regard; as did Sir Thomas More his, upon resigning the seals in

[1] This and the following number may be considered as *prefatory* to the rest; since they set forth the utility of the work, and also plead in some measure, for the form and manner of it.

B   1532;

1532, to the Lord Mayor of London and his
fucceffors in office [2].

I have fometimes thought, that thefe objects
of mirth, however ftrangely and unnaturally
they became fo, might yet be made fubfervient
to good purpofes among the *great*; among
kings, minifters, and all who govern and bear
influence with men. In the firft place I would
propofe, that the term of *fool* be difcarded, and
that of *jefter* only retained. *Fool* implies a perfon deficient in underftanding; but natural
deficiences and imperfections muft never be
made objects of mirth. Again, thefe *fools* in
reality have not been fuch natural fools, as
fome have imagined: on the contrary, if they

---

[2] Herbert's Hift. of Henry.—Angeli was a *fool* of this
fort in France. He had been a follower of the great Condé,
and was given by him to the king; yet was far from wanting wit. He was once fome time in company, before he
began to play *the fool:* when, M. de Bautru (who was the
wit of the court) entering, "I am glad," fays he, "you
"are come; I was afraid I fhould have been alone." *Menagiana.*—By his addrefs in pleafing fome, and in awing
others, he made them all tributaries; and amaffed fo much
money, that M. de Marigni faid, "Of all the fools who
"had followed Monfieur the prince, Angeli was the only
"one who had made his fortune." *Ibid.*—Boileau's ftarved
poet complains, that Angeli in preferment outftripped all
competitors, of what merit foever:

Et l'Efprit le plus beau, l'auteur le plus poli,
N'y parviendra jamais au fort de l'Angeli.

SAT. I.
were

were not the wifeft perfons at court, which yet
might fometimes admit a doubt, they have often been wifer, and known better what they
were doing, than many who have laughed at
them. The appellation of *fools* therefore is
improperly applied to fuch.

Let me now fet forth, what ideas I would
include under the term *jefter*; by **whom**, then,
I do not mean **a** pérfon, who is **merely** to raife
a laugh, by doing abfurd and ridiculous things :
none of our kings have been fo poorly attended, but who have abounded with fervants
qualified for this. By a *jefter*, I mean one, who
fhould mix *utile dulci*, the ufeful with the pleafant; who fhould inftruct, at the fame time
that he diverts; **and, if** the freedom may **be**
allowed me, who fhould make the king *wife*
as well as *merry*.

For this purpofe I would have him endowed
with ftrong original powers, cultivated with letters, and thoroughly practifed in the ways of
men. Nor fhould his letters confift in a fimple knowledge of languages, or in critical and
philological matters; for thefe **of** themfelves,
though they excite admiration among the ignorant, yet leave the underftanding as poor as
they find it : but I would have them to confift of
hiftory, philofophy, and other branches of fcience and literature, which tend to make **men**
knowing **in** human nature **and human** life.

Thus accomplished, a jester may not only be diverting, according to the original institution of his place, but useful also and instructing in a very superlative degree.

By profession, he is a manufacturer and dealer in apophthegms, proverbs, aphorisms, maxims, and *bons mots* of every kind : all which are not only highly calculated for wit and amusement, but (in the opinion of the wisest men) the most efficacious means of conveying knowledge. Seneca says, that " even rude and uncultivated " minds are struck, as it were, with these short " but weighty sentences, which anticipate all " reasoning, by flashing truths upon them at " once ;" and he relates, that Agrippa, the minister of Augustus Cæsar, used to own himself much indebted to that of Sallust, *concordiâ parvæ* **res** *crescunt, discordiâ maximæ dilabuntur* [3] *:* a pithy **sent**ence indeed, and which the good people of old England would, at all times, do well to ponder. Plutarch drew up and digested a collection of apophthegms for Trajan, and Erasmus did the same for a German prince; in the dedication to whom, after observing how finely fitted these close and pointed sentences are for instruction, he adds, that they are " singularly accommodated to " the situation and exigencies of a prince, who

[3] Epist. 94.

" has

" has not time to read Plato, Aristotle, and
" other voluminous writers upon government,
" laws, manners, &c."

Now with such instruments as these, managed judiciously and with address, a jester may produce surprising effects : nay, Bayle has not scrupled to say, that " a sentence, taken " from Livy or Tacitus, is capable of saving " a nation, and perhaps has saved more than " one [*]." It is very well known, that war, peace, and other important national events, have often originated in secret from very minute and (as would be thought) inadequate causes; while the reasons, publicly given out, have been merely ostensible. But a jester, such a one as I mean, is or may be often within the cabinet. He may therefore *instruct* his master, as I have said ; but he may do more : he may also in some measure regulate and direct his passions, and greatly influence his political conduct, while his apparent object shall be only to divert him. There was a jester among the household of Charles I. who was brought before the council, and with much solemnity discarded from court, for pointing his raillery at archbishop Laud ; but many knowing ones have thought, that, if the king had discarded

[*] Project for a Dictionary.

the

the archbishop instead of the jester, his affairs
might have ended better than they did.

Dioclesian, a Roman emperor, made the difficulty of reigning well to consist chiefly in the
difficulty of arriving at the real knowledge of
affairs. "Four or five courtiers," said he,
"form themselves into a cabal, and unite in
"their counsels to deceive the emperor. They
"say what will please their master; who, be-
"ing shut up in his palace, is a stranger to the
"truth, and forced to know only what they
"think fit to tell him[s]." Now the jester will
be sure to prevent or dissipate all this darkness
and obscurity: he will be a perpetual intelli-
gencer to his master: he will daily and hourly
laugh him into true ideas of persons and
things, and lead him gradually to see them as
they are[6]. Thus royalty will be guarded
against many evils: it will not be misled by
either flattery or abuse; but taught to lay the
due stress, and no more, upon whatever shall
be said for or against itself. These and innu-

---

[s] Vopiscus in Aureliano.

[6] This was what the famous *Carvalho* so much dreaded
from the lively and witty Count *d'Obidos: Il craignoit,* says
the historian, *que ses bons mots ne fissent à la fin quelque impression sur l'esprit du Monarque, & ne parvinssent peut-être à
lui ouvrir les yeux.* Memoires de Carvalho, Marquis de Pom-
bal. Tom. II. p. 35.

merable

merable other benefits will be obtained, and all in the way of mirth and pleasantry.

Upon the whole then, agreeably to my idea of a jester, many might be glad to see this personage re-established at court, and a proper stipend assigned to his office [7]. If he produce the effects I have specified, well and good: and, let the worst happen that can, it will be only adding one more to those many places and pensions, which, being of no great use or ornament to the kingdom, must unavoidably create disaffection and complaint; unless we could suppose the English of the same humour with the subjects of a duke of Savoy, who, being asked " how they could bear their heavy " taxations?" replied, *We are not so much offended with the duke for what he takes from us, as thankful to him for what he leaves us* [8].

[7] Yet a certain writer seems to think this in no wise necessary : " The last *jester* we had at court," says he, " was " in the licentious reign of Charles II. Since that time our " manners have been so gradually refining, that our court " at present is full of patriots, who wish for nothing but " the honours and wealth of their country ; and our ladies " are all so chaste, so spotless, so good, so devout, that " there is nothing for a *jester* to make a *jest* of." Yorick's *Sentimental Journey.*

[8] Lord Herbert's *Life*, p. 110. 1770, 4to.

II.

OF QUOTATIONS FROM OTHER WRITERS, ESPE-CIALLY THE ANCIENT GREEK AND LATIN.

IN quotations, as in all other things, men have run into extremes. Some writers have quoted moſt abundantly, in order (as ſhould ſeem) to make an oſtentation of learning; with one of whom La Mothe le Vayer, though himſelf a great quoter, appears to have been much fatigued: "God grant you," cries he, " to become leſs learned"—*Dieu vous faſſe la grace de devenir moins ſcavant.* Others have ſcarcely quoted at all, as Locke and Hoadley, with ſome of an inferior kind, who perhaps have hence affected to paſs for original writers, that needed no extraneous helps: and indeed, in books of mere reaſoning, all quotation to many may ſeem impertinent.

La Bruyere has animadverted upon the for-mer extreme: he complains of books being crowded ſo with quotations, as to be hardly any thing elſe; of citing Ovid and Tibullus at the bar, Horace and Lucretius in the pulpit: where, ſays he, " Latin and ſometimes Greek " are the languages choſen to entertain the " women and churchwardens with [9]." And,

---

[9] Charact. *De la Chaire.*

doubtleſs,

doubtless, nothing can be more absurd and ridiculous than this : by this an author's sense, if peradventure he has any, is almost oppressed and smothered under his learning; and, as Ovid said of a girl overloaded with dress and ornament, he is so garnished out with foreign materials, as to be, in truth, the least part of himself. Mean while, as Bayle observes upon Bruyere, " it is to be feared, that the very op-
" posite custom of not citing at all, into which
" we are fallen, will make learning too much
" despised, as a piece of furniture entirely use-
" less [10] :" and he has elsewhere mentioned, as
" one principal cause of neglect in the study
" of the Belles Lettres, that a great many wits,
" real or pretended, have, with an air of dis-
" dain, run down the custom of citing Greek
" authors, and making learned remarks, as so
" much pedantry, and fit only for a col-
" lege [11]."

It is however certain, that many pleasing as well as useful purposes may be served by quotations, judiciously made and aptly applied. It is pleasing to know, while contemplating any subject, what other writers, men of name and abilities, have thought and said upon it : and then the variety, which the frequent introduction of new personages (as I may call them)

[10] Dict. Bouchin. Note B. [11] Meziriac. Note C.

creates, will greatly contribute to enliven attention, and thereby keep off wearinefs and
difguft. With the Greek and Latin authors
the claffical reader is always entertained: " Mr.
" Clarke's book of coins is much above my
" pitch," faid the learned Markland to his
friend; " but I read it with pleafure as his,
" and *becaufe of the quotations from the ancients,*
" which are numerous ".

But quotation is ufeful, as well as pleafing,
to confirm and illuftrate the fentiments of a
writer; and efpecially in works, like this of
ours: where the great object is, not fo much to
teach men things of which they are ignorant,
by defcanting in detail and at large, as to re-
mind them of what they know; not fo much to
make men read, to borrow Montefquieu's ex-
preffion, as to *make them think.* For this, the
citing of authorities, and dealing in perfonal
anecdotes and apophthegms, feem perfectly
well calculated: for, however it be, men frequently paufe and dwell upon *names,* who
would haftily and inadvertently fkim over
things. Nay, let the reafoning be ever fo clofe
and found, it fhall often pafs for little more
than declamation; while the name of fome admired author, efpecially if he be dead, fhall
arreft the imagination, and make all the im-

---

¹² Bowyer's Mifcell. Tracts, p. 524.

preffion

preſſion which is neceſſary to produce conviction[11].

Again, the practice of quoting from other
writers, and eſpecially from the Greek and Roman authors of antiquity, is uſeful, inaſmuch
(as above hinted) it muſt give ſome counte-
nance and ſanction even to *letters* themſelves :
letters ! neglected, declining *letters !* and with
them declining all that is wiſe, and excellent,
and beautiful, and poliſhed. How would an
aſtoniſhed *macaroni* ſtare, to be aſſured, that the
civilization of kingdoms is founded upon *letters* ; and that, in proportion as theſe are cultivated, ſo is nearly the progreſs of mankind
from their moſt rude and ſavage ſtate, up to
that perfection of elegance and refinement,
which beameth forth from his all-finiſhed and
refulgent perſon ! I ſpeak according to the
gentleman's own idea of himſelf.

Laſtly, were the practice of quoting once
received and eſtabliſhed, this great advantage
would farther accrue to letters, *viz.* that it
would reduce the bulk of ſcribblers, with
which they are diſgraced. Nothing is more
common in theſe days, than for men to begin
to write, and affect to be authors, not only before they underſtand Greek and Latin, but be-

---

[11] *L'authorité peut ſeule envers les communs entendemens,*
ſays Montaigne, *et poiſe plus en langage peregrin.* Eſſais,
III. 13.

fore

fore they have any real or accurate knowledge
of Englifh. It is enough for them, if they can
fpell with tolerable exactnefs : for this accom-
plifhment, joined with fuch materials as magazines, reviews, and other public prints fupply, is ufually the ftock in trade; with which
authors now as well as critics fet up. In fhort,
writing is become a mere manual operation ;
and books are made every day by men without genius, without letters, who are but barely
fufficient to tranfcribe, at the moft to compile.
Upon which account it might well be wifhed,
that every one who prefumes to write, efpecially upon matters of religion and government,
(for in romance and moral painting it is not
neceffary) fhould be obliged to fupport his
meaning, once at leaft with fome Greek, and
once with fome Latin, citation; and fhould
produce at the fame time a true and well au-
thenticated teftimonial, that thefe citations
were not furnifhed by another, but *bonâ fide*
his own act and deed. A teft of this fort
would give a mighty check to fcribbling [14];
and fave reams of paper, which are every moment going to perifh—*peritur_æ parcere chartæ.*

[14] " The world has got fuch an appetite for reading,"
fays our learned printer, " that it fwallows every thing
" which is offered to it. Carelefs readers have made care-
" lefs writers ; and, amidft a multiplicity of books, I every
" day fee barbarity creeping in." Bowyer's Mifc. Tracts,
p. 281.

Upon

Upon the whole, therefore, let us not condemn, and affectedly avoid, the citation of authors; falsely delicate, falsely fastidious. Let us recollect, that the greatest and most respectable writers have done this: that *Cicero*, *Plutarch*, *Seneca*, *Bacon*, *Montaigne*, and *Montesquieu*, left nothing unborrowed from others, which might serve to embellish their own writings; and that the things thus borrowed may, if skilfully applied, have not only all the energy of their old situation, but all the graces of invention in their new one. And why should they not? *there being no less wit in justly applying the thought of another, than in being the first author of that thought* [15]. At least, so says *Mr. Bayle*; whom I have quoted the more freely upon this topic, because he was a very great wit, as well as a very great scholar.

III.

OF THE ANCIENT STATE OF LETTERS IN ENGLAND.

THERE was a time in this kingdom, when *letters* were so low, that whoever could prove himself, in a court of justice, able to read a verse in the New Testament, was vested

[15] Dict. Epicurus. Note E.

with

with the higheſt privileges; and a clergyman, who knew any thing of grammar, was looked upon as a prodigy [16]. In thoſe enlightened days, a rector of a pariſh, as we are told, going to law with his pariſhioners about paving the church, quoted this authority as from St. Peter—*paveant illi, non paveam ego*; which he conſtrued, *they are to pave the church, not I:* and this was allowed to be good law by a judge, who was an eccleſiaſtic too. Alfred the Great complained, towards the end of the ninth century, that " from the Humber to the " Thames there was not a prieſt, who under- " ſtood the Liturgy in his mother-tongue, or " could tranſlate the eaſieſt piece of Latin [17] :" and a correſpondent of Abelard, about the middle of the twelfth, complimenting him upon a reſort of pupils from all countries, ſays, that " even **Britain**, diſtant as ſhe was, ſent her ſa- " vages to be inſtructed by him"—*remota Britannia ſua animalia erudienda deſtinabat* [18].

If the clergy had then, as they are ſaid to have had, all the learning among themſelves, what a bleſſed ſtate muſt the laity have been in ? And ſo indeed it appears : for there is extant an old act of parliament, which provides,

---

[16] *Ordinati ita literaturâ carebant, ut cæteris eſſet ſtupori, qui grammaticam didiciſſet.* Matth. Paris, anno 1061.

[17] Aſſer. de geſtis Alfredi.

[18] Abelard. Op. p. 217. Paris, 1616.

that

that *a nobleman shall be entitled to the benefit of his clergy, even though he cannot read :* and another law, cited by Judge *Rolls* in his *Abridgment,* sets forth, that " the command of the " sheriff to his officer, by word of mouth, and " without writing, is good; for it may be, " that *neither the sheriff nor his officer can write* " *or read* [19]."—Who can say, that such halcyon times may not return ? When we contemplate the ignorance and dissipation of the *great,* whom the *little* are sure to follow : when we consider their not only neglect, but even contempt, of *letters* ; their gambling, and low amusements ; their luxury ; the avarice, meanness, and selfishness, which prevail among them—when we consider all this, and more, can we forbear to exclaim, that *signs following signs lead on the mighty year* [20] ?

IV. A

[19] Many charters are yet extant, where persons of great eminence, and even kings, have affixed the sign of the cross, because not able to write or read—*signum crucis manu propriâ pro ignoratione literarum :* whence the term of *signing,* instead of *subscribing.* Du Cange, in voce *Crux.*

[20] I take the above causes to be equal to the effect, and should be sorry to forebode it from that splenetic and selfish humour only, with which some *literati* have been vehemently affected. *Respice, oro, rem literariam,* said Bentley to his patron, in the dedication of his Horace, 1711 ; *afflictam sanè atrocitate licentiâque temporum, atque ægrè admodum ex ingruentis barbariæ diluvio caput fessum exserentem :*

that

IV.

A LETTER OF DEAN SWIFT TO HIS CURATE [21].

"SIR,   Dublin, April 2, 1723.

"I WRIT to you a month or two ago, to
"let you know, that I had a perewig
"made for you, out of the hair I had from
"you; to which I added more hair given me
"by a lady: the making, and some other hair,
"which the perewig-maker was forced to put
"in, cost twelve shillings. It is a dark pere-
"wig, and is not worth above thirty shillings;
"but will be good enough on ordinary occa-
"sions, and is well made. I desire you to let
"me know, how I could send it to you. I sup-
"pose my letter miscarried. Pray write me
"an answer. My humble service to Mrs.

that is, the learning of Dr. Bentley was not likely to be
rewarded with an archbishopric, for a bishopric (I suppose)
would scarcely have sufficed. With the like spirit Joseph Sca-
liger, admiring the early progress of Caspar Barthius in
letters, said, *natum esse adhuc unum æternitati ingenium, quod
si ad maturitatem perveniret, literas aliquandiu vivere posse.*
But Barthius, after living 71 years, died so long ago as
1658; yet letters are still alive. Blount, *Cens. Author. in
Barthio.*

21 *'Tis my chief wish, my joy, my only plan,*
To lose no drop of this immortal man.
"Warburton;

" Warburton: I hope your whole family is
" well. I am

" Your most faithful humble servant,

" JONATH. SWIFT."

To the Rev. **Mr.** *Warburton,*
  at Maherafelt.

Mr. Urban, from the same desire to preserve
every *drop of a man of genius,* hath inserted in
the Gentleman's Magazine, for June 1785, the
following letter from Mr. Chambers to his
amanuensis, Mr. Macbean.

" Mr. Macbean,
" I want all the apparatus, that I used in
" correcting the new edition of my book, to
" be brought to Cambury house. I fancy you
" can guess pretty nearly what it is. The
" principal thing is the case with shelves and
" papers on them: on the top of this I left,
" I think, almost every thing else I wanted;
" particularly a number of books, I believe
" ten or twelve, and an index wrapped in
" thick brown paper. The first volume of the
" Dictionary too, I was at work upon, should
" be sent: it is cut in two, the letter A
" by itself. I am sorry to give you this

C   " trouble,

" trouble, but know not how to get the things
" without you.   I am

"   Your assured friend and servant,

"   E. CHAMBERS."

These are the *drops of men of genius*, the *drops of immortal men*. Should a taste, however, prevail for **collecting** and preserving these *drops*, as from the reception they meet with is much to be feared, every one must see, that genius, and sense, and wit, and learning, will not **only by** degrees be stifled and oppressed, **but finally** overwhelmed and lost, under **an inundation of** impertinence and rubbish [22].

[22] " The present age," says a very acute writer, " has " manifested an uncommon relish for all such reading as ne- " ver was read."—Alluding to the miscellanies or voluminous collections **of** *every thing*, which dail**y come forth,** he compares them to the " tree of Nebuchadnezzar's dream, in " which was *meat for all* ; and as this meat," says he, " is " of light digestion ; or rather, as it is found to pass off easily " without admitting or requiring any digestion at all, **an** " inexhaustible fund may be necessary **to** feed, though **it** " **cannot** satisfy, an unfathomable curiosity."   Letter to *Warton*, upon his edition of *Milton*'s Juvenile **Poems,** p. 40. 1785, 8vo.

V. OF

V.

OF ABUSES IN FEMALE DRESS [23].

I LATELY saw a print of a lady of quality, sitting to the operations of a *friseur*,
with these words written under: *The folly of*
1771. But this folly was far from being the
production of 1771: it is indeed of ancient
standing, and hath probably prevailed more or
less in all ages of the world. We trace it dis-
tinctly to the Christian æra; for St. Peter,
speaking of the adorning of women, would not
have it to be that "outward adorning of *plait-*
"*ing the hair*, or wearing of gold and **fine**
"cloaths, but the hidden ornament of a *meek*
"*and quiet spirit*, which" (I presume, from
the scarcity of it) "is said to be of *great*
"*price*."

Tertullian and Cyprian, early fathers of **the**
church, have left professed discourses against
the luxury of female dress, and specify among
other things the spurious ornaments of the
head. Synesius, a Christian bishop of the fifth

[23] This was first printed in 1780, with this motto:
Auferimur cultu: gemmis auroque teguntur
Omnia. Pars minima est ipsa puella sui. OVID.

century,

century, defcribes a bride, as " walking about
" like Cybele *with turrets* on her head [24]." The
heathen writers alfo have noted this extravagance; and Juvenal, particularly, mentions the
orders or ftories of this kind of architecture [25].
Thus you might follow thefe head-dreffes, with
fmall intermiffions, through the writers of
every age down to the prefent. They prevailed in France in the 15th century, when,
fays one of their hiftorians, " the ladies were
" exceffive in their drefs, and wore wonder-
" fully high and broad horns; having on each
" fide two ears fo large, that it was impoffible
" for them to come through a door [26]." This
was about 1428, when Conecte, a monk,
preached furioufly againft them: whofe preaching, however, had nothing near the effect of a
fingle word of Lewis the XIVth, in 1699, which
brought them down in an inftant; and which
fhews, as Bayle obferves, that, " if crowned
" heads knew their ftrength in this refpect, or
" would ufe it, they might avail more than
" all the preachers upon earth [27]."

The form and ftructure of head-dreffes, now
in fafhion with us, are known to all; and, if

---

[24] Epift. III.

[25] Tot premit ordinibus, tot adhuc compagibus altum
Ædificat caput.————   Sat. VI.

[26] Argentre, Hift. de Bretagne, liv. x.

[27] Dict. Conecte, Note E.

they

they were not, I could not defcribe them. I
muft needs wonder, in the mean time, at that
ftrange propenfity in the fex, to difguife and
make themfelves fo different, from what their
Creator defigned them to be. *God never made
his works for man to mend*, might any one fay;
but our ladies are far from thinking thus : on
the contrary, to judge from their perpetual
employ, they fhould feem perfuaded, that their
very exiftence has no other object, end, or
meaning, but to improve their natural felves
by artificial decorations [28]. This they fometimes do, as at prefent, by high heads and high
heels ; and in both incur the guilt, which Tertullian imputed to the tragic actors of his age :
" The Devil," fays he, " mounts them on buf-
" kins, in order to make Jefus Chrift a liar,
" who has faid, that *no one can add a cubit to
" his ftature :*" which he elfewhere applies to
the ftructure upon the head [29].

At other times, inftead of lengthening, they
take a fancy to dilate and broaden themfelves
by fpacious hoops and expanding draperies :

[28] Like fome artifts mentioned by Hogarth, who have
" contrived ornaments to correct the *poverty of nature*; as
" they exprefs themfelves." *Analyfis of Beauty*.

[29] Tragædos Diabolus cothurnis extulit, quia nemo poteft
adjicere cubitum unum ad ftaturam fuam. Mendacem facere vult Chriftum. *De Spectac.* c. 23. & *de Cultu Virgin.*
c. 7.

under which *rotunda* form, Addifon fomewhere
compares them to the dome of an Egyptian
temple, and pleafantly fports upon what he calls
the idol of the place. I know indeed, that the
hoop-petticoat is fuppofed to have been introduced as a matter of convenience, as well as
ornament: but I know too, that it perfectly
coincides with that prevailing paffion in the
fex, of fwelling themfelves beyond their natural
fize. The proportions of the human form are in
like manner deftróyed, by pinching in and contracting the waift, as the Chinefe women do
their feet. Both practices are equally abfurd,
and unnatural; but the former is more pernicious, as it lays a foundation for innumerable
ailments.

Painting the fkin is another art they ufe to
improve their perfons, in which alfo they have
the teftimony of a primitive doctor againft
them; who affirms it " contrary to the will of
" God to ufe paint, or black the hair, becaufe
" the Lord has faid, *thou can'ft not make one*
" *hair white or black*[30]." I am not yet fufficiently

---

[30] **Cyprian**, *de Habitu Virginum*.—Powdering the hair,
though not ufually numbered with the *artificialities* of drefs,
is certainly as much fo as any of them: and this is pernicious not only to the individual, by ditching up the pores
and obftructing perfpiration, as painting does, but to the
community alfo at large; inafmuch as it converts immenfe
quantities

ently deep in the myftery of the *cork rump*, to
be able to give any accurate defcription of it;
but every body knows, that it was invented
upon the fame principle, and calculated for
the fame purpofe, of *mending* God's works by
the arts of men [31].

And, as if to difguife was to perfeċt the *fex*,
are not their *interiora* made to keep pace with
their outward *manœuvres?* I mean, are not
their tempers, fpirit, **and inward** feelings, all
as artificially modelled, and as ftudioufly con-
cealed, as their perfons in the manner defcribed
above?—When Mifs fets out for boarding-
fchool, fhe ufually takes leave of fimplicity and
truth of appearance. She is no longer to look,
fit, fpeak, or **do** any one thing, as nature direċts,
and as fhe ufed **to do** it; but to **regulate** all
her movements, and adjuft all her attitudes,

---

quantities of the beft flour into dirt, while the bulk of the
people are feeding upon the worft. To what purpofe are all
our cautions againft withholding, monopolizing, and ex-
porting grain, while **this** moft finful wafte of **it continues**
and is encouraged?

[31] This Cyprian calls *adulterating* the works of God, and
then goes on: *cutem medicaminibus ungunt, genas rubore ma-
culant. Difplicet illis nimirum plaftica Dei. Quam autem in-
dignum nomine Chriftiano faciem fiċtam geftare, effigiem mentiri!*
It is curious to fee this good father, figuring them to his
imagination as rifing from the dead, with all thefe artificialities about them: *an cum ceruffa, et purpuriffo, et illo ambi-
tu capitis, refurgatis?* Ibid.

according

according to difcipline and rules of art. She is not to confider what fhe really *is*, or what fhe ought to *be*, but how fhe will *appear* ; and thus, by the way, is gradually led to enjoy nothing for its own fake, but only fo far as it excites *admiration* in others [32]. She muft learn to counterfeit and diffemble every affection of the heart [33]. She muft know how to rejoice and to grieve, without any emotion at all : and, on the contrary, to feem as cálm and as cool, as the fnowy top of Ætna, without ; though perhaps, like this fame vulcano, there may be very warm, unruly, tempeftuous doings within.

Now, under all this cumberfome affectation of drefs and manners, which leaves no will, no fentiment, no principles, no character,— may not one fay, with the poet, that *the real girl is the leaft part of herfelf?* We have a

---

[32] " The wanton defire of *admiration*," faid one very knowing in her department, " ruins more women, than " any other weaknefs the fex is fubject to." *Con. Phillips's Apology.*

[33] It was (I fuppofe) this fpirit of artifice and diffimulation, which made the celebrated Mad. de Maintenon efteem her own fex infinitely more dangerous than ours, " Be circumfpect," fays fhe to a young female friend, " in " your connections with women. You had better be feen " with fome men at an opera, than with fome women at a " fermon :" *foyez circonfpecte dans vos liaifons avec les femmes ; il vaut mieux etre vue a l'Opera avec tel homme, qu' avec telle femme au fermon.* Lettres,

coarfe

coarfe vulgar proverb, as indeed ours chiefly are, that " Joan is as good as my lady *in the* " *dark* ;" but trick out Joan as artificially as my lady, and darknefs in the cafe will be no ways neceffary. Joan will, *then*, be as good as my lady *in the light:* that is, Joan and my lady being equally difguifed, their fpecific differences will be as little perceived at mid-day, as they would at midnight.

I have only to caution my reader, not to fancy me fuch a favage, as would decry all culture of body and mind. On the contrary, I would have both the one and the other improved and adorned, as much as may be; but . I would have this done naturally, and unaffectedly. Inftead of *artilifing* nature, to fpeak like Montaigne, I would have us *naturalife art*. While we co-operate with nature, we cannot labour too much in the cultivation of ourfelves; but, when we force or rather contradict her, by fubftituting a fantaftic piece of mummery in her ftead, then, far from mending this *form divine*, as we prefumptuoufly imagine, we do indeed degrade and fink it below *human* [34].

[34] *The human form divine.* Milton.

OF FINE GENTLEMEN: WITH THE CHARACTER AND DESCRIPTION OF AN UPSTART.

EXTRAVAGANCE is now become fo effential to a *fine gentleman*, that young heirs
are almoft trained to believe, they cannot be
fine gentlemen without it. For an heir apparent
of 3000l. a year, 20 or 25,000l. of principal
is not now deemed too much, to carry him
through the heats and excentricities of youth:
as if a fupernumerary fum was needful to
purge the paffions, or like zeft to work out the
ferments, which predominate in the conftitution at this feafon of life. Thus profufion is
become an effential of a man of *honour* [35]: a
young fellow cannot be of the *ton* without it;
and œconomy, or any degree of prudence, is
utterly incompatible with that largenefs of
foul, which, while it fquanders thoufands upon
the *turf* or at *Arthur's*, perhaps reluctantly af-
fords half a crown to diftrefs.

[35] By *honour* is not here meant that quality, which dif-
fers nothing from honefty, except in its being difplayed in
a more gentleman-like form ; but only that empty phan-
tom, which often fupplies the want of honefty.

Full

Full of these sublime ideas, an insolent formerly lamented, in my hearing, that the circumstances of his house had destined him to a profession; for that " himself was the *gentleman*
" of it. He had indeed brethren of profes-
" sions, and liberal professions too, who were
" able and accomplished, as well as honest and
" worthy men; but, then, they were not *gen-*
" *tlemen.* They wanted that freedom of spirit
" and humour, which *elevates* above accounts,
" calculations, and other minute and grove-
" ling attentions: they wanted that easy, care-
" less, sauntering habit, which is so very be-
" coming, because it sits so very naturally, upon
" *gentlemen* who have nothing to do. There
" was a method, a littleness **of** management,
" favouring of pedantry and the schools, in all
" **they** did : and, though likely to get well
" enough through life by playing a safe game,
" yet they would never win a prize, any more
" than other dull fellows *snatch a grace, beyond*
" the drudgery and *rules of art.*"—What pity
it is, that there was only one *gentleman* in this
worthy family! **who, to** cut short his history,
as he lived an extravagant, so he died a bankrupt; to the very sincere affliction of his *un-*
gentlemen brethren [36].

Thus

---

[36] It is recorded of Democritus, that, by the laws of his country, **he** was not entitled to burial with **his** forefathers;
because

Thus far of men liberally born, and liberally educated : but there are others, who, though neither the one nor the other, yet parade and figure in the shape of *gentlemen* ; and, in this money-getting age, are by far the commoneft character of the two. I heard one of thefe *pieces of mechanifm* obferve, with much affectation, that *his* misfortune was to *have a tafte* ; that this misfortune had been increafed, by keeping too much *good company*, and feeing too much of life *upon the large fcale* ; and that what ftill added to his expences, were the obligations he lay under to cultivate the *little people* (fo this upftart called them) about his villa : for it will eafily be imagined, that he was not without the low ambition of being *popular* [37]. Now who, do you think, this extraordinary perfon was ? I will tell you.

He was the fon of a cockney in low life, who, by cow-keeping and the help of a milk-

becaufe he had fpent his patrimony, and thereby loft his rank. What an admirable inftitution ! But a *noble* fpendthrift, with us, is fo far from being degraded, that on this very account he is ufually deemed an object for a penfion : to fupport the form of quality, after the fubftance is gone.

[37] Does ever grub or caterpillar live to put forth wings, and be a butterfly ? 'Tis ten to one but the fpirit of popularity feizes him. Yet what is this fpirit of popularity, even among fuperior compofitions ? 'Tis the love of doing foolifh things, for the fake of being admired by foolifh people.

board,

board, had scraped together enough to leave him independent of trade; but who, retaining the spirit and manners of his original meanness, which is often the case with those who rise to sudden riches, gave him no education above that of the vulgar. Coming however to his inheritance, he determined to be a *gentleman*; and, first, he applied to *Pearce*, a taylor of prime and fashionable *goût*, who made him at once a *gentleman* in dress: which, by the way, is no small advance; for this, with the *æs triplex frontis*, that " front of threefold brass," in which this pupil was singularly happy, will procure admission to the first personages of the kingdom, and *no questions asked*. Then he applied to tradesmen, manufacturers, artists: who, from their several departments, made him a *gentleman* in houses, furniture, and apparatus of every kind: and then he got the whole bespangled with pictures and *virtù*.—I had almost forgot to mention, what is a very capital article in the construction of these *new* gentlemen; and that is, a library [38]. For this he ap-

---

[38] Fielding, in his *Voyage to Lisbon*, mentions one Boyce, a blacksmith at Gosport, who, by smuggling and other honest arts, became possessed of 40,000l. This accomplished person, after procuring abundance of fine things, concluded with having a *library*; and, accordingly, sent an order to a bookseller in London, for 500l. worth of his *handsomest* books.

· plied

plied to *Payne*; and *Payne* made him a *gentle-man*, with regard to books. *Payne* talked to him of original ftandard authors, which he *muſt not be without*; of rare and curious copies, in the fineſt preſervation, and moſt elegant bindings: and thus at length furniſhed him with a collection, **in all** languages, of far from inconſiderable value. **They** might, **if properly** painted, as well have been of wood ; for their poſſeſſor had no more pretenſions to learning, than he had to taſte,—or than a mere obſerver of rites and **ceremonies** has to religion. In ſhort, he knew no language but his own ; and **that** no better than the women who ſwept his rooms [39].

Did not I rightly call this ape of elegance and magnificence a *piece of mechaniſm?* and are not many *fine gentlemen,* thus *mechanically* formed ?

---

[39] Lucian conſidered this taſte for book-buying, as ſo ſure a ſymptom of an illiterate fellow, that he joins the two characters together. Theſe book-gentry ſhould ſeem to think, like the man who bought Orpheus's harp, that it would make admirable muſic of **itſelf,** without any ſkill or knowledge in a performer ; **or** him, who purchaſed Epictetus's lamp at a vaſt ſum, in hopes of having with it Epictetus's wiſdom ; or, laſtly, like thoſe wild Indians, who believe, that they inherit not only the ſpoils, but the abilities of any great enemy, they have the luck to kill. *Lucian.* Πρὸς Ἀπαιδεύτον.

Not for himself he sees, or hears, or eats;
*Artists must chuse his pictures, music, **meats.***

To be sure: the artists furnish the taste, as well as the object of it. Mean while, this destination of men to situations and objects, for which they are unfit, is no small detriment as well as nuisance to society. Many of these *fine gentlemen,* who are at least useless burdens to the earth they encumber, might have done good service in the menial offices and arts of life. The only service they do, under this forced and unnatural character, is the transferring of property, which by prodigality they sometimes abuse, into the hands of men, who may rightly use it; and thus justifying Providence, whose ways are constantly to educe good from evil.

P. S. I am not sure, that my *upstart* is equal to the purchase of a borough: else I should have mentioned a seat in parliament as one of the qualifications, by which these gentry rise to *greatness.* The Herald's Office, however, was not neglected, a coat of arms having **been his** first acquisition; and we are just informed, that, to render his name illustrious after death, he hath ordered his funeral to be in the style and manner of the late Richard Ruffel's, Esq: —500l. for a monument, and 4l. yearly to have it brushed by the sexton.

VII. OF

VII.

OF MAKING A FIGURE: WITH TWO PICTURES OF HUMAN MEANNESS.

I HAVE read of a fquib, which was reprefented burfting with this motto under it,
peréam dum luceam—" let me perifh, if I do
" but fhine." The fame motto will do for all,
who diffipate their fubftance by *fhining* or *figuring* with fhew and equipage.

All mankind would *make a figure*. To afpire
to ftations above us, is a maxim univerfally
adopted; yet perhaps the trueft wifdom and
the fureft happinefs is, to cultivate well the
rank in which we are born. Why fhould any
man covet to raife and diftinguifh himfelf farther, than his real well-being may make neceffary [40] ? A mark of diftinction is, in general,

no

[40] When an hufbandman claimed kinfhip with Robert
Grofthead, Bifhop of Lincoln, and thereupon requefted
from him an office, " Coufin," faid the bifhop, " if your
" cart be broken, I'll mend it; if your plow be old, I'll
" give you a new one, and even feed to fow your land:
" but an hufbandman I found you, and an hufbandman
" I'll leave you." *Fuller's Holy State*, p. 25. The bifhop
thought it kinder (as fhould feem) to ferve him in his way,
than to take him out of his way: and perhaps Stephen
Duck,

no better than a mark for human malice to fhoot at.

There are various ways of *making a figure*, according to *Lord Melcombe.* In a mean traffick with the Duke of Newcaftle for court-preferment, the meaneft perhaps that ever was trufted upon paper, he fays—" The Duke muft
" think, that 2000*l.* a year would not make
" my fortune, with one foot in the grave;
" that, as to rank, I have as much refpect for
" the peerage as any man; but that in my fi-
" tuation, without fucceffion or collateral, a
" peerage to me was not worth the expence of
" new painting my coach." He told the Duke, neverthelefs, that, though he *had one foot in the grave*, he was *determined* to *make* fome fort of *figure* in life: " I earneftly wifh it may be un-
" der your Grace's protection; but, if that
" cannot be, I muft *make* fome *figure.* What
" it will be, I cannot determine yet: I muft
" look about me a little, and confult my
" friends; but fome *figure* I am refolved to

Duck, the threfher, had been better provided for, if, inftead of being firft penfioned and afterwards ordained, he had been endowed with ten acres of land, and fuffered to threfh on. By turning the laborious threfher into an inactive parfon, they brought lunacy firft, and then fuicide, upon a man, who might otherwife have enjoyed himfelf with two cows and a pig, and ended his days in ferenity **and** eafe.

D 					*" make."*

" *make*."—Ovid and Horace, though related to
a court, have both expreſſed themſelves, as if
to live and die unknown were the firſt of arts:
certainly to do ſo would be better, than to *make*
ſuch a *figure* as this. Should it be aſked, on
what this contemptible perſon grounded his
pretenſions, he tells you, that he *had a good
deal of marketable ware, parliamentary intereſt*;
and by boroughs could inſure ſix members of
parliament. Yet the Duke ſeems to have valued
him according to his real merits; for the King
would not receive him to any mark of his favour. Pages 297. 299. 308. 315. of the *Diary
of George Bubb Dodington, Lord Melcombe, by
Henry Penruddocke Windham*. 1784, 8vo.

Though this *Diary* every where diſplays that
mean, baſe, and villainous ſpirit, which, without any regard to connections and obligations,
ſubmits to court and flatter the *powers that are*;
though it ſhews its author to have been wholly
directed by motives of avarice, vanity, and
ſelfiſhneſs; yet I entirely think with the editor,
that Lord Melcombe, far from ſuſpecting any
inference from it diſhonourable to himſelf,
meant it as an apology for his political conduct. So different, as he adds, is the moral
ſenſe of courtiers from that of other men!
Editor's Preface.

To put things of a ſort together, let me ſub-

join

join another picture of human meanness, taken from the *Memoirs of Madame de Pompadour.*

When this lady became mistress of Lewis XV. all France paid her their court; and persons, who had decried her birth, afterwards claimed a relationship to her. The following letter to her, from a gentleman of a very ancient family in Provence, will shew to what intense meanness human nature is capable of descending.

" My dear cousin,

" I was ignorant of belonging to you, till
" the king had nominated you Marchioness of
" Pompadour: then an able genealogist proved
" to me, that your great grandfather was my
" grandfather's cousin in the fourth degree.
" You see by this, dear cousin, that there is a
" real consanguinity between us. If it is your
" pleasure, I will send you the genealogical
" tree of our relationship, that you may pre-
" sent it to the king. My son, however, your
" cousin, who served with distinction for some
" years, would be glad to have a regiment;
" and, as he cannot hope to obtain it by his
" rank, I pray you to ask it from the king as
" a favour."

HER ANSWER.

" SIR,

" I shall embrace the first opportunity of re-
" questing the king to grant your son the re-

D 2   " giment

" giment you defire ; but I have in my turn a
" favour to afk of you, which is, to permit me
" not to have the honour of being your rela-
" tion. Family reafons hinder me from be-
" lieving, that my anceftors have been allied
" with the ancient houfes of the kingdom."—
She adds, in her narrative, that fhe fhould
" put the half of France to the blufh, were
" fhe to mention all the letters fhe had re-
" ceived, full of the moft abject fubmiffions,
" from the firft families in the kingdom." *An-
nual Regifter* for 1766.

VIII.

OLD AGE NOT DESIRABLE.

THE *Gerocomicé,* or art of prolonging life
to old perfons, is afcribed to Herodicus,
one of Hippocrates's mafters ; who is cenfured
for it by Plato [40], and I think very juftly. For,
why fhould people be made anxious to live,
when they can in reality no longer enjoy life ?
when they are foon to be a burden to themfelves and all about them ?

[40] In Republ. l. 3.

Gaffendus

Gassendus is said to have lamented, while the physicians were bleeding him to death, that he " perished in a fresh and vigorous old " age 41;" but I know not how to believe it of him : Gassendus was too wise for this. A man of sixty-four, as Gassendus nearly was, however unimpaired in either body or mind, may justly be reckoned, according to Horace's idea, *conviva satur* ; and to any offers made him might then, as I should think, with sincerity reply, that he had indeed *had enough of every thing.*

Is it not astonishing, that such men as Bacon and Descartes should engage in so wild and unphilosophical an attempt, as that of extending life beyond its natural boundaries ? Bacon, aware of objections, affects to apologize for it ; but his apology is so absurd, that one might almost suppose him not in earnest. " Though the life of mortals," says he, " be " nothing else but a mass and accumulation " of sins and sorrows, and though they, who " aspire after an eternal life, set but small va- " lue upon a temporal ; yet the continuation " of works of charity is not to be despised

41 Possem hic viri semper lugendi mortem dolorosam toti Europæ, immo mundo, recensere, nimio illo remedio sanguineo ; et verba ab ejus ore deprompta referre, quibus ante obitum fassus est, *se nimio obsequio periisse, et ad inferos cum viridi adhuc et stante senecta descendisse.* Petri Borelli Observat. Phys. Med. cent. 3. observ. xi.

D 3

" even

" even by us Chriftians." *Hift. of Life and
Death.*

IX.

AGAINST THE MARRIAGE OF OLD MEN.

ALCESTES, aged 72, was lately married to
a fecond wife.   Were I advifed to take
another wife, under the mean and unmanly
profpect of being *coddled* now I am old [42], my
reply would be in fome fuch terms as thefe :—
" My dear Sir, I am greatly obliged by your
" attention to my happinefs, but (with your
" leave) I will referve the little ftrength
" and fpirits I have remaining for the better
" fupport of my old age.   Secondly, though
" I am not fo old as Alceftes, I am old enough
" to have contracted many ways and humours,
" which, being by habit become natural, can-
" not now be contradicted without making me
" unhappy : but they would be contradicted
" by new connections, or any new fyftem of
" living.   Thirdly, if a man has any decent

---

[42] To be *coddled*, is not only to be nurfed and humoured
like a child, but to be made a fool of in every fenfe of the
word : the common fate of men, who marry when they are
old.

" pride

" pride remaining, he will difdain to be efti-
" mated merely as a *convenience :* but an old
" fellow cannot be accepted of in marriage
" from any other motive. Laftly, I have lived
" long enough to have but one general object;
" and that is, to bear the growing infirmities
" of old age, and to wait my diffolution, with
" a fpirit and temper as peaceful, as refigned,
" as contented, and as ferene, as may be. I
" am, therefore, determined to continue as I
" am."

Mean while, and to return once more to the
fubject, if an *old* man will fo far forget himfelf
as to marry, he fhould (above all things) avoid
a *young* wife; left, as Bayle expreffes it, " he
" expofe his forehead to a fhameful and very
" uneafy difgrace." A young man is not exempt from this misfortune; how fhould an
old ? *If thefe things happen where the wood is
green, what can be expected where it is dry ?* Befides, if he efcape the thing, he may be haunted
with the idea: that is, he may *fufpect* himfelf
to be a *cuckold,* though he really be not; which
is perhaps a greater evil, than to *be* one without *fufpecting* it.

P. S. Alceftes, I hear, is juft ftruck with a
palfy; brought on, as the phyficians whifper,
by the unnatural drudgery, to which his fates
had configned him.

X. A

X.

A CAPITAL DISTINCTION OF THE RATIONAL
FROM AND ABOVE THE BRUTE CREATION.

A SIMPLE-minded country wench, in Wor-
cefterfhire I think, was lately driving a
cow to be bulled; when, lo! the bull was gone
aftray, or abfent at leaft. Upon this, the poor
girl took mightily on, and at length fell a crying; when a perfon who was near afked, why
fhe cried, fince the bull was fure to be found
again : " Aye," fays the girl, " but then it
" may all be gone over with the cow; for
" that *they* are not like *us Chriftians* [43].

XI.

OF THE DIGNITY OF THE HUMAN NATURE,
abfolute.

BEFORE Anaxagoras, who lived above
2000 years ago, the univerfe was fuppofed
to confift of matter and its modifications : but
Anaxagoras introduced mind or fpirit; and

[43] Brought to us by a fafe hand.

matter

12

matter has since been considered as only the *caput mortuum* of the universe. This idea of mind, or Νꜫς, was greatly cultivated afterwards, and made at length so entirely the essence of man, as if body was almost a disgrace to him. The Platonists exalted and refined it to such a degree, that Plotinus was actually ashamed of being found in the body—αἰσχυνόμενος ὅτι ἐν σώματι εἴη [44]; insomuch that he could not speak with temper of his family, parents, or country: and, when statuaries and painters would have taken his image, he rejected the proposal with contempt and indignation. The idea has been uninterruptedly transmitted down; and the following passage shews, that our Sir Thomas Brown was not a little infected with it. " I " could be content," says this philosopher, " that we might procreate like trees without " conjunction, or that there were any way to " perpetuate the world, without this trivial " and vulgar way of coition: it is the foolish- " est act a wise man performs in all his life; " nor is there any thing that will more deject " his cooled imagination, when he shall con- " sider, what an odd and unworthy piece of " folly he hath committed [45]."

Mean while, this sublime and spiritual idea

[44] Fabric. Bibl. Græc. l. iv. c. 25.
[45] Religio Medici, Part II. sect. 8.

of the human nature hath been far from being universally received. I might quote Montaigne and other eminent writers against it; and the Worcestershire wench, in the last article, did most certainly not entertain it.

XII.

OF THE DIGNITY OF THE HUMAN NATURE, *relative*.

BY the dignity of human nature, men usually mean the pre-eminence of the human above other natures. But every nature has its dignity, *sua cuique dignitas*, whether human or brutal, according to the distinction; as every man in society, from a king to a peasant: that is, a propriety and even respectability of character are appropriated and belong to each, in their several situations and connections. So that, were the lion to say to the hedge-hog, or the lobster to the oyster, " I am above you, or " the dignity of my nature is greater than the " dignity of yours," would he not talk absurdly? Yes, he would; but not a jot more absurdly, than if man should say to the elephant, " I am above you;" not a jot more

absurdly,

abſurdly, than if a duke ſhould ſay to one of
Jonas Hanway's chimney-ſweepers, "I am
"above you."

Fantaſtic wretched animals, might a weep-
ing angel interpoſe, ceaſe to be vain and inſolent. You are, all of you, made by the ſame
hand, of the ſame ſtuff, and for the ſame purpoſe of filling ſome department in the univerſal
ſyſtem. You are, all of you, parts of one
whole, where there is neither *above* nor below;
and though, to accommodate ourſelves to
worldly ideas, ſome parts are ſaid to be made
for honor, others for diſhonor, yet you are all
of equal dignity, all of equal honor.

XIII.

KEEP WITHIN YOUR BOUNDARIES.

"I DOUBT, whether exceſſive laughter
" becomes men who are mortal," ſays
Bruyere: *je doute que le ris exceſſif convienne aux
hommes qui ſont mortels* [46]. He might as well
have doubted, whether it became a monkey to
ſkip about and play tricks, becauſe poor jackoo
was ſome time or other to return to the earth,
from whence he came.—That prodigious ſage

[46] Charact. de *l'Homme.*

perſon,

perfon, the late Lord Chefterfield, who, among
other ways and means of cultivating the
graces, advifed his fon and pupil to intrigue
with the dames of Paris,—*he* could not bear
the idea of laughing. He thinks, that *fmiling*
may be permitted to a wife man; but fhould
be forry if it could be faid, that, " fince he
" came to the full ufe of his reafon, he had
" ever been *heard* to laugh [47]."

What pity it is, that, inftead of cultivating
their nature well, men fhould fo often attempt
vainly and fantaftically to foar above it,—
fhould want to be angels before their time!
Thus, we have feen Plotinus above [48], afhamed
to find his foul amidft the *fæces* of matter;
and our Sir Thomas Browne, reprobating the
act of generation as very debafing. Agreeably
to which latter idea, another fublime philofopher hath declared " the noblenefs of the foul
" of man to be fuch, that fuch grofs enjoy-
" ments are exceedingly *below* her : and, there-
" fore, even nature hath taught her to *fneak*,
" when fhe, being heaven-born, demits her
" noble felf to fuch *earthly drudgery* [49]." Yet
this faid Sir Thomas Browne did at length
condefcend to *fneak*, and to demit his noble
felf to this faid *earthly drudgery :* for he took a

---

[47] Lett. 112.   [48] No XI.

[49] Dr. Henry More. See Norris's *Theory and Regulation*
of Love, p. 173.

, wife,

wife, with whom he lived one-and-forty years, and by whom he had no lefs than ten children. Stupendous fall! She was, however (as we prefume to have been recorded by way of ex-cufe), fhe was " a lady of fuch admirable fym-
" metrical proportion to her worthy hufband,
" both in the graces of her body and mind,
" that they feemed to come together by a kind
" of *natural magnetifm* [50]."

XIV.

OF GOVERNMENT, AND ITS VARIOUS FORMS [51].

ALL the difputes about government, and its various forms, feem to have arifen from thefe two particulars: firft, from men's view-ing human nature, each through different me-diums, or in different lights; and, fecondly,

[50] Whitefoot.
[51] This No is taken from *The Irenarch of Dr. Heathcote,* pag. 199, 1781, 3d edition: and, if we have tranfcribed a little freely from this writer, it is becaufe we would make more public fome *general* matters of importance, which he hath treated in a fhort clofe way, agreeably to our plan, **but** which muft eafily efcape notice under the *particular* title of his book.

from

from their confidering it as ftationary in its mòde, or of manners always the fame.

Hobbes believed human nature to be very bad : that there was no innate benevolence in men, no focial principle to hold them toge- ther ; but that all were naturally in a ftate of war with one another. *Hobbes* therefore con- tended for the moft abfolute form of govern- ment, as deeming no chains too ftrong for the reftraining of fuch a favage : *Hobbes* was, in fhort, for having him double-ironed. *Shaftef- bury*, on the other hand, thought highly of hu- man nature : he afcribed to it a *moral fenfe*, or inftinctive feeling for what is reafonable and benevolent ; and fuppofed, that the human kind, if not corrupted by education, would as naturally be virtuous, as a fig is fweet : *Shaftef- bury* therefore would approve a republic, or that form of government, which grants the moft to private will. *Locke*, who thought hu- man nature neither fo bad as *Hobbes*, nor fo good as *Shaftefbury*, fuppofed it ; *Locke*, who was neither fo timid as *Hobbes*, nor yet any thing near fo firm as *Shaftefbury*—for let it be remembered, that, in difquifitions of this fort, bodily temperament availeth much [52]—

Locke,

---

[52] Men derive their opinions, civil and religious, chiefly from temperament : yet Hobbes, in queftions of religious

concern,

Locke, I say, was led to that mixed and mode-
rate form of government, under which he
wrote, and to which his principles of governing were meant to be adapted. And thus men
vary in their ideas of civil policy, each con-
ceiving his own to be *the best;* the very archetypal pattern or standard, which every nation and people should aspire after: and hence
the many *Utopias,* with which the world hath
been presented [51].

Were the question put to me, what form of
government I think *the best?* my reply would
be, *that,* which is *best* adapted to the nature,
temper, and manners of a people. Could the
spirit of virtue be kept up, and the manners
remain fixed and uniform, as by education and
discipline anciently at Sparta, a well instituted

concern, was a most uncommon and striking exception to
this general truth; " the boldness of his opinions and sen-
" timents forming a remarkable contrast to the timidity
" of his character." HUME.

[51] These ideal governments have been called, as we say,
Utopias, or *No-wheres;* and they have been called so very
truly, for they have never existed out of the imaginations,
which formed them. But they may also, with a peculiar
propriety, be styled, in my Lord Bacon's terms, *Idola Spe-
cûs,* if we may extend the meaning of those terms a little;
since, if not actually *idolized* by their framers, they have always been contemplated with a more than *Narciffean* fondness. This fondness is finely strictured by Lucian, when he
represents Plato as quitting an Elysium, for the sake of
living in his **own** dear *republic:* ἐν τῇ ὑπ᾽ αὐτῶ ἀναπλασθείσῃ
πόλει οἰκεῖν. **De** Vera Hist. L. 2.

republic,

republic, or whatever might be deemed the freeft form, would certainly be the moft eligible ; becaufe, under fuch a form, human perfection and human happinefs would be carried to the higheft pitch they are capable of attaining.   But where, for want of education and difcipline, the manners are fubject to change— where there is what has been called a *progreffion of manners*, there government muft alfo change, and together with the manners affume a different form: and it is poffible, that, agreeable to their manners in the different ftages or periods of this *progreffion*, the different forms of government, fpecified above, may be fuited to the very fame people.   Does not the hiftory of ancient Rome give us reafon to fuppofe fomething like this ?

Upon the whole, the *beft* government for fociety is like the *beft* good for individuals. Confidered as general abftract ideas, or archetypal ftandards, they are *both* fantaftic and vifionary ; and politicians and philofophers may fearch for ever, without finding them : for, as all government muft be the beft, which is beft accommodated to the circumftances and manners of its people ; fo that muft be the *fummum bonum* to individuals, which is beft adapted to their refpective temperaments and difpofitions. And who does not fee, that, in both thefe cafes, the variety of *beft* governments and of *beft*

goods

goods may be conceived to be almoſt infinite [54] ?

XV.

OF THE PROMULGATION OF LAWS.

IN 1729 was paſſed an act, to prevent bribery and corruption in electing members of
parliament; when the legiſlators provided alſo,
that the ſaid act ſhould be *publicly known
and promulgated*, by ordering it to be read
openly at proper times and places. It were to
be wiſhed, that the ſame proviſion might accompany all other laws and ordinances; the
promulgation of which is ſo little regarded, or
rather ſo totally neglected, that, ridiculous as
it may ſound, the people of England, in general, know nothing of the laws, which they
themſelves are ſaid to make.

No nation has been more free to make laws,

[54] The *ſovereign good* has been compared to the *panacea,*
or univerſal remedy, and aptly enough; the one being as
fitted to procure *all* people *health,* as is the other to procure
all people *happineſs.* The *ſovereign* form of government
would be juſt as well fitted to the various manners, as the
others to the various temperaments and conſtitutions of
mankind. In ſhort, they are all chimæras, and without
exiſtence.

E   than

than the English [55] :—they have indeed been too free; and we may almost say with Tacitus, *ut antehac flagitiis, ita nunc legibus, laboratur*—but many nations have been more attentive to the promulgation of their laws. The Athenians, for this purpose, had their νομοθέται; whose province it was to have their laws written upon a tablet, and fixed up at the statues of the heroes, called ἐπώνυμοι, that the people might have them in contemplation, even before they were proposed to the assembly. The promulgation of Roman law was by clear and legible characters, in some frequented public place : *claris literis, unde de plano recte legi possit, ante tabernam scilicet, vel ante eum locum, in quo negotiatio exercetur; non in remoto loco, sed in evidenti* [56].—And hence Caligula contrived to fix up laws, *minutissimis literis et angustissimo loco*; as a *ways and means* of raising money upon the

---

[55] *Pickering's* edition of *The Statutes at Large*, from Magna Charta in 1225 to 1784 inclusive, consists of above thirty volumes in 8vo, besides the index volume : three-and-twenty of which have been enacted since the Revolution in 1688, and ten of these since 1760, when George III. began to reign.—Henry VII. says Lord *Bacon*, " may justly be " celebrated for the best law-giver to this nation, after Ed- " ward I. : for his laws are deep, and not vulgar ; not made " *upon the spurre of a particular occasion for the present*, but " out of providence for the future, to make the estate of " his people still more and more happy." *Hist. of Henry* VII.

[56] Digest. xiv. 3. 11. ſ. 3.

people,

people, who, from not difcerning and being
apprized of, incurred forfeitures by offending
againft them [57].

But neither in great characters nor fmall, neither in public places nor private, are the laws
of England promulgated to the people of
England. They are not even advertifed, as
common pamphlets are. They may indeed be
had from the fhops, and read, in fome time
after, among the *Statutes at Large*, by men of
the profeffion, and a few others ; but the mul-
titude are left to know them as they can, or (to
fpeak more properly) not to know them at all.
In fhort, when I confider the egregious ignorance of the people of England touching their
laws, it calls to my mind that period in the
Roman government, when " the Calendar was
" fo profound a myftery, that application was
" ufually made to a few lawyers in the fecret,
" in order to know the days of pleading [58]."

[57] Sueton. in Vit. § 41.

[58] Cicer. ad. Attic. vi. 1.—et pro Muræn. § 11.—This
may feem ridiculous, but certainly is not more fo, than what
was actually tranfacted among ourfelves the very laft year ;
when, in many of our public prints, we had the names of two
lawyers tacked to an interpretation of the act for a horfe-
tax : as if a meaning, which fhould have been obvious to
every farmer in the kingdom, could not be drawn from it,
without the affiftance of thefe profeffional gentlemen ; who
yet, after all, were not in general thought fufficiently gifted
for the tafk affigned to them.

XVI.

OF REPRESENTATION IN PARLIAMENT.

THE term *reprefentative* feems lately to have
deviated from its original fignification and
import: for we hear of fome, who confider
themfelves as " nothing more than the *at-*
" *tornies* or *delegates* of their *conftituents* ; and,
" regardlefs of their own, pride themfelves in
" acting according to the *fenfe* of thefe con-
" ftituents only." But this feems a very degrading idea of a reprefentative, and furely ex-
hibits him under a moft fervile point of view.
A reprefentative in parliament is a perfon, de-
puted by individuals to execute their portion
of the public bufinefs in the national council
or affembly, and vefted by them with full and
complete powers in order thereunto. In this
fituation, he is to ufe his beft judgment towards knowing and afcertaining, and his beft
endeavours in promoting, what fhall be moft for
the national good ; and this, without any retro-
fpective view upon his conftituents, or any regard to their *fenfe* of affairs : for it may be,
either that the *fenfe* of thefe conftituents cannot
be conveyed to him, or that they may have no
fenfe to convey.

And

And that this independency of the reprefentative is fuppofed by the conftitution, appears
plainly from hence, *viz.* that the powers with
which he is invefted, are not revocable at pleafure, or before the expiration of the term for
which they were given ; even though they
fhould be employed, not only againft the *fenfe*
of his conftituents, but even againft the national weal itfelf.—How far fuch an ordain-
ment of things is eligible, I fay not: but I fay,
that, if a reprefentative be nothing more than
a perfon, who fits in the Houfe of Commons
to fpeak the *fenfe* of a certain number of people,
as he receives it by the poft out of the country,
he is no better than a tube, an organ-pipe, a
kind of wind-inftrument, which fends forth
found mechanically.

XVII.

OF A REPRESENTATIVE IN PARLIAMENT.

" THE *greateſt* ſlave in a kingdom is gene-
" rally the king of it," ſays a certain
writer[59]. I am tempted, upon well-grounded
concluſions, to except a repreſentative in parliament, reſiding among his conſtituents, and
immediately depending upon them : who, whether you regard the attentions he pays, or
the compliances he ſubmits to, may (I think)
moſt juſtly be deemed, if not indeed the *greateſt*, yet certainly the *ſmalleſt*, of ſlaves.

XVIII.

ELECTIONEERING.

APRIL 1784. The Ducheſs of *D.* has mixed
with the mob of Weſtminſter, and is can-
vaſſing for Fox. Alas ! ſhe little knows what
kind of theatre ſhe has entered upon. Liſten

---

[59] Maxims, Characters, and Reflections. 1768, 8vo. Nº
397.

to the *Canaille*, and learn what they say of her:
look into the print-shops, and see how she is
painted. What billinsgate, what caricature!
Yet the *Canaille* are only tools: they are employed by people, who, by the curtesy of
England, are not of the *Canaille*. Retire, my
dear unthinking Duchess! Though thou wert
clean and pure as an angel, they will make
thee dirtier and filthier than even Gulliver
under the Yahoos.

XIX.

UPON JUSTICES OF THE PEACE[60].

SIR,   March 14, 1785.

IN your Advertiser of the 11th, you have a
short paper *upon the police*, in which it is
asked, whether " *Justices* are still to make a
" *trade* of *justice* ?" and where it is insinuated,
that one great obstacle to an amendment of
the *police* is this very *trade*. The *police* and the
Justices do most certainly, both of them, want
to be amended; and this, not within the bills
of mortality only, but even to the remotest
corners of the kingdom.

[60] This is taken from the *Public Advertiser*.

Lord

Lord *Coke* hath faid of this magiftracy, that " the whole Chriftian world hath not the like, " if it be duly executed." 4 *Inft.* 170. It fhould feem then, as if it had not been *duly executed*; for it is really aftonifhing, with what fupreme contempt and even averfion this order of magiftrates hath, from time to time, been treated. Sir *Thomas Overbury* fpeaks of a " country gentleman as a thing, out of whofe " corruption a juftice of peace is generated." *Characters.*—Lord *Bacon*, in his *Apophthegms*, mentions a *wife Juft-afs*, who, being compelled to thruft a delinquent out of his office, faid, " thou fhalt go, *nogus vogus*;" meaning (poor gentleman!) *nolens volens*.—Bifhop *Francis Godwin*, preaching about the fame time upon Dives and Lazarus, obferved that, " though " the fcriptures had not expreffed plainly who " **Dives was,** yet by his cloaths and his face " he might be bold to affirm, he was at the " leaft a Juftice of Peace," &c.[61]—Thefe were in the reigns of Elizabeth and James, when thofe we call *Trading*-Juftices now, went by the name of *Bafket*-Juftices; as if men, who could do nothing without a prefent, yet who " for " half a dozen of chickens would difpenfe " with a whole dozen of penal ftatutes." So a Member expreffed himfelf in the Houfe of

---

[61] *Harrington's* View of the Church, p. 167.

Commons, as Sir Symonds D'Ewes relates in his Journals, *Anno* 1601.

The Author of *Hudibras*, who lived under Charles I. and II. mentions a Justice of Peace as " one, who has a patent for his wit, and un-" derstands by commission [62]."—Lastly, the late *Henry Fielding* hath represented his bro-ther Justices as a very low order of beings surely, when, speaking of one who was about to " execute Justiceship, which, says he, is a " syllable more than Justice," he adds, " but " luckily the clerk had a qualification, no " clerk to a Justice of Peace ought ever to be " without, namely, some understanding in the " law of this realm [63]." The magistrate here meant was the furious *Squire Western*; and really, when such images occur, a little harm-less mirth must be forgiven. I have never con-

---

[62] *Butler*'s Remains, 1759, 8vo.

[63] *Fielding* does not seem to have been apprised of the expedient since found out, to remedy the defect here alluded to. It is now become a custom, in the country at least, for two or more Justices to meet at an alehouse, and to station an attorney amidst them; who, while he officiates osten-sibly as a clerk, is in reality the first magistrate in the room, by being as it were a light to lighten the rest. The great inconvenience to which this contrivance stands expo-sed, is, that, should any mischance befal the attorney, *si quid humanitus ei accideret*, here's an assemblage of lumina-ries extinguished at once.

templated

templated one of thefe wild-looking[64], bluf-
tering, overbearing ignorants, amidft his pea-
fants at a village-meeting, without feeling an
impulfe to accoft him, in the language of Te-
rence,—*eone es ferox, quia habes imperium in bel-
luas?* but, alas! I might as well accoft him in
the Chinefe.

Mean while, notwithftanding the ridicule to
which the above honeft gentlemen feem to
have been obnoxious,—who probably had little
knowledge of any kind but what related to their
horfes, their dogs, and *the game,* and who acted rather from the authority of fquirefhip, than
the authority of law,—yet they were not in general *Bafket*-Juftices, but abftained from even
the idea of lucre: whereas *now* nothing is
more common than to fee perfons obtruded
upon the public as magiftrates, who are not
only as ftupid and as ignorant as men can be,
but whofe fituations and circumftances do not
fet them above the temptation of *trading.* And
they are obtruded at random; as much at random as alehoufes are licenfed; that is, without
any regard to ufe in the thing, or character in
the perfon.

Spirit of Reformation! thou art careful about

[64] —— *rudis fane bonarum artium, et robore corporis ftolide
ferox.* Tacitus.

many things; when wilt thou carry thyfelf into the department of Jufticing, which is at leaft one of the things needful?

PHILODICUS.

Yes, Philodicus, *fi quid humanitus ei accidederet*; that is, in plain Englifh, " if the at-" torney fhould come to be hanged." A mif-chance, indeed, that he may at leaft deferve, when we confider the impofitions and extortions he will almoft be fure to practife: for it is hardly conceivable, that any attorney of character and credit fhould fubmit to engage in fo humble a fervice.

Mean while, as Philodicus is fo fenfibly touched with *abufes*, why would he not give us fome idea of a *reform?* which, however, feems to lie in the fmalleft compafs. Inftead of Juftices *made at random*, and without regarding either *ufe in the thing* or *character in the perfon*, let fit and proper perfons be chofen at fit and proper diftances; and, inftead of taking fees, which are juft what is demanded [65], let a fettled ftipend be paid to the office of each magiftrate by treafurers of counties, and levied upon parifhes as other rates are. Were fome

[65] A clerk of the peace is finable 10l. if he neglect to expofe conftantly in the Seffions-Room a table of the fees; and a juftice-clerk 20l. if he exacts more than due. We know it: but can it be expected, that a poor, ignorant, affrighted peafantry fhould *indict* and *fue?*

such

such regulation as this to take place, what is now a dirty *trade*, would become a liberal *service*: the spirit of litigiousness among the people, which this trade has so much contributed to inflame and keep up, would be discountenanced and checked; and, in short, the police throughout the kingdom be corrected and amended,

---

XX,

OF THE INEFFICACY OF LAWS WITHOUT EDU-CATION, OR REGULATED MANNERS.

QUID leges sine moribus vanæ proficient! says *Horace*: and it is an exclamation that has, or might have, been made in all ages and nations of the world. We in England have an ecclesiastical, as well as civil, establishment for the security of good manners; but neither separately, nor conjunctly, have they ever effectually performed their business. The truth is, that this famed *alliance between church and state* hath not had the promotion of good manners for its object, so much as might be wished; the parties having rather attended to the promotion of their respective rights and privileges,

privileges[66]. And hence, we are sorry to say, the terms of this *alliance* have been on both sides but ill observed; for, when either hath prevailed over the other, there hath always been an end of the *alliance*.

But, suppose the ballance of power to have been preserved between them, and that they had unanimously made *good manners* their object; yet neither **would** this have availed, without a previous attention to these manners by education **and** early discipline:

> *Eradenda cupidinis*
> *Pravi sunt elementa; et teneræ nimis*
> *Mentes asperioribus*
> *Firmandæ studiis.* **Hor.**

Without education, **all the** solemn pompous exterior of civil and ecclesiastical establishments, all the laws and ordinances upon earth, will not be able, for any long time, to keep mankind in decency and order: experience has ever shewn, that *manners*, as they degenerate, will sooner or later prevail against them. " The laws of education," says Montesquieu, " are the first we receive, and should have re- " spect to the principles and spirit of the go- " vernment we live under: as they prepare

---

[66] Lord Bolingbroke calls this *an ancient and close alliance between secular and ecclesiastical tyranny.* Oldcastle's Remarks.

" us

" us to be citizens, each individual family
" fhould be governed conformably with the
" plan which comprehends them all [67]."

It was on this article, that Plutarch fo juftly
preferred Lycurgus to Numa ; the latter having paid no attention to youth, in his fyftem
of legiflation, but left them to be educated at
random, and juft as accident, or the caprice
of parents, might direct : ἐπὶ ταῖς τῶν πατέρων
ποιησάμενος ἐπιθυμίαις ἢ χρείαις τὰς τῶν νέων ἀγωγὰς [68].
And what powerful effects education wrought
at Sparta, the long duration and hiftory of its
government fufficiently declare : *Lacedæmonii
foli toto orbe terrarum feptingentos jam annos am-
plius unis moribus, et nunquam mutatis legibus,
vivunt* [69]. The laws were not changed, becaufe
the manners were not changed ;—for the laws
muft depend upon, and be fubfervient to,
the manners—and the manners were not

[67] Comme *les loix de l'éducation* nous préparent à être
citoyens, chaque famille particulière doit être gouvernée
fur le plan de la grande famille qui les comprend toutes.
De l'Efprit, &c. iv. 1.

[68] *In Vit.* Numæ.

[69] Cicero *pro Flacco*, § 26.—When one obferved, that
the Spartan government lafted thus, becaufe the kings
knew how to govern ; " yea rather," fays Theopompus,
" becaufe the citizens knew how to obey." *Multum habet
momenti principis integritas, fed multò plus civium recta infti-
tutio.* Erafmi Apophth. p. 55. Amft. 1671.

changed,

changed, becaufe education and difcipline held them fixed and uniform [70].

But in other nations, fuch as ours for inftance, where *morals* in educating are little cultivated, and mere *accomplifhments* chiefly regarded, manners will never obtain any fixed and regular form; but exhibit that variegated and motley appearance, which muft needs refult from individuals, differently trained, and differently fafhioned. And thus the body focial, compofed of heterogeneous and diffonant materials, as it were, which do not kindly mix, and confpire to form a whole, will generate ill humours, fermentation, and diforder within; and thefe operating furely, though perhaps flowly, will gradually corrupt, and finally diffolve it.

---

[70] Ἐπεὶ δ᾽ ἓν τὸ τέλος τῇ πόλει πάσῃ, φανερὸν ὅτι καὶ τὴν παιδείαν μίαν καὶ τὴν αὐτὴν ἀναγκαῖον εἶναι πάντων, &c. *As there is one end in view in every city, it is evident, that education ought to be one and the fame in each; and that this fhould be the objeḉ of the public, not of individuals, as it now is, when every one takes care of his own children feparately. And their mode of educating is particular alfo, each inftruḉing his children as he pleafes; though, what all ought to be engaged in, ought to be common to all. For this the Lacedæmonians may be praifed; fince they give the greateft attention to education, and make it public.* Ariftotel. Polit. VIII. 1.

XXI. an

XXI.

AN APOLOGY FOR DR. JAMES'S FEVER-POW-
DER [71].

" QUONAM *fato fieri*"—by what unac-
countable perverfenefs in our frame
does it happen, that we fet ourfelves fo zea-
loufly againft any thing *new ?* The Fever-Pow-
der grew into repute about the year 1750; and
it was no fooner in repute, than the phyficians
began to perfecute, as fome time after the chemifts began to counterfeit, it. Two fets of
men, therefore, might be confidered as inimical to it, the phyficians by their invectives, the
chemifts by their adulterations; and the latter
would difgrace it more effectually than the
former, by being the occafion of numbers to
perifh, whom the genuine powder would have
cured. It was, it feems, fo natural to expect the
perfecution of fuch a powder, that one of the
profeffion may almoft be thought to have actually foretold it. " Can any one," fays he,
" behold without fcorn fuch drones of phyfi-
" cians, that, after the fpace of fo many hun-
" dred years experience and practice of their

[71] This N° is taken from the *Univerfal Biography*, in
12 vols. 8vo. *art.* JAMES.

" predeceffors,

" predeceffors, not one fingle medicine hath
" yet been detected by them, that hath the
" leaft force, directly and *per fe*, to oppofe,
" refift, and expel a continual fever ? Should
" any by a more fedulous obfervation pretend,
" or make the leaft ftep towards, the difco-
" very of fuch remedies, their hatred and envy
" would fwell againft him, as a legion of devils
" againft virtue: whole focieties would dart
" their malice at him, and torture him with
" all the calumnies imaginable, without ftick-
" ing at any thing that fhould deftroy him
" root and branch: for he, who profeffes a
" reformation of the art of phyfic, muft re-
" folve to run the hazard of the *martyrdom* of
" his reputation, life, and eftate[72]." Dr. Mor-
ton, who has faved millions of lives, as James
obferves, by pointing out the ufe of the *bark*,
complains of the oppofition which was made
to that medicine : " It is an undoubted truth,"
fays he, " that there were many villainous
" flanderers every where, efpecially in London,
" who wickedly and artfully confpired to fup-
" prefs the rifing reputation of this febrifuge;
" left, by this *fhort method* of curing fevers,

[72] The Art of curing Difeafes by Expectation. By Gi-
deon Harvey, M. D. Lond. 1689, p. 196.

F   they

" they should lose opportunities of picking
" the pockets of their patients[73]."

It should seem, as if an inventor was in a similar situation with the citizen of old, who could
not propound a law, without an halter about
his neck. Nay, indeed, in a worse situation,
as having a more certain fire-ordeal to go
through : for the law might pass, and the pro-
pounder escape hanging; but the novelist, or
innovator, as they call him, is sure to be persecuted. The efficacy of James's Powder is, we
presume, as well established by matter of fact,
as the efficacy of any medicine that ever was
hit on : but, alas! what is matter of fact against
prejudices and passions ? and, especially, when
these prejudices and passions are inflamed and
heightened by interested and selfish motives.
There was once a violent dissention between
Peripatetics and Galenists about the origin of
the nerves; the former deducing them from
the heart, the latter from the brain. A Ga-
lenical anatomist of Venice happened to be
performing at a lecture upon the subject,

---

[73] " Verissimum quidem est, non defuisse nefarios quos-
" dam detrectatores ubique, præsertim Londini, qui dolo
" malo consilium ceperunt de hujus febrifugi fama præma-
" turè supprimenda; ne, scilicet, hac succincta methodo
" febres obtruncandi, ægrotantium crumenas emulgendi
" occasio tolleretur." Pyretologia, Lond. 1692, p. 121.

when

when a noble Peripatetic, his antagonist, was present; and he proceeded with more than ordinary care, because he had the conviction of this Peripatetic particularly in view. He dissected with accuracy each minute part; and, laying open the root out of which the nerves grew, publicly exhibited its situation in the brain. Upon which, turning to his antagonist, he asked, "if he was at length convinced, that "the nerves sprung from the brain, and not "from the heart?" who, after some pause, "allowed indeed the fact to be so very plain "and obvious, that he could not but have "assented to it, *if Aristotle had not declared the* "*contrary* [74]."

But what are the objections to this justly famous Powder? Why, some (it is said) refuse

---

[74] This story is told in the Systema Cosmicum of Galilæus, who was himself an illustrious example, to shew how feeble a thing even a matter of fact is, against theory and hypothesis supported by an establishment. When Copernicus revived the ancient astronomy, which made the sun, not the earth, the centre of the planetary system, it was said, by way of objection, that Venus *then* must undergo the same phases with the moon. This Galilæus afterwards discovered by his telescope to be the real matter of fact; but this *real matter of fact*, being adverse to received opinion, exposed him to the cognizance of Pope Urban VIII. who proscribed him as an heretic, and threw him into prison; whence he was not released, till he had formally abjured what **he had seen** with his eyes.

to

to give it, becaufe they know not what it is: and indeed, once in my hearing, an old country apothecary (than whom exifteth not, in general, a more felf-fufficient [75] creature) declared himfelf, with much confcientious formality, to this purpofe:—*he did not know*, forfooth, *of what it was compounded*. He had better have faid, that he was afraid it might hurt the fale of his drugs [76]: and then, though he would have faid nothing more than what every body knew, he would at leaft have fpoken fenfe. For, did the dotard know the conftituent parts, or of what any thing was compounded? Suppofing integrity and philanthropy to be any way concerned, his bufinefs was, not to difpute captioufly about *principia* or primogenial par-

---

[75] " In country-towns, where no phyfician ufually re-
" fides, *apothecaries*, efpecially thofe in years, look upon
" themfelves as perfect *Hippocratefes* in knowledge and ex-
" perience." Dr. Stevenfon *on the Gout*, p. 137.

[76] " An objection to my Powder, and a very ferious one,
" is, that it has a tendency to impair the trade of apothe-
" caries. I am certain, that this is the true reafon of all
" the oppofition made to its ufe, and to me as the author
" of it. The phyficians, that have lifted under the apothe-
" caries banners, have meanly deferted the caufe of the
" public." James's Vindication of his Powder, p. 99.—
But *all* have not *lifted under the apothecaries* : for *fome* avow
its efficacy, and prefcribe it openly ; while *others*, to whom
the fpirit of *martyrdom* is not vouchfafed in fuch abundance,
though they affect to difcountenance, ufe it under a difguife.

ticles,

ticles, but to fearch anxioufly and curioufly into facts or effects; and, if the Powder was
found to operate as reprefented, to give it at
all adventures, let it be compounded of what
it would. I could not fubmit to engage upon
this occafion; elfe I might have referred this
apothecary, as I would fome of his betters, to
Hippocrates, the father of them all: who, far
from difdaining and fcornfully rejecting without examination, advifes practitioners to examine every thing; and " to enquire of all,
" phyficians or not, if in any cafe they know
" of any thing ufeful [77]." And, furely, with
good reafon; fince, as a late phyfician obferved,
" even ignorant people, not knowing the the-
" ories of the learned, nor therefore mifled by
" them, have fometimes followed, what is not
" unfrequently a better guide, traditional ex-
" perience [78]."

Another objection to this Powder is, that it
is *empirical*. If by *empirical* they mean a medicine that has been *tried* or *experienced*, as the
word according to its Grecian origin imports,
fo it ought to be; elfe it may be good for nothing, or even hurtful, for any thing that is

[77] Μὴ ὀκνέειν παρὰ ἰδιοτέων ἱστορέειν, ἤν τι δοκέει ξυμφέρον. De
Præceptis.—" Empirici & vetulæ fæpenumerò in curandis
" morbis feliciùs operentur, quam medici eruditi." Bacon de **Augm**. Scient. lib. 4.
[78] Mufgrave on **the** Nerves, ch. 6.

known,

known. But they do not mean this : they mean, that it is not agreeable to *Pharmac. Londinenſ.*; that it is below the dignity of *liberal prac- tice* [79]; and that, in ſhort, it is not an orthodox medicine. For there is an orthodoxy in phy- ſic, as well as in divinity; and a man may be an heretic with the profeſſors of either, if he ſhall offend againſt their reſpective eſtabliſh- ments, by advancing any thing *new*, or incon- ſiſtent with them. Let, however, what will become of orthodoxy, truth in all caſes ought to prevail; and eſpecially, as in the preſent, where the ſafety and lives of men are at ſtake : for, as *James* himſelf writes, " if the dignity " of phyſic, like that of Moloch, is to be ſup- " ported by human ſacrifices, it is the duty " of every civil ſociety to treat both the art " and its profeſſors like the Knights-Templars, " who, for their tranſcendent villainies, were " extirpated from the face of the earth [80]."

Another circumſtance, which hath been ur- ged to diſgrace the Powders (and the laſt I ſhall mention) is, that it " hath no *ſpecific* effi- " cacy in the cure of fevers, and that other

---

[79] Dr. Donald Monro hath dedicated his " Prælectiones " Medicæ," printed in 1776, 8vo, to the College of Phy- ſicians, in theſe terms : " Collegio Regio Medicorum Lon- " dinenſi, *medicinæ liberalis* cultori & patrono."

[80] Vindication, &c. p. 98.

" medicines

" medicines will do as well [81]." We verily believe, and our faith is grounded upon matter
of fact, that it hath *specific* qualities; that it
will cure fevers more effectually, and (as all
own) more speedily, than any other medicine:
but, were this not so, and were it only of equal
efficacy with others, there is surely something
very ungenerous and malign in the cavil. For
what does it amount to? why, it amounts to
this, *viz.* that Dr. James is a busy, forward,
presumptuous fellow, for labouring to distin-
guish himself by being useful in his profession;
and ought particularly to be discouraged, hated, and persecuted, for aspiring after a *specific*,
which none of his fraternity had been able to
discover. Thus I recollect an Athenian voter,
a notable wiseacre doubtless, who, when asked
why he thought Aristides deserving of banish-
ment, replied, " that for his part he knew no-
" thing of Aristides, but that he had no notion
" of his pretending to be *just* above others:"—
*se ignorare Aristidem, sed sibi non placere, quod
tam cupidè elaborasset, ut præter cæteros* Justus
appellaretur. Nepos.

To conclude: if **James** did not live to see
his Powder received, and its use adopted, *uni-*

[81] " Certè medicamentum melius non est quam *tarta-*
" *rum emeticum,* aliaque medicamenta à medicis quotidiè
" adhibita; nullam enim vim *specificam* ad febres profli-
" gandas possidet." Monro's Præl. Med. p. 62.

F 4 *versally,*

verfally, he only experienced what all advancers of *new* things experienced before him; unlefs we may except Harvey, the difcoverer of the *blood's circulation*; who is faid by Hobbes to have been " the only one, that con- " quered envy in his life-time, and faw his " *new* doctrine eftablifhed :—*Harveius folus*, " *quod fciam, doctrinam novam, fuperatâ invidiâ*, " *vivens ftabilivit*. Præfat. ad Element. Phi- " lofoph."

XXII.

AGAINST THE ABRIDGMENT OF LABOUR.

To the Society for promoting Arts and Sciences.

GENTLEMEN,   March, 1773.

A SOCIETY for the advancement of arts and fciences may certainly have many curious and fome ufeful objects, but I cannot think that the abridgment of human labour fhould be one of either fort. For, what is the end of fociety at large? It is not, that one man fhould batten in wealth and luxury, and that nine hundred ninety and nine fhould ftarve under wretchednefs and poverty; it is, that all fhould enjoy the comforts adapted to each

man's

man's station and condition. But the bulk of mankind muſt live by labour; and, if by any contrivances they are deprived of this labour, how are theſe comforts to be procured?

I have ſomewhere read of a famous printer, who went from Holland to Conſtantinople, and carried with him preſſes and types of all ſorts, in order to introduce the art of printing there. The Vizir hearing of it, ordered the printer to be hanged, and all his apparatus to be deſtroyed; declaring it *cruel, that one man, to enrich himſelf, ſhould take their bread from eleven thouſand ſcribes, who gained their living by their pens.* The execution of the printer favoured of Turkiſh manners, and was indeed ſavage. I like the conduct of that Roman Emperor better, who, when a mechanic undertook to carry ſome large pillars into the Capitol at a very ſmall expence, made the artiſt a handſome preſent for his device, but refuſed to accept it, ſaying, that he *muſt ſuffer the poor people to live* [82].

The principle, however, from which both Vizir and Emperor acted, will always deſerve attention. When nations are got to their height of civilization, as we ſay; when wealth and luxury prevail; when arts and ſciences flouriſh; then they naturally abound with people. Then

[82] Sueton. in Veſpaſ. § 18.

every

every trade is crowded, every profeffion over-
charged; and, as Seneca complained with regard to the Romans in his time, " they have
" indeed too much of every thing:" *omnium*
rerum intemperantiâ laborant [83]. At fuch a period, methinks, it would be rather doing fervice to increafe, than to diminifh, human labour. Our corn is ground by wind and water.
Suppofe that fome wonderful mechanic could
invent and fabricate fuch a fyftem of machi-
nery, that all our lands fhould be cultivated,
and all our manufactures carried on, by wind
and water too; what would be the effect?

There has been a projector of this kind at
Leicefter, in the frame-work-knitting way;
and the knitters have rifen, and pulled his ma-
chine to pieces. I am greatly fhocked at tu-
multuous affemblies and violence : they are
fure to generate a fpirit of infurrection and
riot ; and it will be in vain to fay to this fpirit,
fo far fhalt thou go, and no farther. Neverthelefs, my heart is made to ache almoft daily by
the complaints of poor fufferers; not only of
fome, who (fuch is the prefent unfortunate
ftate of our provifions) cannot procure the
common comforts of life, even with all their
honeft induftry ; but of others alfo, who could
procure them, if they could but procure em-

---

[83] Epift. 106.

ployment.

ployment. Yet, furely, the labourers and manufacturers are not thofe, who ought to be folely, or perhaps even the moft, alarmed at any contrivances to abridge labour; for if thefe fhall come to have nothing to do, every body knows at whofe expence they are to live.

Mean while, it is not in the nature of things, that all times fhould be the fame. If we do fuffer any little hardfhips under the prefent, let us bear them with patience and contentednefs; in full affurance, that God, in his good time, will enable the inftruments and minifters of his government to remove them.

I am, Sirs, yours, &c.

P. S. That the ftrength of any kingdom is in proportion to its populoufnefs, is a favourite axiom with many; and it may be admitted, *always provided*, that objects can be found for the hands to be employed. But the abridgment of labour will not ferve to this purpofe. Nothing hath conduced more to the abridgment of labour, than the late rage in fome countries of inclofing open fields, and thereby converting much of arable land to pafturage. Yet this may be borne, nor will any great inconvenience be felt, while trade or manufactures can employ the hands which are not wanted in agriculture. But fuppofe a deathblow to be given to trade (and let us remember,

ber, that all things, which have a beginning, will fooner or later have alfo an ending) what is to become of the innumerable manufacturers? Will the populoufnefs of a nation *then* be the ftrength of it? Will it not rather be a moft oppreffive burthen?

XXIII.

TO THE FOUNDERS, PROPRIETORS, AND MANAGERS OF THE PANTHEON [84].

GENTLEMEN,

WHEN you conceived the defign of your magnificent ftructure, you undoubtedly had in view the reception and amufement of thofe chiefly, who are diftinguifhed by their birth and fortunes. The very title fets forth your purpofe: for *Pantheon* is compofed of two Greek words, which fignify a receptacle for all the Gods; and originally expreffed a temple in ancient Rome, which the Deities then in fafhion were fuppofed to honour with their prefence.

[84] This Number was printed in the *St. James's Chronicle* of March 21, 1772; and was occafioned by a rumour, that the proprietors of the *Pantheon* meant to confine it to *the quality*, and to exclude *the people*.

From

From the heathenifm of the name, you have been imagined by fome to have defigned it only for thofe who have rejected the Chriftian religion, in oppofition to thofe who ftill retain it : but this conftruction is altogether invidious. Befides, the fcheme would have been quite impracticable ; fince fome few Chriftians, at leaft, would have been fure to creep in, under one difguife or other, in fpite of all your care to keep them out.

Others have drawn a different conclufion from your title, but in my humble opinion equally remote with the former from your true intent and meaning. Thefe, far from fuppofing you to confine yourfelves to any particular rank and character, have on the contrary fuppofed you ready to admit all characters, not excluding even the worft; fuch as gamblers, cheats, whores, and debauchees of the very firft and moft illuftrious magnitude. And they affect to fuppofe this, becaufe the ancient *Pantheon* was prefenced with characters not unlike ; for even whores, and fharpers, and debauchees were found among its Deities.

But we have, happily for us, no fuch characters among thofe, to whom yours is dedicated. Your *Pantheon*, gentlemen, is dedicated to the very flower and quinteffence of the kingdom ; to thofe who muft be called, if any can be called, the Gods and Goddeffes among the

sons of men.   And I wish you had recollected
this speech of Quartilla, the priestess of Pria-
pus, in Petronius: *Utique nostra regio tam præ-
sentibus plena est numinibus, ut facilius possis deum
quam hominem invenire*; that is, "certainly our
"part of the town abounds so with Deities,
"that you may sooner find a God than a
"man." It would have graced your frontis-
piece very well : and there would have been a
striking propriety in it, on your assembly-
nights especially.

But could any doubt remain about the de-
signation of your *Pantheon*, the following cir-
cumstance shews, that you intended it for this
superior order of beings.   For it is sufficiently
known, that as soon as it was finished, and ripe
for consecration, you very judiciously, as well
as very sublimely, appropriated this ceremony
to their High Mightinesses, the Peeresses of the
Realm.   You vested in them solely the power
of the keys ; the power of admitting and excluding whom they, in the plenitude of their
wisdom, should or should not deem worthy of
the honour.

And sorry am I to say, that this measure of
yours, however wisely conceived and deeply
projected, has taken for you a most unfortunate turn.   By aiming rather officiously to
please the Lords, you have exceedingly diso-
bliged the Commons.   These deride you :
they

they confider your overture to the Peereffes, as a ftroke of the moft fervile adulation; and they deteft you, as a company of fawning fyco-phants, who are willing and ready " to rufh " headlong into flavery" *(in fervitium ruere,* as Tacitus expreffes it) without awaiting that gradual progreffion of manners now prevail-ing, which at long run are fure to introduce it. And what is worfe and more mortifying than even this, while the Commons fpurn at your contempt of their lower order, the Peereffes do not feem to have a fufficient *reffentiment* of the homage you have paid them.

Should this unfortunate conftruction of your good meaning defeat the ufe and intent of your magnificent pile, as it is generally believed it will; fhould your *Pantheon* become in con-fequence unfafhionable and unfrequented, you will have nothing left to do, but to convert it into a church; and for this you have an il-luftrious precedent. The ancient *Pantheon* at Rome was converted into a church by Pope Boniface IV. in the year 607, and confecrated to the Virgin Mary, and All Saints, under the name of *Sancta Maria Rotunda.* Indeed no-thing was more common, in the early ages of Chriftianity, when the converfion of the hea-then world was pretty well advanced, than to give Chriftian names to heathen temples, and to appropriate them to Chriftian ufes; juft as they

they gave Chriftian names to heathen rites and ceremonies, which they alſo adopted and employed in the Chriſtian myſteries.

However, gentlemen, let what will happen, you need not be in any mighty panic. The worſt I ſuppoſe you have to fear, is, that the public may at length **be** brought to aſcribe to you more money than **wit ;** and that **indeed is** very likely to happen.

I am, Gentlemen,

Your humble ſervant,

The Man of the Hill.

XXIV.

UPON " NOLO EPISCOPARI."

IN the Dedication of Balguy's Sermons **to** the King, his Majeſty's goodneſs is acknowledged " both in naming him to an high ſta-" tion in the church, **and in** allowing him to " decline **it.**" The writer, from whom I learn this, aſks, whether there be " another inſtance " upon **record** of a *Nolo Epiſcopari*, declared " in good earneſt [85] ?" **Yet** why ſhould it ſeem

[85] St. James's Chronicle, 16 April, 1785.

wonderful,

wonderful, that a man of near feventy years of
age, who has always enjoyed independency and
his own humour, and has a fund for contemplation and happinefs within himfelf, fhould refufe to facrifice eafe and leifure, and fubmit to
the reftraint of crowds and bufinefs? But thus
it is, that men make one another, as they ufually make their God [86], according to the ftandard and image of themfelves: what they feel
poffible or practicable within themfelves, *may*
be done; while all above their feelings or conceptions paffes for vifion, and not *in rerum na-
turâ* [87].

Is there a woman who could refufe " a title,
" a ribbon, a pompous equipage, and a great
" eftate?" Impoffible, would the general reply
be; becaufe the generality of women could
not refufe them. Yet, when Mrs. Vigor was
congratulated by her female friend, upon the
profpect of marrying a gentleman with thefe
accomplifhments, " Can you," faid the fpirited
dame, " can you have fo mean, fo contempt-
" ible a thought of me, to imagine, that

---

[86] Almoft all mankind are, in one fenfe, *Anthropomor-
phites*: for, though they may not all fuppofe the Deity of
human form, or to have a body like ours, yet each is apt to
afcribe to him his own ideas, temper, paffions, prejudices,
&c.

[87] *Quæ fibi quifque facilia factu putet, æquo animo accipit;
fupra, veluti ficta pro falfis ducit.* Salluft.

G   " thefe

" thefe alone would be of any weight? It muft
" be either a fordid foul, or a very trifling
" mind, that can be charmed with what is fo
" often the decoration of a fool or a knave [38]."

XXV.

THE CURE OF LOVE.

O QUANTUM eft in rebus inane! " Oh
what vanity in human things!" Damon
dies for Cælia, or (which is worfe) lives in
mifery. Rhafes, an Arabian phyfician, hath faid,
in his treatife upon the *Prefervation of Health,*
that " concubinage is an excellent cure for
" perfons defperately in love:" but, however
efficacious a remedy this might be with Ma-
hometans, it cannot even be mentioned among
Chriftians.

Did Damon ever hear what the woman at
Lincoln faid, as fhe was coming from the minfter, after having been married? She thanked
God, moft devoutly, that " the troublefome
" bufinefs of love was *now* at an end."—Will
this be any eafement to Damon's paffion? But,
if this fhould not fuffice, let the following re-

[38] See her *Letters from Ruffia.*

cipe

cipe be tranfcribed from Lord Bacon's Apophthegms : I mean, if the very grave reader will .
permit. " A wife, in bed with her hufband,
" pretended to be ill at eafe, and defired to
" lie on her hufband's fide. The good man,
" to pleafe her, paffed over her ; not, how-
" ever, without being fomewhat detained in
" the tranfit. She had not lain long, before
" fhe wifhed to lie in her old place again ;
" and urging her hufband to repafs the road he
" came, *I had rather*, faid he to her, *go a mile*
" *and an half about*." Apophth. 45.

XXVI.

YOU HAD BETTER LEAVE THEM TO FIGHT IT OUT.

A CERTAIN old Roman, being come to
Greece as Proconful, affembled the philofophers at Athens, and offered to affift in fet-
tling their difputes, and in bringing about at
laft an *agreement* in their opinions : upon which
" they all *agreed*," fays Tully, " in laughing
" at him for his pains [89]." This was pleafant,

[89] De Leg. I. 20.

and.

and no harm enfued ; but it is far from ending thus in general.

To interfere with parties who quarrel, with what good meaning foever, is always a nice and delicate affair ; and, inftead of effecting the fervice intended, is ufually rewarded with contempt or ill treatment. *Pray, neighbour, don't beat your wife thus*, faid the man in the play, who humanely interpofed upon a brute of a hufband: *But,* fays the wife, turning fhort upon him, *fuppofe, Sir, that I have a mind to be beat : what bufinefs is that of yours ? Aye, Sir,* continued the hufband, **what bufinefs is** *that of yours ?* And thus the ftorm increafed, till the poor peace-maker was fairly driven off[90].—Human nature, contemplated upon a larger fcale, fhews itfelf precifely thus. In the civil wars of France between the *Frondeurs* and *Mazarins,* the famous Chriftina of Sweden " had a " ftrong defire to interpofe. She offered her " mediation," fays the hiftorian, " which no " body wanted. She wrote to the Prince of " Condé, to the Parliament, to the Duke of " Orleans, *&c.* The Cardinal did not thank " her ; the Queen was ftill lefs fatisfied ; and " the public opinion was, that by intermed- " dling in an affair, which no way concerned " her, fhe had acted contrary to decorum, and

---

[90] Moliere, *Malade Imaginaire.*

" to

" to her dignity. Hence the cool reception
" she met with at the court, when she passed
" through France after her abdication [90]."

XXVII.

OF VANITY AND LYES.

VANITY and lyes are often joined together
by Solomon; and what so naturally ac-
companies *vanity*, as *lyes?* The vain man's aim
is, upon all occasions, to appear *bigger than the
life*, as the painters say; and his immediate object,
like that of Bayes in the Rehearsal, to *elevate* and
surprise. For this sole purpose he will not only
tell the most stupendous lyes about himself, his
family, his fortune, &c. but he will also perform actions, from which even self-preservation
should naturally restrain him : and I have seen
an aspirant after this sort of celebrity, gallop
on horse-back down a flight of stone stairs,
purely to make me wonder how he durst do
it.

[90] Henault, *Chron. Abreg.* anno 1653.

XXVIII

A CURE FOR LYING.

MENDOSUS was a conftant and notorious liar; fo notorious and fo conftant, that (as ufually happens) he did not gain credit, even when he fpake truth. Sometimes he lyed, in order to defame, and therein gratify a fpirit of malignity; at other times for intereft, and to gain fome advantage; at other times he would tell *incredibilia* and *portentofa*, merely from a paffion to *elevate* and *furprife*: and, in fhort, the habit was fo predominant and ftrong, that he would lye without any view or meaning conceivable. Once upon a time, however, a quack undertook, by a fingular *noftrum*, to cure this evil quality, all inveterate as it was; and with the faireft propofal of *no cure no pay*. The recipe was adminiftered in the form of a pill, with a direction to the patient to grind it well with his teeth, left the virtues of it fhould efcape for want of maftication. After champing and champing fome time, he afked the quack, what the deuce he had given him? for that it feemed very nafty; and, taking it out of his mouth, whether from its afpect or its favour, pronounced

it

it to be a *t—d. Truth, by G—*, says the quack, and claimed his pay : but the cure was only momentary, for the patient (as was **said**) immediately relapsed.

XXIX.

A MAN OF HONOUR.

MONS. VOLTAIRE, observing upon certain *dramatis personæ* in Congreve's Plays, says, that " their language is every where that " of *men of honour*, but their actions are those " of knaves : **a proof, that he was perfectly** " well acquainted with human nature, and " frequented **what we** call **polite** company [92]." So that the arrantest scoundrel, the blackest and most detestable villain, by frequenting polite company, and pretending to an higher and more refined integrity, may be denominated **a** *man of honour.* What a perverse and ridiculous use of **words, which convey an** idea just the contrary to what **they** express !—" We " know very well," says Bruyere, " that an " honest man is a man of honour ; but it is " pleasant to conceive, that every man of ho-

[92] Letters on the English Nation, 19th.

G 4

" nour

" nour is not an honeft man [93]."   Pleafant indeed; but this is not the worft : fociety fuffers
from this abufe of terms.   " By feparating the
" *man of honour* from the man of virtue," fays
Hume, " the greateft profligates have got
" fomething to value themfelves upon ; **and**
" have been able to keep themfelves in coun-
" tenance, though **guilty of the** moft fhame-
" ful and dangerous vices.   They are debau-
" chees, fpendthrifts, and never pay a farthing
" they owe : but they are *men of honour*, and
" therefore to be received as *gentlemen* in all
" companies." *Ita noftri mores coegerunt.*

XXX.

OF JESTING AND FROLIC, AS WELL AS JESTING UPON SERIOUS OCCASIONS AND SERIOUS MAT-TER; AND OF DAVID HUME, ESQ. SO FAR AS HE IS CONCERNED IN THIS.

DULCE eft defipere, " 'tis delightful to play
the fool," fays Horace : Scipio was the
boy, **and even Cato** would unbend; as if it

[93] *On connoît affez, qu'un homme de bien eft honnête homme ; mais il eft plaifant d' imaginer, que tout honnête homme n'eft pas homme de bien.* Charact. *des Jugemens.*

                                                    were

were not right " to be wife at all hours," *om-*
nibus horis fapere. Very well : play the fool,
be the boy ; but remember that you do thefe,
as Horace adds, *in loco*—that is, " at proper
" times, and before proper perfons." For, if
the gay and frolicfome humour, however innocent, be fuffered to expatiate at random and
at large—before fools who cannot, or malevo-
lents who will not, underftand it—you may afterwards hear comments upon it, which will
ftrangely furprife you. Yes, your fooleries
may be magnified into crimes ; and you may
have fact as well as meaning imputed to you,
of which 'tis likely you never thought : for, as
in Shakfpeare,

> *You* do not *act*, who often *jeft* and laugh :
> 'Tis old but true, *ftill fwine eat all the draugh.*

An habit of jefting leads into many fcrapes :
but the moft ferious furely that ever attended
it, is one recorded by Speed in the reign of
Edward the Fourth ; when a citizen in Cheap-
fide was executed as a traitor, for **faying**, that
he would *make his fon heir to the Crown*, though
he only meant his houfe, which had a crown
for its fign.

Jefting in illnefs, or **at** the point of death, is
reckoned not barely indecent, but almoft profane : as, when one, who was proceeding to
the gallows, advifed his conductors not to carry
him

him through such a street, lest a merchant, who lived there, should arrest him for a debt; or, as when a dying Catholic, upon the priest's approaching for extreme unction, and asking where his feet were, which pain it seems had made him pull up, replied with seeming gravity, *at the end of my legs*. And numbers, I doubt not, have had hard work to reconcile Sir Thomas More's piety with his mirth upon the scaffold; namely, in desiring the executioner to put his beard aside, since " *It* had " not committed any treason." They have thought, perhaps, that, as we come whining *into* the world, so it is decent to go whining *out* of it [94].

There is, however (and it ought to be noted) an extreme opposite to *whining*, which is no less **weak and** unmanly; and that is, an *affectation* of mirth **and** gaiety at this solemn period—for solemn, **at** least, it most certainly is. Hume ne-

---

[94] *Partridge* seems to have approved of this: for, when *Jones*, in a fit of despair, resolved for the army, and to die as soon as might be in the field of glory, *Partridge* shrunk with horror under the idea. " I know," said he, " we " must all die; but then there's a great difference be- " tween dying in one's bed, a great many years hence, " like a good Christian, with all our friends crying about " us, and being shot to-day or to-morrow like a mad dog; " or perhaps hacked in twenty pieces with a sword, and " that too before we have repented of our sins." B. xii, ch. 3.

ver appears to me under a more unphilofophic
attitude, than when he fports about Charon at
the clofe of his life. Was this to fhew, that
he died a philofopher as he had lived; and
could ridicule the dreams about futurity, with
which others are haunted, at this trying crifis?
—There was certainly fome bravado, fome *parade of magnanimity*, in this; as I fufpect there
was, when, fpeaking of his laft illnefs, which
was a diarrhœa of more than a year's ftanding,
he fays, that, " were he to name the period of
" his life, which he fhould moft chufe to pafs
" over again, he might be tempted to point
" to this later period[95]." Is this conceivable?
—*Scire tuum nihil eft, nifi te fcire id fciat alter?*
Is philofophy then nothing, unlefs exhibited
oftentatiouſly to the public?

XXXI.

OF REFORMATIONS[96].

THE work of reformation, in church and
in ftate, hath long been agitated; and,
doubtlefs, there are many things in both, that

[95] Life by himfelf.   [96] From *The Irenarch.*

may

may well be thought to want it. Some, however, averſe from reforming, think it more expedient to *temporize* with prevailing manners
and cuſtoms; and would rather acquieſce under, than attempt a correction of, the numerous irregularities and evils with which we
abound. This may be juſt and good, as well
as wiſe and politic, in certain ſituations : yet,
if we mean any thing when we talk of human
perfection and human happineſs, it muſt ſurely
be right to correct errors and abuſes; nor can
reformation poſſibiy be deemed unreaſonable,
always provided, that the reformers, amidſt
their zeal, will ponder well the materials, *the
ſtuff,* they have to work upon [97]; leſt, being
hurried on by viſions, and ideas of a perfection
not to be attained, they produce greater evils
than thoſe they would remove.

In the laſt century, by puſhing the ſpirit of
reforming too far, greater evils were produced
than the reformers had it in their view to remove. Reſiſtance was made to the encroach-
ments of regal power, and made ſuccefsfully :
but did the ſpirit of reforming reſt here? No;
it proceeded till the monarchy was deſtroyed.

---

[97] *Mens humana, ſi agat in materiam, naturam rerum con-
templando, pro modo materiæ operatur, atque ab eadem determi-
natur.* Bacon.—And is not this as neceſſary in the world of
ſpirit, as in the world of *matter?*

And

And what followed then ? Why, anarchy fucceeded monarchy ; a republic, fuch as it was,
fucceeded anarchy ; a protectorate fucceeded a
republic ; and, finally, the nation, having reel-
ed to and fro from one form of government
to another, and having found no reft under
any, recurred at length to a monarchy, more
arbitrary even with their own confent, and
more pernicious in its confequences, than that
which had been abolifhed.   But to proceed.

The objects of reformation are, *manners, opinions*, and *eftablifhments*.   On the article of
manners, enough has been written : enough to
fhew, that *manners* cannot be reformed by *laws*,
but only by education, or an eftablifhed fyftem
of early difcipline [98]. With regard to *opinions*, I
am free to own, with Mr. *Bayle*, that " there
" are no truths fo minute, but what are wor-
" thy to be promoted ; no errors fo trifling,
" but what had better be corrected than re-
" tained. But, when the circumftances of time
" and place will not fuffer novelties to be pro-
" pofed, though ever fo true, without occa-
" fioning a thoufand diforders," I muft alfo
concur with Mr. *Bayle* in fuppofing, that " it
" were much better to let things remain as
" they are, than undertake to reform them ;
" fince the remedy would be worfe than the
" difeafe [99]." To which I may add, that, after

[98] See No LIII.   [99] Dict. Arminius, Note E.

all

all the reformation which can be made, every man will have, becaufe every man muft have, his own *opinion* ftill. Ιδιοσυνκρασία is defined by a certain phyfician *humorum illud* **peculiare** *temperamentum, unde fua eft cuique fanitas, fuus cuique morbus:* and might he not have added, if his fubject had required it, *fua cuique indoles, fua cuique OPINIO?*—To fuppofe that any man fhould think as I do, is to fuppofe that man organized as I am; that he has received the fame temperament, the fame nutriment, **the fame education,** and (which includes all) **the fame modification, with** me, in every in-**ftant** of his duration: in one word, it is **to** fup-pofe, that *be* is what *I* am. Why not expect from him a conformity of features, as well as a conformity of opinions, with mine? the for-mer, as fhould feem, being juft as much in his power, as the latter. ·

With regard to *eftablifhments*, I fuppofe my-felf to diffent from thofe, whom the fpirit of reforming agitates the moft, only in this; that, whereas they would have the principle of re-formation to operate at *all* times, and in *all* fituations of things, I would limit and confine it **to** *certain* times and *certain* conjunctures. " There is a time for all things," fays a great reformer : " it is *not every conjuncture* which " calls with equal force upon the activity of " honeft men; but critical exigencies now and

then

then arife ([98])." As therefore, on the one hand, I would not, with a *Leviathan* ſpirit, aſſert the rectitude of *maintaining* at all events whatever was eſtabliſhed ; ſo, on the other, I would aſſert the wiſdom and expediency of *tolerating*, not only imperfections, but even evils, in an eſtabliſhment, until thoſe evils can be removed without producing greater. And I ſeem to aſſert this upon the ſureſt foundation ; becauſe the principle of reformation, unleſs reſtrained by this qualifying clauſe, will never ſuffer the world to remain in quiet. As ſurely as no eſtabliſhment can be perfect, ſo ſurely will reformers never be wanting to diſturb it ([99]). I know

---

([98]) Mr. Burke.—See to what an extent Eraſmus carried the idea of waiting for *conjunctures*, in the buſineſs of reforming religion. *Scio quidvis eſſe ferendum potius, quam ut publicus orbis ſtatus turbetur in pejus : ſcio pietatem eſſe nonnunquam celare veritatem ; neque eam quovis loco, neque quovis tempore, neque apud quoſvis, neque quovis modo, neque totam ubique promendam.* Epiſt. 501.

([99]) The world can never remain in peace, becauſe ſectaries and fanatics will every where think it a duty to diſturb it :—

> And prove *their* doctrine orthodox
> By apoſtolic blows and knocks ;
> Call fire, and ſword, and deſolation,
> A godly thorough reformation :
> Which always muſt be carried on,
> And ſtill be doing, never done ;
> As if religion were intended
> For nothing elſe but to be mended.
>
> HUDIBRAS.

the

the difficulty of afcertaining the crifis, when reformation is to commence;—this muft be determined by the circumftances of time and place—yet I cannot forbear to think as I do: and, if I am in error, it muft be my love of peace and good order that has mifled me. " Very many perfons," fays Mr. *Bayle*, " will " inflexibly adhere to this maxim, That it is a " leffer evil to bear with abufes in church and " ftate, than to cure them by remedies which " will overturn the conftitution in church and " ftate [100]." **I muft** own myfelf to be one of thefe perfons: and am ready to fay, with the good Bifhop *Hall*, that *fome quiet error may be better than fome unruly truth* [101]; or, as *Erafmus* had faid before him, *mihi adeo eft invifa difcordia, ut veritas etiam difpliceat feditiofa.*

But it fhould feem, as if reformations in the **ftate** were far more eafy and far more practicable, than reformations in the church; and, accordingly, a worthy perfon hath lately exhibited a plan, very elaborately drawn, for *parliamentary independency* and *oeconomical reformation* [102]. I was affected with uncommon pleafure **at the report** of this plan, which (I thought) **was ftriking** directly at the root of the thing: for *true patriotifm*, as a great ftatefman obferved

[100] *Dict.* CASTELLANUS. Note Q.
[101] Decad. VI. Epift. 7.
[102] Burke's Speech, &c. on Feb. 11, 1780.

moft

moſt juſtly, *can have no foundation, but fruga-*
lity [101] ; and vain will be all attempts to render Members of Parliament *independent*, till
they can be cured of their extravagancies, and
prevailed on to be *oeconomiſts*. But, to my
very great grief as well as ſurpriſe, the plan of
reformation, here propoſed, has no reſpect at
all to the oeconomy of parliament-men, but
only to the expences of certain departments,
connected with and dependant on the court;
as if great and important ſavings might thence
be made to the nation. Too great ſavings cannot be made to the nation: the nation ſtands in
need of all that can be ſaved : and what Mr.
Burke advances, under this general idea, hath
a real foundation in reaſon and equity. I only
doubt, whether the honourable gentleman, in
purſuing this idea, doth not *contemplate* upon
too ſmall a ſcale, when he would reduce the
expences of royalty to the accuracy and preci-
ſion of private oeconomy. I doubt, alſo, whether the ſavings from this reduction would be
indeed of ſuch capital and eſſential importance,
as is imagined. And, laſtly, I doubt moſt of
all, whether, with our preſent manners, even
government itſelf could make the reformation
propoſed; that is, whether ſuch reformation be
really *practicable.*

But here, Mr. *Burke* hath been before us:

[101] Lord Bath, in *Swift's Letters.*

H   " I know,"

" I know," fays he, " it is common for men
" to fay, that fuch and fuch things are per-
" fectly right,—very defirable, but unfortu-
" nately not practicable. Oh, no, Sir, no:
" thofe things, which are not practicable, are
" not defirable [104]. Indeed? But, is not *parliamentary independency* defirable; and does it
thence follow, that it is attainable? *Parliamentary independency* muft be according to parliamentary manners; which, if we may truft the
reprefentation of thofe who knew them well,
are by no means favourable to it, at prefent.
The late Lord *Chefterfield*, fpeaking of Sir
Robert Walpole, delivers himfelf on this wife:
" Money was the chief engine of his admini-
" ftration, and he employed it with a fuccefs,
" which in a manner difgraced humanity. He
" was not, it is true, the inventor of that
" fhameful method of governing, which had
" been gaining ground infenfibly ever fince
" Charles II.; but, with uncommon fkill and
" unbounded profufion, he brought it to that
" perfection, which at this time difhonours and
" diftreffes this country, and which, if not
" checked *(and God knows how it can now be
" checked)* muft ruin it [105]." The late Lord
Bath, apologizing to *Swift* for defifting " to
" ftruggle againft corruption," declared " the
" whole nation to be fo abandoned and cor-

[104] *Speech*, &c.   [105] *Characters*, &c.

" rupt)

" rupt, that the Crown can never fail of a ma-
" jority in both Houſes of Parliament.—I am
" convinced," ſays he, " that our conſtitu-
" tion is already gone ; and we are idly ſtrug-
" gling to maintain, what in truth has been
" long loſt [106]."

Now, are things really ſo as theſe noble
Lords have repreſented them, or are they not?
for we preſume not to decide. If they be ſo,
why then, ſurely, this reformation in parliament, ſo confeſſedly *deſirable*, is not, however,
ſo confeſſedly *practicable* [107].—And whence, after all, ſhould *independency* ariſe ; or, were it
once upon its legs, how ſupport itſelf? " Can
" a nation, venal, vicious, and corrupt, long
" preſerve its liberty ? Liberty, to be reliſhed
" and preſerved, requires noble, brave, and
" virtuous ſouls : otherwiſe, it degenerates in-
" to licentiouſneſs, and ends by becoming the
" prey of a maſter who can purchaſe it. A
" people, without manners, is not made to be
" free : true liberty muſt be accompanied with

[106] *Swift's Letters.*

[107] No diſcouragement is here meant to any attempt towards reformation : duty as well as policy ſhould put us
upon reforming whatever can be reformed. We may mo-
derate evils, if we cannot remove them : and this perhaps
is all, the worthy perſon aims at ; governing himſelf by the
old rule, " of aſking too much, in order to obtain enough"
—*iniquum petere, ut æquum ferat.* Quintil. IV. 5.

H 2 " a love

" a love of equity, humanity, a deep senfe of
" the natural rights of men. Feelings of this
" kind can only be the fruits of a liberal and
" virtuous education ; far different from that
" narrrow and fervile mode of educating,
" which now prevails in every country. What
" then can be wanting to complete the hap-
" pinefs of a people, who glory in the beft
" and freeft conftitution ? What remains to be
" defired by a nation, into whofe ports the
" riches of the world find their way ? This re-
" mains to be defired : a generous education,
" integrity of manners, true notions of juftice ;
" in a word, difpofitions and appetites, oppo-
" fite to that ardent and unquenchable thirft
" after *filthy lucre*, the abundance whereof is
" fit only to ftifle and extinguifh virtues the
" moft noble, the moft ufeful to fociety.

  " People of Britain, whence thefe continual
" alarms ? thefe factions which tear you, thefe
" dark and fplenetic humours which devour
" you ? The treafures you accumulate, far
" from confirming your happinefs, are to you
" a never-ceafing fource of trouble. How is
" it, that, in the very bofom of liberty and
" abundance, we fee you deep in reverie, un-
" quiet, and more diffatisfied with your lot,
" than the meaneft and moft contemptible
" flaves ? Learn the true caufe of your anxieties
" and your fears. The love of gold never
                   " makes

" makes good citizens. Liberty cannot be
" firmly eftablifhed, but upon equity; or
" bravely defended, but by virtue. Leave to
" defpots the foolifh and deftructive glory of
" making conquefts, and be content with en-
" joying the bleffings of nature in peace. Cul-
" tivate then, O Britons, reafon and wifdom:
" employ yourfelves in perfecting your go-
" vernment and your laws. Fear luxury, fatal
" to manners, fatal to liberty: dread fanati-
" cifm, political and religious. So fhall your
" fortunate Ifle become the model of nations,
" and your liberty fhine propitious to all the
" people upon earth [108]."

XXXII.

OF LIBELS [109].

CONCERNING Libels and Libellers, much
hath been faid, and much hath been done.
Indeed too much, as I am free to think; and I
have often wifhed, that the public perfonages

[108] Une nation vénale, vicieufe, corrompue, peut-elle
donc long-tems conferver fa liberté? &c. Syftême Social.
Part II. ch. 6.

[109] Lord Bacon calls Libels, " the females of fedition;"
as if the fcolding, or tongue-part of the conflict, were performed by them. Hift. of Henry VII.

of the realm would not be quite fo tender-fibred and irritable, with regard to what is faid or written about them.

The famous Reformer Calvin told Francis I. that " there would be no fuch thing as inno-" cence, either in words or deeds, if a fimple " accufation was fufficient to deftroy it :" *nullam neque in dictis, neque in factis, innocentiam fore, fi accufaffe fufficiat* [110]. Now, if this be really fo, as I verily believe it is : if cenforious criticifm, detraction, and calumny, muft more efpecially accompany men, engaged in the tur-bid fphere of active life; and if nothing can fe-cure from thefe, but imbecility, infignificancy, indolence, or obfcurity,—of all which I am moft firmly perfuaded,—what is fatire and a-bufe ? no criterion, furely, of innocence or guilt : nothing, or it may be nothing, but the fermentations and ebullitions of human pre-judices and human paffions [111].—Befides, the profecution, or (which they will always call it)

[110] In Dedicat. Inftitut.

[111] What is fcandal? It is, as thus very juftly defined, *Sermo fine ullo certo auctore difperfus, cui malignitas initium dedit, incrementum credulitas ; quod nulli non, etiam innocentiffimo, poffit accidere :* that is, " a vague and fcandalous report, " from no certain author, invented by malice, and nurtured " by credulity ; and which" (contrary to the proverb of *no fmoke without fire)* " may be propagated of the moft in-" nocent man alive." Quintilian, V. 3.

the

the persecution, of Libellers can never produce any other effect, but to give weight and confequence to both the Libel and the Libeller: that of Tacitus being univerfally true, *punitis ingeniis glifcit auctoritas*. Nay, there is no occafion for *ingenuity*, if that idea be included here, to give a luftre to the profecution : fince nothing is more frequent, than that writers of neither fenfe, nor wit, nor learning, nor honefty, become, by being profecuted, poffeffed of them all.

Philofophers have from time to time held out to poor fufferers in this way (I mean, to thofe who have wept under the fmart of fatire) certain *medicamina mentis*, certain fpecifics to render the mind callous and infenfible to this fort of correction ; and one of them, I think, prefcribes the following *recipe* : " Whenever " you labour under defamation, or whenever " any thing falfe is reported to your difcredit, " confider, that it is not *you*, but fome imagi- " nary perfonage, to whom the imputed in- " famy belongs." But this feems nothing near fo efficacious, as the virulence and malignity of the cafe may require. For if *Robert*, miftaking in the dark, fhould fall upon the fhoulders of *Richard* with a cudgel, would the impreffions be lefs forcible, or the fenfations lefs lively, becaufe *Richard* might not be the perfon, for whom the favour was intended ? There is more good fenfe, if not fo much

H 4 fubtlety,

fubtlety, in the faying of Auguftus; who,
when urged by his fon-in-law to purfue this
race of fcribblers, replied, " Don't indulge
" a fpirit of refentment againft thefe our ad-
" verfaries; it is quite fufficient, that we are
" not in a fituation to be hurt by any one :"
*fatis eft, mi Tiberi, fi hoc habemus, ne quis nobis
malè facere poffit* [112].

But, neither does this entirely pleafe me :
for, firft, this Emperor derived his boafted
fecurity from ufurpation and tyranny; and,
then, he afterwards became himfelf a fevere
profecutor of libellous productions [113]. The example of Timoleon is more perfect in its kind.
This wife and virtuous man, being wrong-
fully accufed in an affembly of the people, inftead of refenting or even taking it ill, thanked the immortal Gods for granting what he had
fo often prayed for ; which was, that " the Sy-
" racufans might have the liberty of fpeaking
" what, and of whom, they would, with im-
" punity [114]." This example is, I fay, more
perfect; but then, alas ! it is too perfect for the
age we live in : it is above the ftrength of men, as
men are now—οἶοι νῦν βροτοί εἰσι. I chufe therefore, upon the whole, to recommend the beha-

---

[112] Sueton. *in Aug.* 51.

[113] *Primus Auguftus cognitionem de famofis Libellis, fpecie le-*
gis Majeftatis, tractavit. Tacit. Ann. I.

[114] Nepos *in Timol.*

viour of the Emperor Conftantine ; who, being importuned to punifh fome feditious perfons, for disfiguring his ftatues by throwing
ftones at them, did nothing more than calmly
ftroke his face, and tell his friends with a
fmile, that he *did not perceive himfelf to be
hurt* [115]. This cold contempt of what men fay
or think, feems to have been the fpecific of our
celebrated Doctor Swift againft impreffions
from the malignity of fcandal, as fet forth in
a poem he has left us ; which, being fhort and
edifying, may as well be here fubjoined.

ON CENSURE, in 1727.

YE wife, inftruct me to endure
An evil, which admits no cure:
Or how this evil can be borne,
Which breeds at once both hate and fcorn.
Bare innocence is no fupport,
When you are tried in fcandal's court.
Stand high in honour, wealth, and wit:
All others who inferior fit
Conceive themfelves in confcience bound
To join and drag you to the ground.
Your altitude offends the eyes
Of thofe, who want the power to rife.
The world, a willing ftander-by,
Inclines to aid a fpecious lye :

[115] Chryfoftom. *Homil.* 20.

" Alas !

" Alas ! they would not do you wrong,
" But all appearances are ftrong."

 Yet, whence proceeds this weight we lay
On what detracting people fay ?
For let mankind difcharge their tongues
In venom, till they burft their lungs,
Their utmoft malice cannot make
Your head, or tooth, or finger ake :
Nor fpoil your fhape, diftort your face,
Or put one feature out of place :
Nor will you find your fortune fink,
By what they fpeak, or what they think :
Nor can ten hundred thoufand lyes
Make you lefs virtuous, learn'd, or wife.

 The moft effectual way to baulk
Their malice, is—*to let them talk.*

XXXIII.

OF THE LIBERTY OF THE PRESS.

" THE Liberty of the Prefs," faith a certain
  writer [116], " is the palladium of all the
" civil, political, and religious rights of an
" Englifhman,"—to which I have no objection : but he contends, that " no particular

[116] *Junius,* in Dedicat. Pref. and Lett. 61.

           " abufes

" abuses ought, in reason and equity, to pro-
" duce a general forfeiture, or to abolish the
" use of it,"—to which I must object very
loudly. I agree, that *abuse* ought not to abolish *use*; but I insist, that this position cannot
be maintained so absolutely, as is here supposed. For, surely, whenever the evils, arising
from the *abuse*, shall *exceed* the evils, which
would arise from *abolishing the use*, then this
use in reason ought to be *abolished*; provided
only, that the *abuse* be incorrigible.

With regard to the Liberty of the Press, I
shall not descant, whether abuses *ought* or *ought
not* to abolish its use: persuaded am I sincerely,
that, if our present manners hold, they most
assuredly *will*. When the Press ridicules openly
and barefacedly the most revered and fundamental doctrines of religion: when the Press, in
political matters, attacks persons without any
regard to things, or perhaps attacks things for
the sake of abusing persons: when the Press
not only wantonly assaults the first characters
in church and state, but even sacrifices the
peace and quiet of private families to the sport
and entertainment of an ill-natured public :—
and is it not notorious, that all this is done
daily [117]?—then, I say, this noble, reasonable,
and

[117] " Such writings the vulgar more greedily read, as
" being taken with petulance and scurrility. They are the
" food

and manly Liberty is degenerated into a bafe, unwarrantable, cruel licentioufnefs ; and this licentioufnefs—determine as logically, and contend as loudly, as you pleafe—will, by an unavoidable confequence flowing from the nature and conftitution of things, fooner or later bring about its deftruction. Things are fo formed, that extremes muft ever beget, and prepare the way for, extremes. Abufes of every thing muft deftroy the ufe of every thing: and if the people grow *licentious* and ungovernable, it is as natural, perhaps as neceffary, for their rulers to increafe their reftraint, and abridge their *liberty*, as for the breakers of horfes to tighten the reins, in proportion as their fteeds fhall fhew an impatience to be managed [118].

It has been faid, that without freedom of thought there can be no fuch thing as wifdom,

---

" food of men's natures, the diet of the times. The writer " muft lye ; and the gentle reader refts happy, to hear " the worthieft works mifinterpreted, the cleareft actions " obfcured, the innocenteft life traduced." *Ben Jonfon's Difcoveries.*

[118] Montaigne looked upon " fcribbling, as the fign of " a licentious age ;" and thought, that " there fhould be " laws againft foolifh and impertinent fcribblers, as well " as againft vagabonds and idle perfons." *Effais,* iii. 9. The misfortune is, that it would be difficult to draw the line betwixt foolifh and wife fcribblers ; and a licenfer, with an *imprimatur,* would defeat the end of all fcribblers, wife as well as foolifh.

nor

nor any fuch thing as liberty without freedom
of fpeech : and, becaufe the latter is true in a
qualified fenfe, and under certain limitations,
the authority of Tacitus has been abfurdly and
even ftupidly obtruded, as a warrant to take off
all reftraint, and allow ourfelves an unbounded
licence, as well in fpeaking as in thinking.
" Rare and happy times," fays he, " when a
" man may think what he will, and fpeak what
" he thinks :" *rara temporum felicitas, ubi fen-
tire quæ velis, et quæ fentias dicere, licet.* Rare
and happy times indeed ! But pray, good
Sirs, what times were thofe, or who has read
of any times, when men were not at liberty to
think as they would? A man may *think as he
pleafes* in the worft times, as well as in the beft,
becaufe thought, as they fay, is at all times
free : but can a man at any time, or under
any government, even the beft, be allowed the
liberty of *fpeaking what he pleafes*, of commu-
nicating himfelf up to the ftandard of his
ideas ? May every man fpeak of every man,
what, for inftance, the fpleen of humour, or the
caprice of imagination, fhall happen to fuggeft ?—But thefe gentry, in truth, know as little of Tacitus, as they do of fociety, and what
it will bear. " If life remains," fays he, " I
" have referved, for the employment of my
" old age, the reign of the deified Nerva,
" with

" with that of the Emperor Trajan ; a work
" more copious, as well as more fafe : fuch is
" the rare felicity of thefe times, when you are
" at full liberty to entertain what fentiments
" you pleafe, and to declare what fentiments
" you entertain." *To declare what fentiments
you entertain :* yes, but of whom, or what ?—
not of every man you meet, or of every thing
that happens : Tacitus underftood human affairs in a different manner : but—of thofe particular reigns, oppofed to former tyrannical
reigns ; when men, far from fpeaking our,
durft fcarcely truft themfelves even with their
own thoughts.

It is remarkable, that the freeft thinkers, as
as well as the freeft fpeakers, have never allowed fuch a licence in theory, whatever themfelves may have taken in practice. " Let us
" feek truth," fays one, " but feek it *quietly*
" as well as freely. Let us not imagine, like
" fome who are called free-thinkers, that
" every man, who can think and judge for
" himfelf, as he has a right to do, has there-
" fore a *right of fpeaking*, any more than of
" acting, according to the *full freedom* of his
" thoughts. The freedom belongs to him as
" a rational creature : he lies under reftraint as
" a member of fociety.—We may communi-
" cate our thoughts only fo, as it may be done

5

" without

" without offending the laws of our country,
" and disturbing the public peace[119]."

And if this be true about things and opinions, shall it not be so, *a fortiori*, when applied to persons and characters? Must a philosopher be circumspect and guarded, when treating of abstract propositions, or discussing speculative points which few can comprehend; while any low, malicious, unprincipled wretch shall be permitted to scatter firebrands indiscriminately in society, and vomit out scurrility and abuse, without justice and without measure? Will any man say, that *the laws of our country are not offended*, and *the peace of society disturbed*, more in the latter case than in the former?—I know it will be asked, where will you draw the line of distinction? how ascertain the point, where liberty ends, and licentiousness begins? and I shall in this, as in many other cases, allow the extreme difficulty of marking boundaries[120], and reducing human affairs to precision and exactness; but I believe nevertheless, that, unless some expedient can be hit upon to correct the very atrocious abuse of the Press, the destruction of its use will be found unavoidable.

[119] *Lord Bolingbroke.*
[120] *Rerum natura nullam dedit cognitionem finium, ut ullâ in re statuere possimus, quatenus,* &c. Cicero.

As

As to any *formed* defign againft the Liberty of the Prefs, about which fome have dreamed, I cannot fuffer myfelf to be at all apprehenfive of it : it is of more ufe and importance to a King of Great Britain, than (if poffible) to any of his fubjects ; and this alone fuffices with me to ftifle and keep down every rifing jealoufy. In abfolute defpotic governments, where the will of the Prince is the law of the country, where all things are adminiftered by force and arms, and where the glory of the *Grand Monarque* is the fole end and object of the monarchy, it matters not much for him to know, what the condition of his fubjects is, and what they fay or think about him : but in a qualified and limited monarchy, like ours, where the King is no more than the Firft Magiftrate appointed by the people, where he is as bound to obey the laws as the meaneft of his fubjects, and where the well-being of thefe fubjects is the fole end of his appointment—furely to fuch a Prince it muft be of the laft confequence to know, as minutely as he can, what is doing in every corner of his kingdom ; what the ftate and condition of his fubjects; whether they enjoy plenty, proportioned to their induftry ; and whether, in fhort, the end of his kingly government be in every refpect anfwered ? All this, I fay, and more, a King of Great Britain

- muft

muſt know as he can : but—how muſt he know it ?

A King, let his *diſcernment of ſpirits* be what it will, let him pry ever ſo acutely into the heads and hearts of thoſe about him, will never be able to pierce through the manifold diſguiſes, which courtiers always know how to wrap themſelves in. By courtiers are not meant thoſe gaudy painted images, which move mechanically about a palace, and are really nothing more than ſo much furniture ; but thoſe, who are entruſted with the great offices, to whom the adminiſtration of affairs is committed, and who for the moſt part manage and direct the reins of government as they pleaſe. And as he cannot diſcover, by any natural ſagacity in *himſelf*, the latent principles of things, any more than the real characters of perſons ; ſo he muſt not expect to receive any *effectual* information from *others*. For, I ſuppoſe, it will be no ſatire upon any particular court, that now is, or ever was, to ſay, that there never was a Prince, who was told by any of his ſervants all thoſe truths, which it concerned him to know. At leaſt this ſeems a propoſition ſo very well grounded, that I do not think the ſevere plain-dealing of a Clarendon, or the honeſt bluntneſs of a Sully, ſufficient to form an exception to it. The Emperor Diocletian made the difficulty of reigning well, to conſiſt chiefly

I ·in

in the difficulty of arriving at the real knowledge of affairs. " Four or five courtiers,"
says he, " form themselves into a cabal, and
" unite in their counsels to deceive the Em-
" peror. They say what will please their maf-
" ter; who, being shut up in his palace, is a
" stranger to the truth, and forced to know
" only what they think fit to tell him [121]."

Now this great hindrance to good government, as Diocletian thought it, is almost, if
not altogether, removed by the justly valued
Liberty of the Press. By means of this, the
lowest subject may find access to the Throne;
and, by means of this, the King has a key, if
I may so call it, to all manner of intelligence:
nor is there any thing, the least important to
government, of which he can remain long un-
informed, unless he designedly shuts his eyes.
It is not meant that he should suddenly adopt,
as real truth and matter of fact, every thing
which may be read in the public prints:

---

[121] *Diocletianus dixit, nihil esse difficilius quàm bene imperare.
Colligunt se quatuor vel quinque, atque unum consilium ad deci-
piendum Imperatorem capiunt. Dicunt, quid probandum sit.
Imperator, qui domi clausus est, vera non novit: cogitur tantum hoc scire, quod illi loquuntur.* Vopiscus in Aureliano.——
" Princes," says Ben Jonson, " learn no art truly, but
" the art of horsemanship. The reason is, the brave beast
" is no flatterer: he will throw a Prince, as soon as his
" groom." *Discoveries.*

and many perhaps may think, that amidst so much misrepresentation and error, so much partiality and disguise, so much indiscriminate scurrility and abuse, he can hardly depend upon any thing at all, or take any measures from such a chaos of truth and falsehood. But of this chaos, were it ten times more so, it is indisputably certain, that very much use, and very many advantages, may be made. The King may be directed to find, what he would never have thought of looking for : more than glimmerings will ever and anon appear, which will enable him to push his discoveries far ; and he will trace from hence many things to their source, which would otherwise have remained for ever unknown. In short, from these public intelligencers, some things will be hinted, others spoken out more freely, others presented in their full glare ; and thus, upon the whole, all concerns of moment will lie open before him.

Wicked and selfish ministers know this so well, that we have often heard of management, in courts very corrupt, to stop up these channels of intelligence to the Prince. They know, that by them a constant commerce, correspondence, and union, as it were, may be maintained between the Prince and his people. They know, that while these are so maintained, they vainly attempt to cabal, and to impose upon their mafter; and if, notwithftanding, they will not tell him all the truth they fhould, yet they dare not abufe him with mifreprefentation and lyes. Why? becaufe difcovery is inftantly at hand, and becaufe difgrace and ruin will tread upon the heels of it. So that, all things confidered, the advantage to the Sovereign from the Liberty of the Prefs is one great fecurity with me for the continuance and prefervation of it; nor, I perfuade myfelf, will its abolition ever be attempted by any King, who knows his true intereft, and purfues the well-being and happinefs of his people, as the fole end and objeft of his reigning.

XXXIV.

OF JURIES.

JURIES, or the trial *per pares*, is an effential part of the Englifh conftitution, being exprefsly fpecified in *Magna Charta*. Yet an author, very learned in the law, " conceives,
" that by this was meant chiefly the trial of
" the barons by their peers; though it hath,
" fortunately for the liberties of this country,
" been expounded to extend to the trial of all
" perfons by a Jury." He thinks that a French
law,

law, by which " all nobles were to be tried
" *par leurs pairs*," made near the time of our
Magna Charta, and by perſons of the ſame order, namely, the nobles and barons in both
kingdoms, may rightly be conſidered as expo-
ſitory of the Engliſh [122]. But, however ancient and conſtitutional their power, there are
not wanting perſons to ridicule and condemn
it. The Scythian Anacharſis, having ſeen the
orators haranguing the people at Athens, expreſſed his ſurpriſe, that " in Greece wiſe
" men pleaded cauſes, but fools determined
" them [123] :" and ſome, with us, think it
equally abſurd, that ſuch ſort of perſons, as
uſually compoſe our Juries, ſhould be made
judges in *matters of law :* they would confine
their judgment, or power of deciding, to the
matter of faƈt.

It is certain, that this latter notion of Juries,
whether well or ill grounded, is by no means
new : for all our law-books inſiſt upon it, as the
prime and eſſential qualification of a Juryman,
that he be choſen out of the *Viſne*, that is,
vicinage or neighbourhood; *de vicineto, ubi
faƈtum ſupponitur*, ſays Forteſcue [124]; becauſe,
as they write, *vicinus faƈta vicini præſumitur
ſcire* [125] : but ſay little or nothing of his qua-

[122] Barrington, *on Ancient Statutes*, p. 29. 3d edit.
[123] Plut. *in Solon.*   [124] *De Laud. Leg.* c. 20.
[125] Hawkins's P. C. II. 23.

lifications

lifications in law; and therefore include only
half the idea of a Juryman according to thofe,
who will have him a judge of *law* as well as
fact.—There is a paffage in Bracton, which
feems to fhew, that, in Henry the Third's
time, it was the duty of the Judge to controul the verdict of the Jury: *fed, cum ad
Judicem pertineat juftum proferre judicium, opor-
tebit eum diligenter examinare, fi dicta Jurato-
rum in fe veritatem contineant, et fi eorum juftum
fit judicium, vel fatuum; ne, fi contingat Judicem
eorum dicta fequi et eorum judicium, ita falfum fa-
ciat judicium et fatuum* [126].—Lord Clarendon
declares himfelf explicitly of opinion, that the
Jury are not to judge of the *law*; and fpeaks
contemptuoufly of Hobbes, for making them
judges of *law* as well as *fact* [127]. I fhould not,
I confefs, have fufpected Hobbes of any biafs,
in favour of the people or their privileges;
and if he has any where expreffed himfelf in-
confiftently with his general fyftem, fo it is:
but he certainly fays, that " thefe twelve men,
" the Jury, are no court of equity or of juftice,
" becaufe they determine not what is juft or
" unjuft, but only whether it be done or not
" done: and their judgment is nothing elfe,
" but a confirmation of that, which is properly
" the judgment of the witneffes [128]." Laftly,

[126] Lib. IV. c. 19.   [127] *Survey of Leviathan*, p. 129.
[128] Works, p. 598. *edit.* 1750.

the

the excellent Montefquieu, if I underftand him, had the fame notion of our Juries : " In " England," fays he, " the Jurors decide, " whether or no the accufed be guilty of the " fact brought before them [129]."

On the other hand, Littleton in his *Tenures* exprefsly fays, that, " if a Jury will take upon " them the knowledge of the *law* upon the " matter, they *may* [130] :" to which Lord Coke agrees, in his comment thereupon. And indeed it is not eafy to conceive, how thefe twelve men can properly bring in a verdict (that is, can pronounce a man *guilty* or *not guilty*) without being judges of the *law* as well as of the *fact* ; becaufe a combination of both thefe ideas is neceffary to afcertain and fix the idea of a *crime*. Sir Thomas Smith, in his *De Republica Anglorum*, has the following paffage in his chapter upon Juries : *Quamprimum jurifjurandi religione obftringuntur Duodecemviri ad facti veritatem dicendam, tum jurifperiti facti fpeciem aperiunt :—ubi res teftibus confirmata, Judex fub verborum compendio propofita a jureconfultis in utramque partem argumenta Duodecemviris alte a capite repetit ; teftium dicta commemorat ; rurfufque facti fpeciem inculcat* [131]. The *fpecies*

[129] *En Angleterre, les Jures décident fi l' accufé eft coupable ou non du fait, qui a été porté devant eux.* L'Efprit, &c. VI. 3.

[130] Sect. 386.   [131] Lib. II. 18.

facti,

facti, the nature, the *specific* nature, of the fact, is, we see, fully and accurately set forth to the Jury : and with reason ; for, without knowing the nature as well as certainty of the fact, how shall they judge of its legality or illegality, its criminality or its innocence ? and, without these, how bring a verdict, or pronounce about guilt [132] ?

XXXV.

OF ENGLISH PATRIOTISM, WITH THE IDEA WHICH FOREIGNERS HAVE OF IT.

WHOEVER should take a view of political *manœuvres* in England, must be ready to suppose it one of the best governed nations upon earth. For why ? he would see all ranks and professions, all ages and sexes, anxious al-

---

[132] There is a curious medal of the famous John Lilborne, who stood a trial under Cromwell ; which, as far as its authority goes, confirms the above notion of the rights of a Jury. The medallion represents his effigies to the life, with this remarkable inscription : *John. Lilborne. saved. by. the. power. of. the. Lord. and. the. integrity. of. his. Jury. who. are. judges. of. law. as. well. as. fact.* Oct. 26. 1649. Evelyn upon Medals, p. 171.—See particularly, upon this subject, a piece intitled, *The Englishman's Right, or a Dialogue about Juries.* By Sir John Hawles.

ways, and sometimes even seditious, for just and right administration in the affairs of state. But this apparent benefit is a real misfortune, as it tends to keep us ever restless and unquiet : and I call the benefit apparent, because, upon a nearer inspection, this zeal for the state will usually be found only a zeal for the zealot ; I mean, that all his pretences and clamours for the Public have, at the bottom, no other object but his own private emolument.—Let me, upon this occasion, call forth a certain anecdote from antiquity, which, while it illustrates and countenances what I say, may by proper meditation be rendered highly edifying : it is, that of more than sixty patriots, or *liberty-men*, who conspired against *Julius Cæsar*, not one, excepting *Brutus*, was believed to have been influenced by the nobleness and splendor of the deed, τῇ λαμπρότητι καὶ τῷ καλῷ τῆς πράξεως, but to have acted solely from interested and selfish motives [133].

The truth of the case is, and almost every one now seems reasonably well convinced of it, that all this bustle and contest among us is [134],

---

[133] Plutarch. *in Bruto.*

[134] This contest hath now for many years so wholly taken up our political leaders, that the police of the kingdom, and all interior regulations, which far more concern our well-being and happiness than *who shall govern*, have been almost totally neglected.

" not *how* the government shall be admini-
" stered, but *who* shall administer it :" *magis
quorum in manu sit,* to use the language of Livy,
quam ut incolumis sit respublica, quæri. And
this is the idea, which foreigners in general entertain of the English. " Very long experi-
" ence proves," says one of them, " that the
" patriotism of those, who oppose the go-
" vernment, hath no other object but to teaze
" the Sovereign, to thwart the measures of his
" ministers, to traverse their best concerted
" projects; and solely, that themselves may
" have a share in the ministry [135]. An English
" patriot is commonly nothing more than an
" ambitious man, who makes efforts to suc-
" ceed the ministers he decries; or a covetous,
" greedy-minded man, who wishes to amass
" treasure; or a factious, turbulent man, who

---

[135] The original goes on, " that is to say, *in the spoils
" of the nation;"* as if to plunder was equally the object
of all who govern.—This writer should seem to have thought
with Themistocles; who, when the people of Athens mur-
mured at exactions, and were importunate for a change of
magistrates, pacified them with the following apologue.
" A fox sticking fast in a bog, whither he had descended
" in quest of water, flies swarmed upon him, and almost
" sucked out all his blood. To an hedgehog, who kindly
" offered to disperse them, No, replied the fox; *for, if
" those who are glutted be frighted away, an hungry swarm
" will succeed, who will devour the little blood remaining."*
Plutarch.

" seeks

" feeks to reftore a fhattered fortune. But
" are patriots of this ftamp formed to take fin-
" cerely to heart the interefts of their country ?
" Accordingly, when they obtain the places
" they wanted, they follow precifely the tracks
" of their predeceffors, and become in their
" turn the objects of envy and clamour to
" thofe they difpoffeffed, who are now again
" the patriots and favorites of the Public : for
" a fickle reftlefs people always believe thofe
" to be their true friends, who are the enemies
" of the perfons in power ; and thus, not a
" jot the wifer by experience, are enfnared
" and taken by the fame popular arts, practif-
" ed upon them in an eternal fucceffion [116]."

XXXVI. or

[116] Une très longue expérience prouve, que dans la
Grande Bretagne le *Patriotifme* de ceux, qui fe montrent
oppofés à la cour ou au parti du miniftere, n'a pour objet
que d'importuner le Souverain, de contrarier les actions de
ces miniftres, de renverfer leurs projets les plus fenfés ;
uniquement, pour avoir part foi-même au miniftere, c'eft
à dire, aux depouilles de la nation. Le *Patriote Anglois*
n'eft communément qu'un ambitieux, &c. *Syftême Social*,
Part II. ch. 6.—Is not the fingle inftance of *Pulteney*, fufficient to cure men of being hallooed, and led on furioufly,
by patriots, *if experience could make wife ? Walpole's* miniftry was oppofed and attacked many years, and *Pulteney*
was at the head of the oppofition : yet no fooner was *Walpole* driven off, than *Pulteney* and *Carteret* entered into
private negotiations with the *Newcaftle* party, who were
men of *Walpole's* meafures ; and, compromifing matters,
Pulteney

XXXVI

OF THE CONDUCT OF EAST INDIA ADVEN-
TURERS.

WHAT is the reason, that men should concur to do *in a body*, what not one individual of them would even think of *single?* The
same, which permits men to act in the Indies,
what in Europe they would shudder at with
horror. An Englishman, a Dutchman, a
Frenchman, a Spaniard, or a Portuguese, sets
out to these regions, in order to make a fortune. When he hath crossed the Line, or perhaps before, he ceases to be any of these, or indeed of any country: in short, he ceases to be
human. As Abbé Raynal says, " he is a do-

Pulteney became Lord Bath, and *Carteret* Lord Grenville.
They took very few of their compatriots with them into
the new-formed ministry : and Lord *Chesterfield*, being one
that was left behind, expressed his resentment thus, in a paper
called " Old England, or the Constitutional Journal, N° 1.
" Feb. 5, 1743."—" This paper," says he, " is undertaken
" against those, who have found the secret of acquiring
" more infamy in ten months, than their predecessors,
" with all the pains they took, could acquire in twenty
" years. We have seen the noble fruits of a twenty years
" opposition blasted by the connivance and treachery of a
" few, who, by all the ties of gratitude and honour, ought
" to have cherished and preserved them to the people."

" mestic

" mestic tiger, again let loose in the woods,
" and who is again seized with the thirst of
" blood. Such have all the Europeans been,
" when arrived at the regions of the new
" world ; where they have been actuated with
" one common rage, the passion for gold [37]:"
and, after being satiated with blood and gold,
they come home in the shape of first-rate
gentry, and are received as humane, just, equi-
table, good kind of persons.

The following is an extract from the *Ga-*
zetteer, dated " East India House, 13 May,
" 1784. The Court of Directors having re-
" ceived intelligence, that some boats with sea-
" poys having been wrecked near Cannonare,
" about two hundred of them were seized and
" detained by the Bibby, notwithstanding re-
" peated applications made for their release :
" and, Cannonare government being on all
" occasions inimical to the Company, General
" Macleod, in order to take satisfaction for
" those injuries, made a capture of the place ;
" in the attack and reduction of which and its
" dependencies the Company's troops merited
" the warmest praises." Upon which, the day
after, appeared this just and spirited comment :
" The Court of Directors have now published,
" and we have it from authority, that the same

[37] Hist. of *European Settlements* in *East and West Indies.*
Book ix.

" system,

" fyftem, which has fo long difgraced us in the
" Eaft, ftill continues to be followed. The
" Bibby, an independent princefs, is to be
" plundered on a weak pretext, but really be-
" caufe fhe is wealthy; and, becaufe the ra-
" pacious invaders of her country may, by this
" fingle ftroke, accumulate the fortunes of
" Nabobs, and return to their native country
" rich enough to invade its juftice. This has
" been for a long time the fyftem of the Eaft;
" and, now that the Company has fecured
" fuch an intereft in the Britifh Houfe of
" Commons, the fame (we are afraid) will be
" continued, till the Englifh race are extir-
" pated in the Eaft."

Refpecting this great and important object,
I fay nothing as a politician, or as a merchant;
but as a man, and a friend to the rights of humanity, I fay, that I wifh *we had no connections
with the Eaft Indies.*—Behold a different fpirit in the Weft, from what thefe adventurers
have cultivated in the Eaft; and how humanely
it operates towards the loweft of our fellow-
creatures, even African flaves: of which the
following extract from the Epiftle, at the yearly
meeting of the Quakers, held in London 1784,
prefents a noble fpecimen.

" The Chriftian religion being defigned to
" regulate and refine the natural affections of
" man, and to exalt benevolence into that

8 " charity,

" charity, which promotes peace on earth, and
" good-will towards all ranks and claſſes of
" mankind the world over—under the influ-
" ence thereof, our minds have been renewedly
" affected in ſympathy with the poor enſlaved
" Africans; whom avarice hath taught ſome
" men [138], laying claim to the character of
" Chriſtians, to conſider as the refuſe of the
" human race, and not entitled to the common
" privileges of mankind. The contempt in
" which they are held, and the remoteneſs of
" their ſufferings from the notice of diſinte-
" reſted obſervers, have occaſioned few advo-
" cates to plead their cauſe. The conſidera-
" tion of their caſe being brought weightily
" before the laſt yearly meeting, friends were
" engaged to recommend endeavours for put-
" ting a ſtop to a traffick, ſo diſgraceful to hu-
" manity, and ſo repugnant to the precepts of
" the goſpel. The report of the meaſures
" adopted in execution thereof, hath afforded
" comfort and ſatisfaction to this meeting; and
" it hath been our concern to recommend to
" our friends, to whoſe care this buſineſs is
" committed, to perſevere in all prudent ex-
" ertions for attaining the deſirable end. And
" it is our earneſt deſire, that none under our

[138] *Beckford*, for inſtance, and other *patriotic* contenders for *liberty* and the *natural rights* of men.

" name

" name may weaken or counteract our endea-
" vours, by contributing in any way to the
" support of this iniquitous commerce [139]."

This was a great and noble motion, and
would have done honour to the best order of
religious, that ever appeared on earth ; and
were the spirit and temper, from which this
motion originated, to be sincerely and univerfally cultivated, how much more happy, becaufe how much more perfect, would man become !

XXXVII.

OF CIVILIZED AND BARBAROUS NATIONS.

MUCH of the European cruelty, perhaps
the greater part, which, to the difgrace of
human nature, hath been practised in the East
and West Indies, originated doubtless from
the *auri sacra fames*, the accursed passion for
gold : but much, I am persuaded, proceeded
also from men's having considered the natives
of those distant countries, as barbarians, sa-

---

[139] " *Negroes for sale.* A cargo of very fine stout men
" and women, in good order, and fit for immediate service,
" just imported from the windward coast of Africa, in the
" ship *Two Brothers*." From a South Carolina Gazette,
July 1784.

vages,

vages, and greatly below the standard of *our*
humanity. This hath been a fatal error; and I
call it an error, because, from all the information I have been able to acquire, the inhabi-
tants of England, whether regard be had to
either *knowledge* or *manners*, may be deemed as
much barbarians and savages, as those of any
other country in the world [140]. And here I
shall not instance from the coasts, where the
Christian people of good Old England consider
the distresses of seamen and the plunder of a
wreck as a *blessing*, and, says Fielding [141],
blasphemously call it such; but will refer to the
inland and nearly central parts, where civilization and knowledge may be supposed to prevail
the most.

I have spent some years in a village of about
two hundred families, consisting of farmers,
manufacturers, and labouring men; and which
hath a parson, a free-school, and the usual ways
and means of improving and adorning human
nature. Meeting one day a farmer, an intel-
ligent skilful man in his way, and observing
him as it were superstitiously attentive to a very

---

[140] Individuals in England may be, and certainly are,
more polite and knowing, than can be found in the countries
alluded to: but *individuals* do not stamp the *general* character of a nation: this must be determined by the com-
monalty, or people at large.

[141] Voyage to Lisbon.

small

small sprig of eldar, I accosted him upon the subject. " Perhaps, Sir," says *Ruff*, " I can " now tell you something, that may hereafter " be of use to you. ' Sir, I rode above thirty " years to L—— market, yet never without " blistering my a—, and *losing leather*, as the " saying is ; but, Sir, since I have put this bit " of eldar in my breeches-pocket, to which I " was advised by my neighbour P—, and " which with God's leave I will never go " without, far from being blistered, I have " not been even chafed or heated." Upon my smiling, as if I did not conceive how this could be—" Sir," says he, " perhaps you may " not believe another thing. John H's pig " got lamed the other day : and how do you " think he cured him ? By nothing in the " world, but only boring a little hole in his " ear, and putting in a small peg about as big " as my eldar." I told him, that these things were perfectly above my comprehension ; and endeavoured to shew him, in language he understood, that there could be no connection between the causes and effects in either case. He was much disconcerted with my spirit of unbelief; and seemed to think me a person, whom nothing could convince.

A few years ago, in this same village, the women *in labour* used to drink the urine of their husbands ; who were all the while stationed, as

.I have

I have feen the cows in St. James's Park, and
ftraining themfelves to *give* as much as they could.
The rationale of this cuftom (that is, the why
and the wherefore) I never could get rightly
explained : it is however become obfolete, if
not exploded ; the patronefs of it, who was a
fuperior perfon in the parifh, having fome time
fince departed this foolifh world.—I will mention but one inftance more ; only begging the
reader not to confider the above as fictitious,
but as matters of fact, that may be afcertained
even by legal evidence.

A young woman in the neighbourhood was
fubject to fits, and during the paroxyfms was fo
unruly, that there was a neceffity of holding
her down by force. To do this more effectually, a very well meaning young man once
fpread himfelf upon her, in the prefence of
many attendants : to whom he foon and fud-
denly exclaimed, as if compelled by infpira-
tion [142], that " the Lord had fpoken to him,
" and that it was the Lord's will he fhould
" marry the patient." Now what emotions
the young man felt within, during this tender
and delicate fituation, I am unable to fay : but,

[142]. There is no interior movement of either body or
mind, but, with weak and enthufiaftic perfons, may pafs for
a divine impulfe : this fhould put us upon our guard againft
delufion, or rather madnefs.

K 2   whether

whether from natural or fupernatural impulfe, he fpeedily married the woman; and the whole affair at this prefent writing is not two months old.—Having this only from rumour, I cannot affirm that all the circumftances were exactly as I have related: however, a divine interpofition is believed upon the whole, and the hand of the Lord to be plainly vifible.

Thefe few fpecimens may ferve to fhew the fuperiority of *knowledge* in *us* enlightened civilized people, to that of Hottentots and other barbarians. How ftands the comparifon with regard to *manners?* Do the former equally tranfcend the latter in *manners* alfo? Let us hear thofe, who feem to have had better opportunities of being informed than ourfelves. For my part, fays a fenfible writer, and as fhould feem traveller, " I have met with peo-
" ple as polite, ingenious, and humane, whom
" we have been taught to look upon as cani-
" bals, as ever I converfed with in Europe;
" and from my own experience am convinced,
" that human nature is every where the fame,
" allowances being made for unavoidable pre-
" judices, inftilled in their infancy by igno-
" rance and fuperftition. And nothing has con-
" tributed more to render the world barbarous,
" than men's having been taught, from their
" cradles, that every nation almoft but their
" own are barbarians: they firft imagine the
                                        " people

" people of diſtant nations to be monſters of
" cruelty and barbarity, and then prepare to
" invade and extirpate them, exerciſing greater
" cruelties than ever ſuch nations were charged
" with.   This was exactly the caſe of the
" *Spaniards* and the natives of *America* [143] :"
and would to heaven the caſe could ſuit no
other people and country !

An ancient writer, who lived when the Romans were the moſt polite and **knowing, clearly**
gives the preference **to thoſe they called bar-**
barians, in point of *manners*. He is ſpeaking
of the Scythians ; and, after deſcribing their
way of life, obſerves, that " juſtice was culti-
" vated and preſerved among them, not by
" laws, but by the ſpirit and temper of the
" people ; that they held no crime more atro-
" cious than theft ; that they had not the ſame
" paſſion for gold and ſilver with other na-
" tions ; and that a moderation, contented-
" neſs, and ſobriety of manners, laid them **un-**
" der no temptation of invading what **was not**
" their own.   **And I wiſh,**" ſays the hiſtorian,
" that the **reſt of the** world **poſſeſſed the** ſame
" ſpirit of moderation, **the ſame juſtice in ab-**
" ſtaining from what **belongs** to others : arms
" would not then commit the ravages they do ;
" nor mankind periſh more by the ſword than

[143] Salmon's Geograph. Grammar, in Pref.

" from

" from the natural lot of mortality. And it
" may seem altogether wonderful, that nature
" grants to savages, what the Greeks cannot
" attain with all their refinement and parade
" of philosophy; and that civilized and po-
" lished manners are exceeded by those of un-
" cultivated barbarism. So much more ad-
" vantageous to the one is an ignorance of
" what is wrong, than to the other a know-
" ledge of what is right [144]."

[144] Juſtitia gentis ingeniis culta, non legibus. Nullum
ſcelus apud eos furto gravius : aurum et argentum non per-
inde, ac reliqui mortales, appetunt. Lacte & melle veſcun-
tur, &c. Hæc continentia illis morum quoque juſtitiam edi-
dit, nihil alienum concupiſcentibus : quippe ibidem diviti-
arum cupido eſt, ubi et uſus. Atque utinam reliquis mor-
talibus ſimilis moderatio et abſtinentia alieni foret ! pro-
fectò non tantum bellorum per omnia ſecula terris omnibus
continuaretur ; neque plus hominum ferrum et arma, quam
naturalis fatorum conditio, raperet. Prorſus, ut admirabile
videatur, hoc illis naturam dare, quod Græci longâ ſapien-
tium doctrinâ præceptiſque philoſophorum conſequi neque-
unt ; cultoſque mores incultæ barbariæ collatione ſuperari.
Tanto plus in illis proficit vitiorum ignoratio, quam in his
cognitio virtutis. Juſtin. II. 2.

XXXVIII. GREAT

XXXVIII.

GREAT EFFECTS FROM CAUSES APPARENTLY SMALL.

SOMEBODY hath called Swift's *Drapier's Letters*, " the brazen monuments of his " fame :" alluding, I fhould fuppofe, to the effect they produced, rather than to any thing extraordinary in their compofition. They are written, as Swift ufually wrote, with abilities and addrefs; but they were far from being the *caufe* of the *effect* that followed. The truth is, and we have Swift himfelf confeffing it, that " the fuccefs of the *Drapier's Letters* was not " owing to his abilities, but to a lucky junc- " ture, when the fuel was ready for the firft " hand, that would be at the pains of kindling " it." *Letters.*—The royal commentator upon Machiavel's Prince, if indeed his Majefty of Pruffia be the author of that comment, makes the change of Queen Anne's Miniftry, and the confequent peace with Lewis XIV. to be *caufed* by a difpute between the Queen and the Du- chefs of Marlborough about a pair of gloves. *Chap.* 25. It might be fo; but it muft have been, juft as the fcratch of a pin upon the cu- ticle may be the *caufe* of a mortification, where

the

the conſtitutional habit is very bad.—I would not ſay therefore, in this and the former in-ſtance, that the Drapier's Letters and gloves were the *cauſes*, but that they *occaſioned* cauſes, already provided, to begin to operate in pro-ducing their effects: which is what ſhould pro-perly be meant, when **great** *effects* are ſaid to proceed *from cauſes apparently ſmall.*

XXXIX.

OF KING'S FRIENDS.

" THE King of France," ſays Machiavel,
" ſuffers nobody to call himſelf of the
" **King**'s party, becauſe that would imply
" there was a party againſt him." *Diſcors.* III.
27.   With us, by affecting to be diſtinguiſhed as *King's friends*, many minute things have crawled up to ſituations, both in church and ſtate, which (to uſe the Poet's language) may reaſonably make one *wonder, how the Devil they got there.*—The King of England has no *enemies.*

XL. Doctors

XL.

DOCTORS DIFFER.

DR. POWELL, in the firſt of his Sermons, publiſhed by Dr. Balguy, 1776, ſpeaking of " abſurd and ſlaviſh principles of govern-" ment, **which now,**" he ſays, " are fled into " everlaſting darkneſs," notes, **that they " left** " their laſt footſteps before the altars of God, " and in the faireſt temples of literature:" meaning *Paſſive Obedience* and *Non-reſiſtance* at Oxford.—But Dr. Miles Newton, in his Faſt-Sermon **before that Univerſity,** 1777, ſhould ſeem to conſider this as a miſrepreſentation and calumny : and, alluding to the doƈtrines of *original compaƈts, power derived from the people,* and the *lawfulneſs of reſiſtance* when ſuch power is abuſed, " ſuch wild, viſionary, enthuſiaſtic no-" tions," ſays he, " have always been **counter-** " aƈted and oppoſed by the **examples and** in-" ſtruƈtions of this **Univerſity :** which may, " without vanity, boaſt, that it has been ſtea-" dier **in its** principles, and ſuffered more for " its conſiſtency, in the ſupport of regal go-" vernment, than perhaps any other place **of** " the like nature in the Chriſtian world." P. 22. See N° XIV.

XLI. THE

XLI.

THE LOVE OF LIFE.

AN old man, fays Æſop, coming home from the woods ſomewhat overloaded, threw down his burthen, and in the anguiſh of fatigue called for death. Death appearing, to know his commands? only, ſays he, to—*help me up with this wood.* Let us not grow peeviſh with life upon every little vexation; that is to ſay, upon every change of the weather. In like manner, Antiſthenes the Stoic being very ſick, and impatiently crying out, Who will deliver me? " This," ſaid Diogenes, preſenting a knife, " very ſoon if thou wilt." *I do not mean, from my life,* replied Antiſthenes, *but from my diſeaſe.*—Montaigne ſays, that there is no condition ſo wretched, which men will not accept, " provided they may live:" and he quotes from Seneca the example of Mecænas, who is there repreſented to have held this language:

Debilem facito manu,
Debilem pede, coxa;
Tuber adſtrue gibberum,
Lubricos quate dentes:
Vita dum ſupereſt, bene eſt.   Epiſt. 101.

                                              Seneca

Seneca calls this, and juſtly, *turpiſſimum votum* ; nor, humbly as I think of human philoſophy, can I perſuade myſelf, that this is the wiſh of men univerſally. Meanwhile, it is certainly the true tone of ſpirit and temper, "neither to "wiſh nor fear to die."

Summum nec metuas diem, nec optes.

Martial. x. 47.

XLII.

MUCH ADO ABOUT NOTHING.

MULTUM agentes nihil agendo, hath uſually been ſaid of thoſe officious, buſy, fluttering things, who are always in a hurry, yet doing nothing : but it may juſtly be ſaid of man in general. Upon what poor uninteresting objects is he perpetually employed, and with what importance and moſt ſerious concern ! "Is that the point," ſaid the philoſopher, looking contemptuouſly down upon the earth, "is that the point, which ſo many nations are "partitioning with fire and ſword [145] ?" When Alcibiades was pluming himſelf upon his nu-

[145] *Iſtudne eſt punctum, quoa inter tot gentes ferro et igne dividitur ?* Seneca.

merous

merous farms and poffeffions, Socrates drily
afked to fee them upon a map of the earth,
which was hanging before them [146]: not unlike
a Grand Seignior, who, enquiring where England was, which *made fo much difturbance* [147],
was defired to remove his thumb, which hid it
upon the map.   In fhort, life, as inftituted and
conducted by mankind in general, is all vanity,
folly, and madnefs; our fpeculations nothing
but a *Comedy of Errors,* our actions *Much ado
about Nothing* [148].

---

[146] Ælian. III. 28.

[147] England, minute as fhe may feem, hath always been
reftlefs, unquiet, *difturbing* ; like **Dryden**'s Achitophel,

A fiery foul, which, working out its way,
Fretteth the pigmy body to decay,
And o'er-informs the tenement of clay.

[148] " It is certain," fays Hume, " were a fuperior being
" thruft into a human body, that the whole of life would
" to him appear fo mean, contemptible, and puerile, that
" he never could be induced to take part in any thing."
The Sceptic.—I cannot think it neceffary to call down angels,
for this contempt of earthly things : I think that men are
fully fufficient for it.   A found underftanding, well and ho-
neftly cultivated, and rightly and duly eftimating what
paffes around him, may eafily withhold a man from *taking
part in any thing.*   I do not call in the aid of Chriftianity,
which is known to **be** more than fufficient.

XLIII. HU-

XLIII

HUMAN NATURE DIFFERENTLY ESTIMATED.

" ALL," says a certain writer, " which can be
" done by a wise man (seeing that by na-
" ture he is appointed to act, for the space of
" 30, 50, or 70 years, some ridiculous silly part
" in this fantastic theatre of misery, vice, and
" corruption) is either to lament with Heracli-
" tus the iniquities of the world, or (which is
" the more cheerful, and therefore I do pre-
" sume the more eligible, course) to laugh
" with Democritus at all the fools and knaves
" upon earth [149]."—Montaigne preferred Democritus's humour to Heraclitus's; " not,"
says he, " because it is more pleasant to laugh
" than to weep, but because it is more scorn-
" ful, and more expressive of contempt, than
" the other : for," adds he, " I think we can
" never be enough despised." *Essais*, I. 50.—
To Brutus, courting him into the conspiracy
against Cæsar, Statilius answered, that he was
" perfectly satisfied of the justness of the cause,
" but did not think mankind so considerable,
" as to deserve a wise man's concern :" agreeably to that of Theodorus, who " would not

[149] Swift's Life by Deane Swift, **p. 206.**

" have

" have a wife man run any rifques for a com-
" pany of fools."—Muretus feems to have entertained a fublimer idea of human importance;
when, having fallen fick upon the road, and
overhearing a confultation of phyficians, who,
fuppofing him an obfcure perfon, agreed at
length *facere periculum in corpore vili*, as they
expreffed it, he cried aloud, " What ! will you
" prefume to make experiments upon one, for
" whom Chrift died?" *Menagiana*. See N° XI.
XII. XIII.

XLIV.

OF GALLANTRY AND DEVOTION.

THE ftrongeft argument againft *devotion*, in
the very high fenfe of that word, is, that
though it may elevate and fpiritualize the
foul, yet it doth not feem to be neceffarily connected with any influence over the body. The
devotee feldom or never finds a difficulty, in
reconciling meditations and prayers to even the
groffeft immoralities: with him fenfuality and
devotion mix cordially together. Margaret,
Queen of Navarre, tells of a young Prince,
who, having an intrigue with an advocate's
wife in Paris, and his way to her lying through
a church,

a church, never paffed that holy place, going
to or returning from this godly exercife, but
always kneeled down to pray, and was very devout [150].

N. B. I take this pious Queen to have been
the fame Margaret, who, upon a complaint
from fome court-lady of being overdone with
what is called family-duty, made an edict, that
" no man fhould know his wife carnally more
" than fix times in one night."

XLV.

OF ANTE-NUPTIAL FORNICATION, WITH A HINT OR TWO FOR ITS PREVENTION.

OSBORN calls this commerce before marriage, a fin againft prudence rather than
againft virtue. Doubtlefs, it is but too natural
to confider the fame act, as no worfe than an
indulgence *before*, which is ufually confidered
as a duty *after*. This indulgence, however, is
againft law and order : the confequences of it
are often productive of mifery : and, therefore,
it cannot be too much guarded againft. But
it is not guarded againft enough ; for only con-

[150] Montaigne, liv. I. ch. 56.

template

template the bufinefs of *courtfhip*, how it is conducted, efpecially among the common people.
A male and female begin to fympathize with,
and feel a fondnefs for, each other : they *court*,
as it is called ; that is, they carefs each other ;
and thefe careffes pafs, not openly and in the
day-time, but in the darknefs of midnight and
moft hidden retirement. Amidft fuch careffing, it
is impoffible to fay, " So far fhalt thou go, and
" no farther,—fo far is innocent, any farther
" is finful." The boundaries of things are dif-
ficultly defined ; and, in the prefent cafe, the
parties often get into the territories of fin, be-
fore they fufpeft themfelves out of the precincts of innocence. **Or, if** they **do** fufpect
and recollect themfelves, after they have paffed
the line, all power of alarming hath ten to one
ceafed; and fo unhappy is their fituation and
condition, that each might juftly fay, were ut-
terance granted, *prudens*, *fciens*, *vivus*, *videnf-*
que, pereo. Such fituations muft be carefully
avoided, unlefs mankind would lead themfelves into temptation.

There is a particular inftance of our police,
which, on this very account, I fhould be pleafed
to fee correcfted and amended. May and June,
in 1779 I think, fourteen *filiations,* or father-
ings of illegitimate children, were made in my
prefence. I was ftruck with the fingularity of
the thing; I mean, at the concurrence of fo
                                        many

many fimilar cafes in thefe two months; which were more in number than what the reft of the year produced. But, upon ruminating, I feemed to trace the caufe to the *Statute Seſſions,* or (as they are commonly called) *the Statutes,* held in October or November preceding: whither all the young men and maidens of the villages refort, for other purpofes, frequently, befides that of being hired. I have fometimes thought, that if at *Statutes,* as well as *Fairs,* **a** public bell were rang **at a** certain hour, as **a** fignal for this fort of gentry to difperfe and take themfelves off, many, very many, good effects would follow. Perhaps the nation might not be fo populous, but a vaft deal of rioting and drunkennefs would be prevented.

XLVI.

ABOVE PAR.

MEAD recommends **a** little excefs or joviality, *now and then* [151]; and, I confefs, I believe it to be as falutary to the mind and affections,

---

[151] Quamvis temperantia omnibus fit utilis, medici tamen antiqui auctores fuerunt, ut qui bene valeret, & fpontis fuæ effet, genio *nonnunquam* indulgens, tam cibum quam potum

folito

fections, as it can be to the body. Shaftsbury somewhere calls company or conversation *an amicable collision*; but, methinks, it should be a little warmed and elevated with wine. I would not rant with Horace, *quid non ebrietas designat*, and so forth? Drunkennefs is an odious and beaftly thing, and as noxious to the mind as to the body: but, to be cheered beyond the natural tone of the fpirits, and raifed to a ftandard fomewhat bigger than the life, may (I fhould think) be attended with good effects upon both. By thus invigorating the vital powers, and quickening for a while the circulation of the fluids, obftruétions may be removed among the *interiora* of the body, as the gathering *fordes* of rivers are occafionally forced down by a ftronger current than ordinary. The immaterial part of us will alfo be benefited equally with the material; aye, perhaps more fo. Frefh ftrength and firmnefs will be given to the fpirits; all thofe *clouds* or vapours, with which the human noddle is, like Shakfpeare's *towers*, frequently *capped*, will be difperfed; the heart and affections will be warmed and exalted; and the whole man will be a better, as well as an happier, being. In fhort, by taking off his atten-

folito abundantiùs affumeret: tutior autem eft in *potione,* quam in *efca,* intemperantia. *Monit. & Præcept. Med.* fub. fin.

tion

tion from folly, vice, care, and mifery, and thus forgetting his fituation a little, he will infenfibly procure a new edition of himfelf [152].— All this, however, if you mean to preferve its efficacy, only *now and then*.

XLVII.

HUMAN PERFECTION NOT IN NATURE.

LORD CHESTERFIELD tells his fon, in one of his letters to him, that he " fhall " diffect and analyfe him with a microfcope, " fo as to difcover the leaft fpeck or blemifh." Lord Chefterfield was not altogether in earneft: fo it is, however, that men ferioufly *diffect* and *analyfe* one another. They overlook the great and good in a character or compofition, and dwell upon foibles, imperfections, and infirmities [153]. But this is bafe, injurious, cruel ma-

[152] " **Liquors,** taken in fuch quantity as *elevates* without " *intoxicating,* **are** the inward cloathing **of the body** in our " foggy, **damp** atmofphere." Dr. Stevenfon *on the Gout,* **p.** 161.

[153] The unfortunate Chancellor Bacon complained, very feelingly I fhould think, of this iniquity in judging. *Iniqua admodum et mifera eft conditio hominum virtute præcellentium, quia erroribus eorum, quantumvis leviffimis, **nullo modo** ignofcitur: qui tamen in hominibus mediocribus **aut omninò late**rent, aut veniam facilè reperirent.* De A. S. lib. 8.

lignity.

lignity. They fhould furvey and examine each
other, as they would furvey and examine a
noble pile of building : not pink and peep about
for afperities upon the furface, or little irregularities among the *minutiæ* ; but contemplate
the magnitude, ftrength, and form of the whole,
with the beauty **and** proportion arifing from all
the parts.   By their way of criticifing and cen-
furing, it fhould feem as if all men were **to be,**
what Paterculus makes the firft Scipio to have
been; who, he fays, " did never, in his whole
" life, either fay, or do, or think any thing,
" but what was highly excellent, and to be
" commended,"—*nihil in vita nifi laudandum aut
dixit, aut fecit, aut fenfit* [154]. Such a ftyle might
fuit the writer, who was to extol the virtues of
Tiberius and Sejanus; but mankind affuredly
are not fo formed : they are a mixture of qualities; and happy is **he,** whofe good fhall be
found to overbalance his bad.

XLVIII.

OF PROFESSIONAL CHARACTER.

RAMAZZINI, a phyfician of Padua, wrote
a book *de morbis artificum*; to fhew the
peculiar diftempers of tradefmen, arifing from

[154] Lib. I. c. 12.

each

each respective trade. Might not a philoso-
phic observer construct a work upon a similar
plan, to mark the specific habitudes and manners of each respective order and profession?

In the course of this disquisition, he would
be led to observe, for instance, that insincerity
in a courtier must be the ruling feature of his
character: and why? because, without allowing
any thing to private humour, principle, or affection, the men of this order accommodate
themselves solely to times and persons.—He
might ascribe lying to an ambassador; because,
being " sent to *lie* abroad for the good of his
" country," as Sir Henry Wotton defined his
office, he preserves a habit of lying, even when
the officiality or duty of so doing may not require it.—A want of moral sense and sympa-
thising humanity would be found in men of the
law; because, paying no regard to the distinc-
tions of right and wrong, but only intent upon
serving their clients, they are led to treat with
indifference, and sometimes even to sport with,
the most injurious decisions against the most
pitiable objects.—The love of gain in all who
traffic; because such have been habituated to
consider money as the chief good, and to value
every man according to what he is worth.—
And, lastly, an open systematical kind of kna-
very in the *honest* farmer; who, without any
regard to value in the commodity, professes to

buy

buy as cheap, and fell as dear, as he can; and who, if you remonftrate againft his offering a horfe or cow for twice its worth, afks you, with a fneer, "whether he muft not do the "beft he can for his family [155] ?"—Would not, I fay, all this be perceived, where profeffional fpirit is not checked and counteracted by natural temperament? And thus through life, and every department of it: where the characters of men would be found in a compound ratio of temperament and profeffion; and be natural or artificial, according to the proportion in which thefe are combined.

XLIX.

OF PERSONAL IDENTITY.

WE are born, it is faid, with the feeds or principles of diffolution in our frame, which continue to operate from our births to our deaths; fo that in this fenfe we may be faid to *die daily*. But, I think, we may be faid to

[155] **Our good** Chriftian farmer, however, may deign to learn a better leffon from an heathen. *Ex omni vitâ fimulatio diffimulatioque tollenda eft: ita, nec ut emat melius, nec ut vendat, quidquam fimulabit aut diffimulabit vir bonus.* Cicero de Offic. III. 15.

die daily in another sense; and that is, in the
change we are always undergoing in our persons, tempers, and manners, which makes us, in
the different stages of our lives, quite different
beings:—which makes, if I may so say, *one self*
to be continually dying, while *another self* is as
continually growing out of it.

Let me illustrate this reflection, by what
gave rise to it.—A boy of three years old was
playing before me the other day, upon whom a
matron gazed with uncommon fondness, because he bears a striking resemblance to what
her own son, who is fifteen, was at that age;
and who, it is certain, would not *now* excite in
her the fondness, that this strange child does.
She owned it was so; and I told her what I supposed to be the reason: *viz.* that she viewed
the little boy as the image of a being, who
once existed, but whom she now considered as
no more; and recollected only with that *deside-
rium* or longing fondness, with which we call
up the images of departed friends or relations.
And, added I, "there is between the two
"objects not the difference which at first sight
"there may seem to be: for your son at three
"years old, whom this little boy resembles,
"was as different from what he is now, as if
"he were a different being. Nay, though a
"being with his name and connections hath
"grown out of him, and still subsists, was he

L 4 not

" not really a different being ? and is not his
" *then-self* dead, as his *now-self* will be twenty
" years hence ?"—It feems to me, that this fentiment and reafoning may be applied to every
moment of our lives : by the continual flux
our material part is in, we are every moment
laying afide *one felf* and affuming *another felf*,
every moment dying and reviving. Death
therefore is not fo much laying afide our old
bodies (for this we have been doing all our
lives) as ceafing to affume new ones.

Let me add another illuftration of the above,
from an affair between two boys, in which
there is nothing fictitious but the names. When
William left London, and went into the North,
he wept at parting with his friend and companion *Tommy*. He enquired frequently and af-
fectionately after *Tommy* ; he longed to fee him
again ; and, after two years abfence, he did fee
him. But he did not meet him fo warmly as
was expected : on the contrary, he looked difmayed, as if difappointed ; and his behaviour
to him was fomewhat cold and diftant. Being
afked the reafon, he replied, that " this was
" not *Tommy*, at leaft the *Tommy* he left ; and
" that he fhould love him as well as ever, if he
" looked more like *Tommy*." The truth is,
Tommy's ftature was increafed, and his features altered ; and *William* no longer acknowledged the identity of his friend, but
                                                    thought

thought him another person ; at least the same
as another person, because not presenting the
idea he had been accustomed to be fond of.
Just so, I suppose, I may love my mother, under
that image which she bore in 1738, when she
died ; but were my mother to be presented to
me, all decrepit and withered with age, as she
would have been now in 1784, I could scarcely
fancy her the lively pretty woman, who used to
caress me, and whom under that form I used to
love. In short, she would appear a new person, a new being ; and, though I might from
reason esteem her as my mother, yet I should
feel none of that love which *instinct* produces.

Upon the whole, therefore, did not Locke
determine rightly, when he made *personal identity* to consist in consciousness ?

L.

OF CONFERRING AND RECEIVING FAVOURS.

SOCRATES, though importuned, refused to
go to the court of Archelaus, King of Ma-
cedonia. Seneca, who has recorded the fact,
says that his ostensible reason was, " not to
" receive favours, which he could not return,"
—*nolle se ad eum venire, a quo acciperet beneficia,*
cum

cum reddere illi paria non poffet : his real one,
" not to go into voluntary fervitude,"—*noluit*
ire ad voluntariam fervitutem [156]. The real one,
certainly : for Archelaus was a bad prince;
and courts are not places of freedom and in-
dependence, even under good ones.—Befides,
the former reafon would, I fhould think, have
been unworthy of Socrates. What ! is no man
to receive a benefit, but who is able to return
it ? If fo, then (as Ariftotle makes him reply
upon this occafion, but furely unphilofophi-
cally) " it muft be as great an affront to con-
" fer a benefit upon a perfon who cannot re-
" turn it, as to injure a perfon who cannot re-
" drefs himfelf [157] :" and then all acts of kind-
nefs, generofity, and charity, muft be banifhed
from among men ; fince one party is no more
at liberty to confer, than the other to receive, a
favour.

How is it, I wonder, that we hear fo many
exclaiming loudly againft receiving favours ?
" I think nothing fo dear as what is given
" me," fays Montaigne; " and that, becaufe
" my will lies at pawn under the title of in-
" gratitude. I more willingly accept of offices
" to be fold; being of opinion, that for the
" laft I give nothing but money, but for the
" firft I give myfelf [158] :" as if, according to

----

[156] De Benefic. V. 6.   [157] Rhetor. II. 23.
[158] Effais, III. 9.

ancient

ancient language, " to receive a favour was to
" fell our liberty,"—*beneficium accipere eft liber-
tatem vendere.* It may be fo in fome cafes, **and**
with fome perfons; and I fhall fo far compro-
mife the matter with Montaigne, that we ought
to be careful, and perhaps fomewhat nice,
from whom we receive favours. But to lay
down the propofition univerfally, and with refpect to all manner of perfons; to fpurn the
very idea of receiving a favour from, or being
obliged to, any one; to think and reafon, as if
fervices conferred and received ought, like
other trading commodities, to be weighed as in
a fcale; to keep an account as of creditor and
debtor; and to dread a balance againft **us** as
much, as if lofs of liberty and imprifonment
were **the** confequence—all this **is** wretched:
'**tis all** faftidious *hauteur*, pride, infolence, de-
noting a fpirit and temper certainly unchri-
ftian, but unphilofophical alfo and impolitic **in**
the higheft degree. And why? Becaufe **it**
would greatly weaken, if not deftroy, **all** that
mutual affection, all that **intercourfe** of kind-
nefs and good offices, fo by **nature** neceffary to
the helplefs, dependant **ftate** of man, and fo
contribut**ing** (if not effential) to his happinefs
in fociety.

LI. law

LI.

LAW AND EQUITY.

JUSTICE, " the miſtreſs and queen of all the virtues [159]," the baſis of all ſocial virtue as well as happineſs, the very corner-ſtone on which ſociety is built—this very juſtice, if exerciſed too rigorouſly, would often be found, amidſt the combinations and entanglements of human affairs, even to border upon injuſtice; inſomuch that the civilians have eſtabliſhed it into a maxim, that " extreme juſtice is extreme " injuſtice,"—*ſummum jus ſumma injuria.*

It ſhould ſeem, therefore, that the magiſtrate, to whom the execution of juſtice is committed, muſt not only *do juſtly*, but (in the language of the Prophet) alſo *love mercy.* I do not mean, that he ſhould ever act otherwiſe than the laws direct, or at any time diſpenſe with the right execution of them; but only, that he be governed therein, as often as he can, by the *ſpirit* rather than the *letter* of them. For in the law, as well as in the goſpel, the *letter* frequently

---

[159] *Omnium domina et regina virtutum.* Cicero de Offic. III. 6.—According to an ancient Greek moraliſt, every other virtue is comprehended in that of juſtice : Ἐν δὲ δικαιοσύνῃ συλλήβδην πᾶσ' ἀρετή 'ſι. Theognis.

killeth ;

killeth; as when any statute, from a new and different situation of things and persons, gradually brought on by course of time and change of manners, enforceth proceedings different from, or, it may be, contrary to, the true original intent and meaning of it. The office, therefore, of a magistrate, a Justice of Peace for instance, should be in part a kind of a petty chancery; a court of equity, as well as a court of justice : where a man, although pursued by *law*, may yet be redressed by *reason*, so often as the case will admit of it; and that will be as often as the *spirit* of any law or statute shall be found to clash with its *letter*.

Mean while, it must be carefully noted, that the magistrate has no power to decide according to equity, when it is opposed to written and positive law, or stands in contradistinction to it : no, not even the Judge, much less the Justice. It is a maxim, *ubi lex non distinguit, nec nos distinguere debemus*; and again, *judicandum ex legibus, non de legibus* : and an ancient pronounced it very dangerous for a Judge *to seem more humane than the law*; φαίνεσθαι φιλανθρωπότερον τῦ νόμυ. The danger consists in its opening a latitude of interpretation, and thereby giving room to subtlety and chicanery, which, by gradually weakening, would in time destroy the authority and tenor of law : for, " though " all general laws are attended with inconve-
" niencies,

"	niencies, when applied to particular cafes;
"	yet thefe inconveniencies are juftly fuppofed
"	to be fewer, than what would refult from
"	full difcretionary powers in every magif-
"	trate." *Hume.*—So that the difpenfation of
equity feems referved, and with good reafon,
not to the Judge who is tied down by his rules,
but to **the law-giver** or fupreme legiflator:
according to that well-known maxim, *ejus eft
interpretari cujus eft condere.* Thus Conftantine
the emperor: *Inter æquitatem jufque interpofitam
interpretationem nobis folis et oportet et licet in-
fpicere.* Cod. l. 14. 1.—See alfo Taylor's *Elements of Civil Law,* p. 90, &c.

It is not meant, therefore, as is faid above,
that the magiftrate fhould ever difpenfe with
law, or act againft it; but only, that he fhould,
as far as he can, temper it with lenity and for-
bearance, when the *letter* is found to run counter to the *fpirit.* For inftance; our ancient
Saxon laws nominally punifhed theft with
death, when the thing ftolen exceeded the value of twelve pence: yet the criminal was permitted to redeem his life with money. But, by
9 Hen. **I.** in 1109, this power of redemption
was taken away: the law continues in force to
this very day; and death is the punifhment of
a man who fteals above twelve-pennyworth of
goods, although the value of twelve pence now

is

is near forty times lefs than when the law was made. Here the *fpirit* is abfolutely outraged by the *letter :* and therefore might not a Juftice, when a delinquent of this fort is brought, en-deavour to foften the rigour of this law; or ra-ther to evade it, by depreciating the value of the thing ftolen, by fuffering the matter to be compromifed between the parties, and, where the character of the offender will admit of it, inftead of purfuing the feverities of *juftice,* by tempering the whole procedure with *mercy ?*— This, and fuch like modes of acting, may be faid indeed to be ftraining points ; but, unlefs fuch points be ftrained occafionally, magiftrates muft often act, not only againft the *fpirit* of the laws, but againft the dictates of reafon, and the feelings of their own hearts.—Sir Henry Spel-man took occafion, from this law, to complain, that " while every thing elfe was rifen in its " value, and become dearer, the life of man " had continually grown cheaper [160]."

Fortefcue has a remarkable paffage concern-ing this law. " The civil law," fays he, " where a theft is manifeft, adjudged the cri-" minal to reftore fourfold ; for a theft not fo " manifeft, twofold : but the laws of England, " in either cafe, punifh the party with death, " provided the thing ftolen exceeds the value

[160]. *Gloffar.* in voce *Larícinium.*

" of

" of twelve pence [161]." But, is not this comparison between *Civil* and *English* law astonishingly made by a man, who was writing an apology for the latter against the former? What? —is it nothing to settle a proportion between crimes and punishments? and shall one man, who steals an utensil worth thirteen pence, be deemed an equal offender against society, and suffer the same punishment, with another, who plunders a house, and murders all the family?—See *Beccaria*, an Italian marquis, *Upon Crimes and Punishments.*

LII.

WHY LAWYERS ARE AVERSE FROM DECISIONS ACCORDING TO EQUITY.

IT has constantly been imputed to the men of this order, that they love to adhere to *law*, in opposition to *equity*; that they had rather kill by the *letter*, than save by the *spirit*; and that they always murmur, and sometimes clamour [162], let reason determine ever so rightly, if she determines otherwise than the law directs. The imputation is not new, or even

---

[161] *De Laud. Leg. Angliæ*, c. 46.
[162] See the P. S. to this Nº.

modern.

modern. The younger Pliny, I remember, in a case where law and equity clashed, determined (as all men would, where they could) according to equity: but tells you, at the same time, how apprehensive he was, lest by so doing he should incur the displeasure of the lawyers. " Hoc, si jus accipias, irritum," says he ; " si defuncti voluntatem, ratum & firmum est. " Mihi autem defuncti voluntas, *vereor quam in* " *partem jurisconsulti quod sum dicturus accipiant,* " antiquior jure est [163]."

A more recent instance will illustrate this still farther. The trials of Sir William Friend, Sir William Parkyns, and others, on the assassination-plot, came on, after the provision of counsel learned in the law (not allowed before) had received the royal assent, but before the commencement of its operation. " I entreat," said Parkyns, " that I may have the allowance " of counsel : I have no skill in indictments : " I do not understand these matters ; nor what " advantages may be proper for me to take. " The new statute wants but one day. What " is just and reasonable to-morrow, surely " is just and reasonable to-day; and your " Lordship may indulge me in this case." But, says the humane author [164], from whom I transcribe this, Holt, Chief Justice, was too good a Judge to suffer the stubborn principles of law

[163] Epist. V. 7.   [164] Principles of Penal Law, ch. xv.

to yield to the milder inferences of equity. *We cannot* (he replied) *alter the law, till lawmakers direct us : we must conform to the law, as it is at present, not what it will be to-morrow : we are upon our oaths so to do* [165].

This, so far as I can learn, has ever been the temper and spirit of the lawyers. They are displeased when things are done, not only against forms, but even without them. They hate, we say, to have points judged and determined by equity : why ? not surely from any natural aversion to equity (for how can this be peculiar to any order of men ?) but from its tending to supersede law. All orders hate, and ever will hate, whatever tends to destroy the characteristics of their profession. Divines hate morality, when opposed to religion ; as physicians hate regimen, when opposed to medicine [166]. The reason is, that morality and regimen,

---

[165] Forster's Crown Law, 230. 232. State Trials, 630, 631.

[166] The present Bishop of Gloucester, in his Fast Sermon, Feb. 1782, is offended at Dr. Adam Smith for saying, that " Mr. Hume approached as nearly to the idea of *a perfectly* " *wise and virtuous man*, as perhaps frail humanity will per- " mit :" and well he may be offended ; for, if this can be without aid from religion, what occasion for a church and bishops ? *Hume's Life.*—Dr. William Stevenson, a physician, complains repeatedly, that he hath been vehemently opposed, or in his own language persecuted, every where by apothecaries : which who will be surprised at, when he is told, that this

said

men, thus circumstanced, tend to set aside religion and medicine; because they represent
them, indirectly at least, as superfluous and un-
necessary. And what can be more mortifying
to a professor, than any thing which tends to
shew, that his profession is an useless, and therefore probably a pernicious, burthen to society?

Human nature, upon this head, is uniform
throughout. Pythagoras, we know, exhorted
every man to reverence himself, as the best pre-
servative against doing any thing below, or unworthy of, himself: αἰσχύνεο σαυτόν, says he, in
the verses called *golden*. Now a man's second
self is his profession; yea, in truth, it is often
his first self: I mean, his natural character is
not only discoloured, distorted, and disguised,
but it is sometimes totally absorbed and swallowed up, by his professional character. All orders of men have reverenced themselves as orders, and perhaps none more than the men of
the law. Sir Edward Coke, in his *Institutes*,
frequently takes occasion to set out the learning and importance of the lawyers: he calls

---

said Doctor would have reduced the whole *Materia Medica*
to these " eight officinals, viz. *Cantharides*, *Tartar Emetic*,
" *Mercurius Dulcis*, *Aloes*, *Sena*, *Jalap*, *Salts*, and *Opium*.
" These, says he, compose all the virtue, all the efficacy, of
" the apothecary's shop: give me these, and the contents
" of all the shops in England (beside) may be poured into
" the streets for me." *Cases in Medicine*, p. 56. 58. 1781,
8vo.

them

them " the fages of the parliament; the very
" life and foul of the King's council." Alfo,
in a fpeech made upon a call of ferjeants, he
compares the *coif* to *Minerva's helmet*, who was
the Goddefs of *Counfel*; and likewife fays, that
" the four corners of their cap import fcience,
" experience, obfervation, recordation [167].

Sir John Fortefcue had exprefied himfelf before in the like magnificent terms, and difplayed
with a kind of oftentation the great advantages
of ftudying the law, as well as the awful dignity
and pomp of its profeffors; and he " thinks
" it a great and peculiar token of the Divine
" goodnefs, *magna et quafi approbata benedictio*
" *Dei*, that from amongft the Judges and their
" offspring have fprung more peers of the
" realm, than from any other order of men
" whatever: which," fays he, " can never be
" afcribed to mere chance or fortune, that be-
" ing nothing; but ought to be attributed to
" the bleffing of God, who by his prophet had
" declared, that *the generation of the upright*
" *fhall be bleffed* [168]." From which pofition,
thefe two corollaries manifeftly arife: firft, that
exaltation to a peerage is a bleffing from Heaven; and, fecondly, that this bleffing may be
obtained by juftice and uprightnefs in the profeffion of the law. And if this honeft Chancel-

[167] Barrington *on Anc. Stat.* p. 406. 3d edit.
[168] *De Laudibus, &c.* cap. 51.

lor's reasoning be good, we are led to think highly of our present chiefs in the law; since it is plain, that the practice of it is in our times, as it was heretofore, frequently the road to peerages and preferment.

P. S. No true man of the profession was ever heard to speak with temper upon the noted case of *Coke*, a gentleman of Suffolk, and *Woodburn*, a labourer, who were indicted, in 1722, upon the famous *Coventry* Act of 22 and 23 of *Car.* II.; *Coke* for hiring and abetting *Woodburn*, and *Woodburn* for the actual fact of slitting the nose of Mr. *Crispe*, *Coke*'s brother-in-law. The murder of *Crispe* was the thing intended; and he was left for dead, being terribly hacked and disfigured with an hedge-bill: but he reco-vered. Now though, by this statute, to disfi-gure, with an intent to disfigure, be felony, yet the bare intent to murder is not so: and *Coke*, who was a lawyer, had the skill and ad-dress (I say nothing of the modesty) to rest his defence upon this point, that " the af-" sault was not committed with an intent to " *disfigure*, but with an intent to *murder*; and " therefore not within the statute."

The court however held, that, if a man at-tacks another with such an instrument as an hedge-bill, which cannot but endanger the dis-figuring of him, and in such attack happens not to kill, but only to disfigure him, he may be indicted on this statute: and it shall be left to

the

the Jury, whether it were not a defign to murder by disfiguring, and confequently a malicious intent to disfigure as well as to murder.
Accordingly, the Jury found them guilty of
fuch previous intent to disfigure, in order to effect their principal intent to murder ; and they
were both condemned and executed [169].

Now, though thefe delinquents were criminal enough, God knows, yet, according to this
ftatute, they were not condemnable ; and the
fame conftructive violence, in the interpretation of laws, might often hang an honeft man
as well as a knave. I am, therefore, here with
the men of the profeffion, though for reafons
probably different from theirs, and wifh that they
had been acquitted ; for I think entirely with
Fortefcue, that " twenty evil doers had better
" efcape death, than one juft man be unjuftly
" condemned :" *mallem revera*, fays the humane Chancellor, *viginti facinorofos mortem pietate evadere, quam juftum unum injuftè condem-
nari* [170].

[169] *State Trials*, VI. 212.   [170] *De Laudibus*, &c. c. 27.

LIII. MAN-

LIII.

MANNERS WILL PREVAIL AGAINST LAWS.

IT hath often been affirmed, and with airs of of high concern, that there is no nation upon the globe better provided with laws than the English; nor any, whose laws are more loosely and negligently executed. The censure, implied in the latter of these propositions, is usually levelled at the magistrate; and it is levelled, as I have always observed, with some degree of peevishness and warmth: *better*, it is said, *to have no laws at all, than to have laws of no effect* [171]. But the magistrate is censured without any just cause,—indeed for neglecting, what it is not at all in his power to perform: and the censure, if traced to its origin, will be found to arise from a very common, but very mistaken supposition, *that laws are sufficient to controul and govern manners*; whereas it is certain, that the very reverse is true, and that *manners will always controul and govern laws*.

The prevalence of manners over the laws in ancient Rome was long complained of, before the destruction of the commonwealth. Plautus

---

[171] —frustra interdicta quæ vetuerant cernentes, nullas potius quam irritas esse leges maluerunt. *Plin. Nat. Hist.* xxxvi. 3.

flourished

flourished about a century and half before the civil war broke out between Cæsar and Pompey; yet the manners in Plautus's time were become so notoriously degenerate, and withal so prevailing against the laws, that he makes even a slave to hold the following language [172]:

Nunc mores nihil faciunt quod licet, nisi quod lubet.
Ambitio jam more sancta 'st : libera est legibus.

* * * * * * *

Mores leges perduxerunt jam in potestatem suam.

* * * * * * *

Neque quicquam lege sanctum 'st : leges mori ser-
viunt.

—But, **not to loiter** upon ancient theatres, let us descend at once to modern; to that particularly, on which we act, and with which alone we are concerned. And here, without rambling over an immense field, let us confine our observations to three or four acts of parliament, which solely respect manners : for these will suffice to shew, that laws will be of little, or rather no efficacy at all, when manners bear strongly and powerfully against them.

By a law, enacted in 2 Geo. II. common swearing is forbidden, as being justly deemed the mark of a very profligate or a very foolish spirit : and the delinquent is fined, according to the rank he holds in society. But is the prac-

[172] *Trinummus,* Act. IV.

tice

tice of it fuppreffed, or even curbed ? Nay, can
any thing prevail more univerfally ? and is it poffible to ftir out, without having our ears every
moment annoyed with it? Very true : but the reafon is, that the *Juftice of Peace*, who has the care
of this, as of almoft all other ftatutes, will not
put it in execution. Say you fo ? Well then,
let us fuppofe this magiftrate, with half a fcore
of fetters or informers, marching forth upon a
vifitation in his diftrict, with a determined purpofe to execute this law againft all, *gentle* as
well as *fimple*, who fhall be found to offend a-
gainft it :—I am obliged to march him out, becaufe, unlefs *per accidens*, no information of this
kind will ever be brought home to him—I afk
now, what reception he would meet with, and
what amendment he would work ? He would
be deemed an officious, troublefome, impertinent perfon : he would be abufed, infulted,
hated : and, as to reformation and amendment,
far from any thing tending thereto, he would
infallibly promote the crime he was endeavour-
ing to correct. He has indeed law to fupport
him, and gofpel too, if that could do any good :
but *leges moribus ferviunt*, the laws give way to
manners : licentioufnefs is eftablifhed, and pro-
fligacy triumphant. So, by an ordinance in
1650, when the righteous ruled the land, it was
made felony in both fexes, without benefit of
clergy, to commit adultery or fornication : but

3   laws,

laws, made againſt manners which will always prevail, of courſe repeal themſelves; and for this particular ordinance, as one pleaſantly obſerves, " it could not have continued long unrepealed, even if Charles II. had not ſucceeded to the throne [173]."

The acts of parliament, relating to alehouſes and tipling, are very explicit, preciſe, and ſtrong : and they are too well known, to need to be enlarged on. But, is it poſſible to put theſe acts in execution ? Shall every man be fined, who is known to be drunk ; and every ale-ſeller deprived of his licence, who may happen to ſuffer irregularities in his houſe ? Not only the manners, but the very police, of the country would oppoſe this. It is believed, with good reaſon, that the Juſtice of Peace cannot, in any ſingle branch of his office, ſerve his neighbourhood more effectually, than by paying a rigid attention to houſes of this ſort; they being indiſputably, as they have ever been deemed [174], the grand ſources of corruption and debauchery among the people : and this atten-

[173] Barrington on Anc. Stat. p. 125.

[174] " In the ſtatutes of this reign, there are ever coupled " the puniſhment of vagabonds, the forbidding of dice and " cards to ſervants and mean people, and the putting down and " ſuppreſſing of alehouſes ; as ſtrings of one root together, and " as if the one were unprofitable without the other." Bacon's Hiſt. of Henry VII.

tion

tion is frequently inculcated upon him by the Judge from the bench. Yet, fhould this magif-trate proceed, as the ftatute directs, againft any of thefe houfes, though ever fo notorioufly and fcandaloufly diffolute, the very loweft officers of the Excife would inftantly erect themfelves in oppofition to him. They would abet the ale-feller, with the ufual infolence of their office; would be ready to gauge the unlicenfed cafk; and plume themfelves perhaps as better friends to Government, for fupporting its revenue, than the magiftrate, whofe procedures have a tendency to diminifh it [175].

It is pleafant enough to confider, that, while Government is making laws for the preventing of drunkennefs, thefe little officious minifters of it are promoting drunkennefs, for the righteous purpofe of ferving Government [176]. But I have

feen

[175] Mandeville was abufed for writing a book to fhew, that *Private Vices were Public Benefits:* that is, that a cor-ruption of manners, though pernicious to individuals, might yet be ferviceable to the State. But, are they not made fo in this cafe, in the cafe of lotteries, which promote a fpirit of *gaming*, and in many other cafes? where we may almoft fay with *Seneca*, that "iniquities are practifed according to "acts of parliament,"—*ex fenatus confultis fcelera exercen-tur.*

[176] Doubtlefs, a more ftriking contradiction cannot be; and a French writer has expreffed himfelf very properly, as well as very pleafantly, upon the fubject. *Une fociété, qui pu-nit les excès, qu' elle fait naître, &c.* that is, "a fociety, "which

feen the thing happen, having indeed experienced it in my own practice ; and it brought to my mind an affair of a fimilar kind, related by Dr. Giles Fletcher, who went in a public character to Ruffia towards the end of Queen Elizabeth's reign. This obferver, fpeaking of the many wicked and barbarous arts, which were ufed by the Czars, to drain and opprefs their people, fays, that " in every great town the em-
" peror hath a drinking houfe, which he lets
" out for rent. Here labourers and artificers
" many times fpend all from their wives and
" children. Some drink away every thing they
" wear about them, even to their very fhirts
" inclufive, and then walk naked : all which is
" done for the honour of the Emperor. Nor,
" while they are thus drinking themfelves
" naked, and ftarving their families, muft
" any one call them away, becaufe he would
" hurt the Emperor's revenue [177]."

Duelling is another good inftance, to fhew the prevalence of manners over laws. " The
" law," fays Mr. Hawkins, " fo far abhors du-
" elling, that not only the principal, who ac-
" tually kills the other, but alfo his feconds,

" which punifhes the exceffes it occafions, may be compared
" to thofe, who have the loufy diftemper : they are forced to
" kill the vermin with which they are tormented, though
" the ill habit of their conftitutions every moment produces
" it." *Syftéme de la Nature*, ch. 12.
    [177] *Of the Ruffe Commonwealth*, ch. 12. Lond. 1591.
                                                        " are

" are guilty of murder, whether they fought
" 'or not[178]:" and the punishment of course is
death. But, in spite of this sanction, strong
and powerful as it is, is not the age of Quixotism coming on again? Does not the humour
rodomontade prevail among the great; and is
it not creeping down, even to apprentices and
attorneys clerks?—I called it Quixotism: and
surely I had reason. Observe the manners of
our present duellists; weigh the principles they
go upon; attend to the ceremonial of their en-
gagements; and tell me then, if any adventures
of the famous Knight of La Mancha are built
upon a more foolish foundation, and accompanied with more solemn yet more ridiculous
rites, than theirs.

Perhaps a stronger instance cannot be
brought, than this before us, to shew the prevalence of fashion, not over laws only, but
over sense, and reason, and equity, and humanity. The duellist is never an amiable, and
oftentimes a bad, composition: but he has *honour* for his sanction and support; *honour*, all-
powerful *honour:* and this vain, unmeaning,
empty word,—this *fine imaginary notion*, as Sy-
phax truly calls it,—is, through the prevalence
of fashion, sufficient to preserve him upon terms

[178] 1 Hawk. P. S. 82.

with

with fociety, and to fecure his reception as ufual amongft gentlemen [179].

Let me fubjoin a paffage from a good writer; which, while it animadverts upon this *particular* inftance of Britifh manners, will ferve to confirm our *general* pofition. " No law will, or " ever can, be executed by *inferior* magiftrates, " while the breach of it is openly encouraged " by the examples of *fuperior*. Does any man " think, that the beft laws againft *duelling* " would have any effeſt, if there was at the " fame time a *duelling* office kept open at St. " James's ? The example of thofe, who fhould " execute laws, or fee them executed, is " ftronger than the authority of thofe, who " make them. The example of Vefpafian did " more towards the reftraint of luxury, than " all the fumptuary laws of Rome could do " till his time; for," fays Tacitus, " *a com-* " *plaifance towards the prince, and a fpirit of* " *rivalfhip in imitating his manners, were of far* " *more force, than any dreaded punifhment from* " *the laws* [180]."

[179] Addifon fpeaks of a *club of duellifts*, but obferves, that, " confifting only of *men of honour*, it did not continue long; " moft of the members of it being put to the fword, or " hanged, a little after its inftitution." *Speɛ̌.* N° 9.

[180] *Obfequium in principem, et æmulandi amor, validior quam pœna ex legibus et metus.* Annal. III. 55.—Cato's Letters.

I will

I will cite but one inftance more; and that fhall be the act, to prevent bribery and corruption in electing Members of Parliament, paffed in 1729. It fhould feem, that no ftatute was ever better guarded, and enforced with ftronger fanctions, than this. The elector fwears, if demanded, that he has not received any thing directly or indirectly, in one fhape or other, in order to give his **vote**: this oath to be adminiftered **by the officer**, who prefides at the poll, on forfeiture of 50l. upon refufal. No perfon fhall be admitted to poll, till he hath taken this oath, if demanded as aforefaid: and if the fheriff, or other returning officer, fhall admit any perfon to **be** polled before he is fworn, if demanded, **he** forfeits 100l.; **as** does alfo the perfon, who fhall vote or poll, without firft taking this oath, if demanded. After this, the ftatute enacts, that every returning officer fhall take an oath, that he hath acted with impartiality, difintereftednefs, and fidelity, in the returns he hath made. And then follows **the** great **and** tremendous claufe, which lays a penalty of 500l. on all perfons, who fhall take money or reward for their votes, as well as on the candidates, who by themfelves or any other perfons fhall give it; and which for ever difables both from voting in any future election, and from holding, exercifing, or enjoying any *office, franchife,* &c. **as** if fuch

perfons

perfons were naturally dead. This, one would think, was going as far as human wifdom could forefee; and muft have been fecurity enough, if any thing could be, againft bribery and corruption in all fuch cafes : yet, what has been the effect ? Every body knows : every body knows, that bribery and corruption have been practifed ever fince, and are now avowed without referve or difguife.

The Minifter, againft whom this act was levelled, was fuppofed to pack his parliaments, and to carry all his meafures by the fingle expedient of corruption. At firft indeed he oppofed it; but, foon dropping oppofition, he affected to co-operate with thofe, who were for it. Aware of the no-effects it would have, the minifterial writers of thofe days ridiculed it under the name of *the golden dream* [181] : and doubtlefs the Minifter laughed at it himfelf; for he abounded with pleafantry, and was of an humour to laugh. He was not learned; and poffibly never heard, how Anacharfis laughed at Solon, for thinking to reftrain avarice and ambition by laws [182] : but he knew human nature and the world, and perceived, no doubt, as clearly as Anacharfis, how little acts of parliament would avail in ftemming the torrent of popular manners.

[181] *Craftfman*, N° 313.　　[182] Plut. *in Solon*.

Overzealous

Overzealous reformers, when they see crimes committed often and with impunity, are apt to grow angry: they blame the magistrate for negligence: they call aloud for severer laws and more active magistrates. But severe laws, instead of reforming, would harden a people: they would make them desperate, and perhaps they might make them rebellious. "It is a "perpetual remark of the Chinese authors," says Montesquieu, "that, the more the seve-"rity of punishments was increased in their "empire, the nearer they were to a revolu-"tion. *The reason is,* says he, *that punish-*"*ments were augmented, in proportion as the* "*public morals were corrupted* [183]."

In short, to punish is to begin at the wrong end. If we would effectually reform a people, we must lay a foundation in discipline and manners. "Good manners," says Tacitus, "did more with the Germans, than good laws "in other countries [184]:" and, among the Spartans, the rigid education of their youth, and the sacred regard that was paid to the regulation of manners, in a great measure superseded the use of laws. "It is an old complaint," says Lord Bacon, "that governments have

---

[183] L'Esprit, VI. 9.—*Videbis ea sæpe committi, quæ sæpius vindicantur,* said Seneca formerly.

[184] *Plus ibi boni mores valent, quam alibi bonæ leges.* De Mor. German.

been

" been too attentive to laws, while they have
" neglected the bufinefs of education [185]:" the
wifeft ftatefmen and the ableft obfervers of human nature have always joined them together,
as the only folid bafis, on which the well-
being and happinefs of a nation or people can
be erected [186].

LIV.

LAWS MUST BE FITTED TO A PEOPLE.

WHEN it was infinuated to Solon, that he
had not given the Athenians fo good
laws as he might have done, that wife and re-
fpectable perfon anfwered, " I have given them
" the beft they were able to bear [187]." *Belle*
parole !

[185] Vetus querela eft, inde ufque ab optimis et prudentif-
fimis feculis deducta, refpublicas circa *leges* quidem nimi-
um fatagere, circa *educationem* indiligentes effe. *De Aug.*
Scient. lib. 1.

[186] " There are two things," fays Polybius, " which
" are effential parts in every government; and thefe are
" the *laws* and the *manners,* &c." Lib. VI. extract 3.

[187] Plut. *in Solon.*—It is remarkable, that Mofes practifed
this conformity with the Jewifh people, by accommodating
certain rites and ceremonies to their ancient prejudices ;—
ritus aliquos, fays Spencer, *longo ufu receptos reformando, eofque*
ad

parole ! " a fine obfervation," fays Montefquieu, " and which ought to be perfectly underftood " by every legiflator [182]." Certainly : how elfe will he be able to adapt his means to his end ? Laws, to produce their effects, muft, like all other things, be fitted to their objects. Would you tame a wild animal from the deferts of Africa, you would doubtlefs adapt your *manege*, as nearly as you could, to the nature of the beaft you had to deal with. The human is reckoned by fome the wildeft of all beafts : but, wild or tame, why not treat him according to his nature, and according to the fituation he may happen to be found in ?

A legiflator therefore, who knows what he is about, who takes aim, as they fay, and does not mean to bolt at random, will not retire into his clofet, and there feign abftract and ideal fyftems of laws and government; but he will look abroad, examine and contemplate well the materials he has to work upon, and direct and regulate all his operations by what he fees. He will not confider only what is true, but what is practicable alfo ; and, if he cannot make men fo perfect as he would, he

---

ad Dei ipfius cultum transformando : ritus enim haud paucos antiquitus ufitatos in novam quafi formam finxit Deus, ut plebis animos, quos ratio non potuit, ufus aut divina συγκαταβασις cultui suo conciliaret. De Legibus Hebræor. L. I. c. 5.

[182] L'Efprit, *liv.* xix. *cb.* 21.

will

will make them as perfect as he can.   When
the Dictator Cæsar was projecting a reformation of abuses and manners among the Romans, his counsellor advised him, to accommodate his measures to their present prevailing
habits and customs, and not to think of " re-
" calling them to those ancient original stand-
" ards and rigid rules of discipline, which in
" the then degenerate and corrupt state of
" their manners, instead of being observed,
" would only be made a jest of [189]:" and who
can say, that he did not advise him well? So,
when a motion for reforming was made to Tiberius, the politic tyrant replied, that " it
" might possibly be better to overlook pre-
" vailing and inveterate corruptions, than ex-
" pose their impotence to the world, by shew-

---

[189] ———— non ad vetera instituta revocare, quæ jampridem
corruptis moribus ludibrio sunt. Sallust. Orat. I. ad Cæf. de
Rep. ord.—But Cæfar does not seem to have profited by this
advice ; for, soon after his return from the African war, he
enacted laws to regulate their dress, equipage, furniture, &c.
but chiefly their tables, and style of eating. Legem præcipue
sumptuariam exercuit : dispositis circa macellum custodibus, qui
obsonia contra vetitum retinerent, deportarentque ad se ; submissis
nonnunquam lictoribus atque militibus, qui, si qua custodes fefellis-
sent, jam apposita e triclinio auferrent. Suet. in Vit. § 43.
More, surely, could not be done to enforce the execution of
any law ; yet it appears to have been neglected, and of no
effect at all. Cæsari certum est Romæ manere ; ne, se absente,
leges suæ negligerentur, sicut esset neglecta SUMPTUARIA.
Cic. ad Att. xiii. 7.

ing

" ing how unequal they were to the reforma-
" tion of them [190]."—The Emperor Galba confirmed the wisdom of this ; for, exerting a spirit of reforming, beyond what the manners of
Rome would bear, he not only failed, but lost
his life, in the attempt : *nocuit antiquus rigor et
nimia severitas, cui jam pares non sumus*, says
Tacitus. Hist. I. 18.

Mean while one cannot, without some surprise, behold certain patriotic leaders among
the Romans, such as Cicero and Brutus, making
a stand for liberty, and vainly struggling to
restore it to a people, whose virtue was entirely
gone, and whose manners were totally relaxed
and dissolute. *Liberty*, says Sidney, *cannot be
preserved, if the manners of the people be corrupt* [191]. But the Roman manners were in a
high degree corrupt ; which made Jugurtha
say, even half a century before, that " Rome
" itself would be sold, if a buyer could be
" found :" *urbem venalem, si emptorem invenerit.*
Sallust.

[190] *Nescio an suasurus fuerim omittere potius prævalida et
adulta vitia, quam hoc adsequi, ut palam fieret, quibus flagitiis
impares essemus.* Tac. Ann. iii. 53.
[191] On Government, ch. 11.

LV.

NOT WHAT SEEMS PERFECT, BUT WHAT IS PRACTICABLE.

THAT wild enthusiastic spirit, which would elevate human nature above her genuine standard, would in like manner push civil society beyond any degree of practicable perfection. The same Plotinus, whom we have already strictured for the former [192], was equally stimulated with a zeal for the latter. It is related by Porphyry, who hath written his life, that he asked the Emperor Gallienus to build and endow a city for philosophers, that should be governed according to Plato's ideas, and be called Platonopolis [193]; and Porphyry adds, that Plotinus would have obtained what he asked, if some malignants at court had not interposed. They probably thought, that the Treasury-money might be more usefully employed: the Emperor, however, might have found some advantage from it, as he would certainly have got rid of all the *Utopians*, the *visionaries* in politics, the statesmen of general abstract ideas; which, when they are suffered to be busy, are a very troublesome order of

[192] No XI.   [193] Fabric. Bibl. Græc. IV. 12.

3

beings:

beings : thefe would all, with one accord, have haftened to Platonopolis.

A certain writer has obferved, that thefe well - meaning fpeculative politicians (for *well-meaning* they are often allowed to be) " are of all others the moft untraccable in go- " vernment, and mifchievous in bufinefs : who " endeavour to deftroy all governments, be- " caufe they are not perfect ; and oppofe all " adminiftrations, becaufe they cannot govern " men by fuch means, as they are not defigned " or formed to be governed by [194]." Cato, formerly, was an offender in this way : he was a " well-meaning fpeculative politician ;" and is recorded to have done mifchief in the Senate at Rome, merely from not diftinguifhing be- tween what *feems perfect* and what is *practicable.* " With the very beft intentions and the clear- " eft integrity," fays Tully, " he fometimes " hurts the commonwealth." And how ? " By " giving his opinion upon all occafions, as if " he were in the pure and incorrupt republic of " Plato, and not amidft the low and degenerate " tribe of Romulus [195] :" contrary to which, as the fame Tully obferves, " a ftatefman muft " confider, not only what is beft in itfelf, but " what is neceffary alfo to times and fitua-

---

[194] *Upon the Origin of Evil.* Letter V.
[195] Tanquam in Platonis πολιτεία, non tanquam in fæce Romuli. *Ad Att.* II. 1.

" tions."

" tions [196]." *Tempori cedere*, that is, to submit
to the time, is a submission, which the statef-
men of all ages have ever found it expedient
to make. Tully lays it down as a capital and
fundamental maxim in politics ; and, speaking
to Atticus of something he had done as the act
optimi civis, he adds, fed *ita* optimi, ut *tempora*,
quibus *parere* omnes πολιτικοὶ præcipiunt. Nor
could even Cæsar himself, though conqueror
and dictator, be exempt from this submission
to the circumstances of affairs : nos illi *servimus*,
says Tully, ipse *temporibus* ; nec ille, quid *tempora* postulatura sunt, scire potest [197].

It is common to blame individuals, when *affairs* go wrong, and it is sometimes right ; but
it is not always so : for the statesman, any more
than other men, cannot act invariably and always as he would : he is often forced along by
a necessary train of things, and obliged to act,
not as he would, but as he can. He may
watch conjunctures : he may avail himself at

---

[196] Non solum ei quid esset optimum videndum est, sed
etiam quid necessarium. *De Leg.* III. 11.—And to this wise
maxim even Cato himself, in a more reasonable mood, and
when common sense prevailed over stoicism, could occasionally conform : for, when the Senate found it expedient to
support Bibulus against Cæsar, in suing for the consulship,
they " made a common purse, to enable him to bribe as
" high as his competitors ;" *ne Catone quidem abnuente*, as
Suetonius says in Vita Cæs. §. 9.

[197] *Ad Att.* xii. **5**.—*Ad Fam.* iv. **9.** *et* ix. **17**.

moments

moments by policy and expedient: he may rightly adapt certain means to certain ends, and sometimes succeed; but he will frequently miscarry: for there are in all governments so many circumstances and contingencies, independent of human foresight and will, that oftentimes the most which the wisest manager can do, is to make the wisest use of incidents as they rise: *quæ casus offert, in sapientiam vertere.* Tacitus [198].

[198] " We may lament the imperfections of our human
" state, which is such, that, in cases of the utmost importance
" to the order and good government of society, we are re-
" duced to have no part to take, which our reason can ap-
" prove absolutely. Perfect schemes are not adapted to our
" imperfect state. Stoical morals and *Platonic* politics are
" nothing better than amusements for those, who have had
" little experience in the affairs of the world, and who have
" much leisure. In truth, all that human prudence can do,
" is to furnish expedients, and to compound as it were with
" general vice and folly; employing reason to act even
" against her own principles, and teaching us (if I may say
" so) *insanire cum ratione.*" Bolingbroke's *Idea of a Patriot King.*

LVI.

OF COFFEE-HOUSE POLITICIANS, AS THEY ARE CALLED.

THERE is no order of men, who are more an object of curious contemplation, than those καρδιογνώςαι, or *knowers of hearts* (for such I think they muſt be deemed, if any uninſpired mortals can be ſo deemed) who are perfectly acquainted with the tempers and principles of Miniſters, whoſe perſons they never ſaw; and can at once, as if by intuition, trace all tranſ-actions in politics to the cauſes from which they ſpring. The famous Cardinal *de Retz*, who was the life and ſoul of the faction he go-verned, and muſt have been privy, if any one could be ſo, to all the moſt ſecret ſprings and movements of it, yet declares, that " there are " inexplicable points in *affairs*, which are ac-" tually ſo at the moment in which they hap-" pen; that they are impenetrable even by " thoſe, who are the neareſt to them : whence " he cannot but wonder at the inſolence of " certain obſcure perſons, who imagine them-" ſelves to have penetrated into the very hearts " of thoſe, who are concerned the moſt in " theſe affairs [199]."

It

---

[199] *J'admire l'inſolence de ces gens de néant, qui s'imaginent avoir penetré dans tous les replis des cœurs de ceux, qui ont en*

la

It is obfervable, that he makes this remark no lefs than four times, while he relates the tranfactions of the *Fronde* in 1651: and, though his animadverfions are levelled at certain low impertinent hiftorians, which infefted his times as they do ours, yet—are they not equally applicable to thofe innumerable ftatefmen fcattered through the land, who affect to know the penetralia of a court, and to trace every idea with as much exactnefs and certainty, as if they had perched upon the pineal gland of the Minifter, at the moment it iffued forth?

Among this order of ftatefmen are your *Doctores Umbratici* ;—for there are fuch doctors in politics, as well as in divinity, law, and phyfic —men, who, fitting *in the fhade* as it were, *fee vifions* and *dream dreams* : that is, form the moft perfect fyftems of governing, if Minifters were but wife enough to attend to them duly. All which may poffibly be amufing, and would be alfo innocent, if kept at home for private ufe ; but the misfortune is, that thefe *feers* of *vifions* and *dreamers* of *dreams* are ever eager and zealous to have them introduced into pub-

---

la plus de part dans les affaires.—Il y a des points dans les affaires inexplicables dans leurs inftans.—Ne doit-on pas admirer l'infolence des Hiftoriens Vulgaires, qui croiroient fe faire tort, fi ils laffoient un feul évenement dans leurs ouvrages, dont ils ne declaraffent pas les refforts ? Memoires.

lic affairs, and fure to grow angry and difaffected, when they are not, in their eftimation,
properly attended to : little confidering, alas!
that what they *fee* and *dream*, is not reducible
to practice, or to be made of any ufe in the affairs of men—*nihil ex iis, quæ in ufu habemus,
aut audiunt, aut vident.* Petron.

LVII.

OF REASON OF STATE, OR STATE-NECESSITY.

WHAT is *Reafon of State*, or *State Neceffity ?*
Why, in truth, neither more nor lefs, ex-
plain them as you will, than an affumed right
to difpenfe with the laws, whenever they ob-
ftruct the meafures of a Prince or his Minifters.
Milton has called *neceffity* the *tyrant's plea.*
Another writer calls it " the great patronefs of
" illegal actions, which politicians have ufed,
" as certain philofophers did Occult Quality,
" though to a different purpofe; this being the
" philofopher's refuge for ignorance, that the
" politician's fanctuary for fin."—Pius Quin-
tus, fays Lord Bacon, could not bear the name
of *Ragioni di Stato*, being wont to fay, that
thefe were the mere devices of wicked men,
wherewith to opprefs religion and virtue: *no-
men ipfum averfatus eft Pius V. folitus dicere, effe
mera malorum hominum commenta, quæ oppone-*
rentur

rentur religioni et virtutibus moralibus [200].—
They had once a term in France, which, if it
had been properly nurtured up and cherished,
would have answered all the purposes of this
reason of State, by countenancing Kings **and**
Ministers in whatever *manœuvres* they might
please to set on foot; and that was, *the public
good.* Thus, the princes of France leagued
against Lewis XI. for THE PUBLIC GOOD : *on
l' appella la ligue* DU BIEN PUBLIC, says Mezeray, anno **1464,** *parce que les princes luy donnoient
ce beau pretexte :* and, in 1475, Edward IV. of
England was preparing a descent upon France
under the same pretext of *public good* [201].—Our
State lawyers, however, reprobate these ideas,
and certainly with good reason : " I know,"
says one of them, " of no distinction between
" *State necessities* and others : our books do
" not make any such distinction : and we find,
" in 3 Car. I. Mr. Serjeant *Ashley* was com-
" mitted to the Tower, for saying, in one of
" his arguments at the bar, that there was a
" *State power*, or law of the State, as **well** as of
" the Country. And the Judges, with respect
" to ship-money, were committed for saying,
" that there was a *State necessity* for it [202]."

[200] De Augm. Scient. l. i.

[201] Comines, anno 1464 and 1475.

[202] Judgment in the case of *Entick* and *Carrington*, C. B.
Michaelmas Term, 1765, delivered by Lord Chief Justice
Prat.

LVIII.

METHINKS, they fhould be called *acts of folvency*; fince they enable men to pay debts, and (which is extraordinary) without money or effects. But to be ferious.—— Acts of infolvency are occafional acts, by which perfons are difcharged from fuits and imprifonment, upon furrendering their all to their creditors[203]. It hath often been agitated, to whom the benefit of thefe acts fhould extend; whether to all indifferently, or only to fome, who could with propriety be deemed proper objects of it? But, though to draw the line, and define boundaries, be generally difficult in human affairs, yet here it feems eafy. Let a court or committee of equity be ordained, to fit at ftated times upon prifoners for debt: and let all, whom *misfortunes* have brought into durance, be releafed; but let *defaulters* or rogues be detained, or otherwife difpofed of according to fome wife police. To think of releafing all, the guilty as well as innocent, would be as unjuft and partial, as it would be weak and impolitic; and were any one to propofe

[203] Blackftone's Commentaries, ii. 31.

this,

this, "perhaps to be *popular*," I should deem him knavish as well as foolish. As deliberate schemes, as ever were concerted for a burglary, have been concerted to gain trust and credit, in order to defraud and rob: and getting into debt, with such concerters, is nothing else but a certain mode of robbing.

LIX.

A DECISION BY THE KING OF PRUSSIA.

THE Amsterdam Gazette, of 13 Feb. 1784, records the following decision by the King of Prussia. A soldier of Silesia, being convicted of stealing certain offerings to the Virgin Mary, was doomed to death as a sacrilegious robber. But he denied the commission of any theft; saying, that the Virgin, from pity to his poverty, had *presented* him with the offerings. The affair was brought before the King, who asked the Popish divines, whether, according to *their* religion, the miracle was impossible? who replied, that the case was extraordinary, but not impossible. Then said the King, the " cul-
" prit cannot be put to death, because he de-
" nies the theft, and because the divines of
" his

" his religion allow the prefent not to be im-
" poffible ; but we ftrictly forbid him, under
" pain of death, *not to receive any prefent hence-*
" *forward from the Virgin Mary, or any Saint*
" *whatever.*"—This, I take it, was anfwering
fools according to their folly, and is an inftance
of wifdom as well as wit.

LX.

EXPERIENCE MAKES FOOLS WISE.

NOT it indeed; no, nor even men, who
are not fools. For inftance, experience
may convince every man, even the wifeft, that
his " judgment conftantly deceives him : is he
" not therefore a fool," fays Montaigne, " if
" he does not diftruft it ?" Very true, Seigneur:
but, pray, how many beings have you known,
who, from this reflection, have become lefs
pofitive in their manners, lefs dogmatical in
their opinions, lefs fudden in their decifions ?
—Experience may fhew every man, that public
rumour *always* lies : that the facts related, however confidently warranted for truths, are often
without any foundation at all, notwithftanding
the proverb *no fmoke without fire* ; but always,

by

by adding or diminishing, disguised and altered from their real selves [204]. Yet, who is there, that hesitates to admit and swallow at once *any* thing said of *any* man, and especially (thanks to the milkiness of human nature) if to his disgrace or detriment [205]?

Another striking instance, where even the wisest men are not taught by experience, may be seen in pages 122 and 123 above, No. XXXV.

LXI.

THE BRAVADO OPPOSITE TO WHAT HE WOULD SEEM.

SOME years ago, at St. George's Hospital, Westminster, two boys underwent each the amputation of an arm. The one expressed just and natural apprehensions of the operation, yet bore it in a firm and reasonable

---

[204] *Fama ne tunc quidem, cum aliquid veri affert, sine mendacii vitio est ; detrahens, adjiciens, demutans de veritate.* Tertullian. Apol. c. 7.

[205] When any thing *bad* is said, human malignity swallows it greedily, and the gulp is delicious; not so, when any thing *good :* this is swallowed, as a medicine is swallowed, and often stays as difficultly upon the stomach.

O

manner. The other defpifed the timidity of his fellow-patient, made extremely light of the operation, and even fet it glorioufly at defiance; yet complained during the procefs **in the** moft womanifh [206] and daftardly ftile, and **was, in** fhort, totally fubdued by it. Upon my feeming greatly furprifed, the furgeon faid, that *it was always fo.* —I **believe it is** fo in other things, as well as courage. Whenever vanity oftentatioufly parades either upon wealth, or knowledge, or learning, *&c. &c.* there fufpicion fhould naturally arife : and why ? becaufe realities are feldom folicitous about appearances, yea, **often not enough** attentive to them ; while wind and emptinefs inflate and *puff.*

[206] This term by right fhould be withdrawn ; for I actually faw a woman, in the fame hofpital, undergo the amputation of a breaft, without complaining at all, fo far as I could perceive. How is it, that the women feem fo much better formed for fuffering than the men ? is it, that they are more trained to expect it as a thing in courfe ?

LXII.

LXII.

OF ACADEMIES OR PRIVATE SEMINARIES.

WHY do people, in the education of their children, avoid public schools, and affect academies [207] ? or some of those choice nurseries for youth, where the gentleman, not for **profit**, but for amusement, and **the** pleasure **of making** pupils more finished, **confines himself to six** or eight, **at** the rate of 100 l. instead of 20 l. a year !—Why ? for the same reason, that many leave the established church, and run to a Methodist meeting-house; in sure and certain-hope of being better instructed by a shoemaker or a weaver, than by a man trained at **a** school and university :—for the same reason, that men leave regular physicians for the sake of quacks or waterologers [208].

[207] By *Academies* are not here meant those public seminaries among the Dissenters, where education is conducted in its best manner ; but schools in **private houses**, which assume the name **of** *Academies*.

[208] "Miss Molitor, just arrived from Strasbourg, embraces this opportunity to acquaint the public, that through long practice with **her** father, Dr. Molitor of Strasbourg, she undertakes to *cure* all those disorders, that are deemed *incurable* by the Faculty. She flatters herself, by *seeing the water* of the patient, to tell if curable or not." *Morn. Chron.* 21 April, 1784.—This, I take it, **is the way** to have business.

There

There may have been, but it has not been my fortune to fee, even a fingle youth accomplifh-ed in letters, and who could fairly be called a fcholar, come forth from any of thefe private feminaries. And indeed, how fhould their mafters teach, what not one in ten hath ever learned?

LXIII.

A COMPENDIOUS WAY TO BE SAVED.

SOME, who defpair of being faved by *Works*, turn Methodifts to obtain falvation by *Faith*. They refemble the *Butler* in Addifon's *Drummer*. Having loft a filver fpoon, he confults a con-jurer; who promifes him the fpoon again, but upon condition, that he fhould " drink nothing " but fmall-beer for a fortnight:" but the Butler, defpairing to " recover it this way, " e'en bought a new one." Thus, it is much eafier to be faved by faith among the Metho-difts, or abfolutions among the Papifts, than by a courfe of moral practice [209]: all finners

---

[209] Churchmen do not inculcate moral practice, as *of itfelf* fufficient to fave, but only as a *fine qua non*; that is, a man cannot be faved without it, his beft endeavours towards moral perfection being neceffary to qualify him for the benefits of Chrift's death.

like

like it better, for the same reason that an epi-
cure or voluptuary had rather be cured by medicine or Bath waters, than submit to abstinence
and regimen.

LXIV.

A VINDICATION OF PARACELSUS.

ONE of the papers, in the *Medical Transac-
tions* just published [210], contains the following paragraph: " If modern times had not
" furnished similar instances, it would have been
" matter of astonishment to us to have heard,
" that Erasmus, the friend, the correspondent,
" and the patient of our excellent Linacer,
" whose great skill in the science of physic he
" extols in several of his epistles, ever consult-
" ed, in his own case, so *wild,* so *illiterate* an
" enthusiast, as Paracelsus appears to have been.
" But it is to be *lamented,* that in matters,
" which relate to physic, even the most sensible
" part of mankind has ever shewn a degree of
" weakness and credulity, easily imposed upon
" by the *self-importance* of those, who know
" how to recommend themselves to the world
" by *bold promises*; and that *diffidence, doubt,*

[210] The publication here alluded to was in 1768, an 8vo;
whence it appears, that this article was drawn up many
years ago.

O 3 " and

." and *hefitation*, which help to conftitute the
" true character of a philofopher, have ruined
" both the fame and fortune of many an excel-
" lent phyfician."—Thefe words are important, and will furnifh, as a preacher would fay,
abundant matter for edification.

Now, though it is not meant to *vindicate*
Paracelfus fully and abfolutely throughout, yet
—hath not this writer's zeal againft him fomewhat tranfported, and carried him farther, than
the matter of fact will in ftrictnefs admit of?
That Paracelfus was *wild* to a confiderable degree, will not be denied; but, whether he was
either fo *wild*, or fo *illiterate*, as he is here reprefented, it is at leaft pardonable to doubt,
becaufe men, neither *wild* nor *illiterate*, have
thought and fpoken highly of him. The writer
quotes Erafmus, as having *confulted him in his
own cafe*: his complaint and *lamentation* are
grounded upon this very fact. If then Erafmus,
though the friend and patient of Linacer, whofe
fkill too in phyfic he hath greatly extolled,
did (as by thus confulting him he certainly did)
fuppofe, that Paracelfus might do what Linacer
had not done—could Erafmus think otherwife
than highly of him?

True it is, that Erafmus hath not fpoken fa-
vourably of phyficians in general; a letter of
his to Warham, archbifhop of Canterbury, beginning in thefe terms: *Incidit Erafmo tuo
periculofa et omnium graviffima cum calculo con-
flictatio.*

flictatio. Deventum in manus Medicorum et Phar--macopolarum, hoc eft, carnificum et harpyiarum, &c [211]. But these and similar strokes regard only the morals of the profession, and in no wise affect his testimony for Paracelsus, whose abilities, as a professor, are the point in question. Others also have spoken in the highest terms of this physician. *Placuit Altissimo Paracelsum misisse,* says Van Helmont, *qui medicaminum altiores præparationes mundo proponeret* [212]: **and** Gerard Vossius speaks of him, as having actually raised chemistry from the dead [213].—But, as we mean to comment a little upon the qualifications and manners of this physician, let us, for the fake of contemplating his history and character the better, draw the chief lines and features of them out, and present them here under one point of view.

PARACELSUS was born, 1493, near Zurich in Switzerland [214]. His father being a physician, he learned from him the elements of his art;

---

[211] Opera. **Tom.** III. p. 164. **L. Bat.** 1706.

[212] De **Ortu** Medicinæ, p. 406. Amst. 1652.

[213] Chemiam, diu sepultam, quasi ab orco revocavit: scriptor, ut de eo nobilissimus Tycho, pluribus oppugnatus quam intellectus. *De Philosoph.*

[214] Boerhaave, Elementa Chemiæ, p. 19. L. **Bat.** 1732.—Histoire de la Medecine, par Dan. Le **Clerc, p. 792.** Amst. 1723.

but,

but, captivated with alchymy, as he grew up, he was placed under the moſt eminent maſters in that way. He then travelled, and viſited al-moſt all the countries and univerſities in Europe; conſulting indifferently, wherever he was, phyſicians, barbers, old women, conjurers, chemiſts, &c. **and** eagerly adopting from any whatever he thought uſeful. About his 20th year, he examined the mines in Germany; then proceeded as far as to Ruſſia : on the borders of which being taken by the Tartars, he was carried to the Cham, and afterwards ſent with that prince's ſon to Conſtantinople ; where, as himſelf relates, he was let into the ſecret of the philoſopher's ſtone. Returning to Europe, he ſettled at Baſil ; and here grew famous, eſpecially after his ſucceſsful treatment of Frobenius, the celebrated printer [215]. By this, he became acquainted with Eraſmus ; and was, in ſhort, ſo highly eſteemed, that the magiſtracy of Baſil made him profeſſor of phyſic in 1527, and ſettled upon him an handſome ſalary. Here

---

[215] Non poſſum polliceri præmium arti tuæ ſtudioque par : **certe** gratum animum polliceor. *Frobenium ab inferis revocaſti,* hoc eſt, dimidium mei : ſi **me** quoque reſtitueris, in ſingulis utrumque reſtitues. Utinam ſit ea fortuna, quæ te Baſileæ **remoretur.** *Eraſm. ad Paracelſ. Epiſt.*—He did not however **ſtay long** at Baſil, but went to Alface, July 1528 : and, rambling afterwards through ſeveral countries, came at length to Saltzbourg, where he died Sept. 1541. *Le Clerc,* p. 801.

he

he read lectures two hours every day, sometimes in Latin, but oftener in German; and here, in a public and solemn manner from the chair, he burned the writings of Galen and Avicenna, though he affected to value highly Hippocrates and the ancient physicians.

"He had," says Rapin, "a profound ge-"nius, but a dark and obscure expression: all "his words were enigmas, and all his discourses "mysteries [216]." Rullandus, a German Physician, formed a dictionary of his new-invented terms, which however did not suffice to make them intelligible. He was thought to have used a familiar or demon, and to have carried it about in the hilt of his sword. It is certain, that he affected to pass for a magician; and did not scruple to teach, that, if God refused to lend his assistance, it was lawful and right to consult the devil [217]. He was prepared also to be an ecclesiastical reformer, and had his singularities in divinity, as well as in physic. He main-

[216] *Toutes ses paroles estoient des enigmes, et ses discours des mysteres.* **Reflex.** sur la Philosoph.

[217] G. **Vossius**, though an admirer of Paracelsus, must yet have looked upon this with horror; since he thought it better to die, than to be cured by charms or magical operations. Similis est quartanæ sanatio, says he, per ABRACADABRA chartæ inscriptum, et collo appensum. Plane autem assentio B. Chrysostomo, qui docet, utut hujusmodi amuleta præstarent quod promittunt, satius nihilominus fore, ut morbo obeamus, quam sic recuperemus sanitatem. *De Philosoph.*

tained,

tained, among other strange things, that " our
" first parents before the fall had not the parts
" necessary to generation; but that they protu-
" berated afterwards, like a scrophulous tumor
" from the throat [218]." His manners were
somewhat savage: he was arrogant and assuming, a mighty boaster, a great promiser. By virtue of his *Elixir Proprietatis*, he undertook to
protract the life of man to any period; but,
while he was deliberating how far to protract his
own, he died, after a few days illness, in his 48th
year. His works are in Latin; but his Latinity,
like his manners, is rather barbarous. They
have been printed more than once [219]: the best
edition, as I suppose, is that of Geneva, 1658,
in 3 vols. folio.

Now, from this general survey of Paracelsus,
what is the idea to be formed of his character? why, undoubtedly, *wildness* appears
to have **been a** prevailing cast in **it.** But,
was *wildness* peculiar to Paracelsus? Was

---

[218] Negabat primos parentes ante lapsum habuisse **partes**
generationi hominis necessarias: *postea accessisse, ut strumam
gutturi.* Vossius, *ibid.*

[219] Guy Patin is quite angry, that printers and presses
should be found for such work ; **and** declares, that they had
better print the Koran. *Avez vous ouï dire,* says he, *que le
Paracelse s'imprime à Geneve ? Quelle honte, qu'un si méchant
livre trouve des presses et des ouvriers ! J'aimerois mieux qu'on
eût imprimé l'Alcoran.* Lettre 58. On the other hand, **Van**
Helmont calls him *Monarcham arcanorum, decus Germaniæ,*
&c. De Ortu Med. **p.** 603. So it is, that doctors differ.

not

not Van Helmont, were not an hundred others,
wild as well as he ?—Take but the bulk of writers upon other subjects ; upon philosophy, upon
divinity, upon metaphysics, particularly : bring
them to the test of reason : examine them well.
You will find, that they abound with wild and
fantastic notions, with vain and groundless con-
ceits ; that some write purely from imagination
and temperament, that others are misled by
prejudice and passion, and that all are constantly losing sight of nature and common sense.
From Paracelsus this censurer " transcribes
" passages, on account of the just observations
" they contain ;" and owns, that, " in the
" midst of the most incomprehensible. jargon,
" he sometimes talks intelligibly [220] :" which
really is as much, as can be said of almost any
writer, upon subjects so abstruse and profound.
Even from Galen; whose name has been founded
so high in the regions of physic, and whose
works are reckoned to contain so many excellent
things ; I say, from Galen will I **undertake** to
produce as solid, full, and elaborate **nonsense**, as
this writer **for** his life can from Paracelsus.
Galen was doubtless an illustrious physician in
his day, and also a very acute and learned man.
Isaac Casaubon hath called him *Criticorum, non
minus quam Medicorum, principem* [221] ; but, if he

[220] Medical Transact. p. 330.

[221] In Athenæum. *Lectori.*

is *now* read by here and there a man, it may
possibly be as much for his language and critical
skill, as for any medical treasures supposed to be
lodged in him.

So much then for Paracelsus's *wildness* : as for
his *illiteracy*, if I may so call it, this may not be
so easily ascertained. I can indeed readily conceive, that he was no critic in Greek and Latin;
but must not hastily pronounce *illiterate* a man,
who has left us two or three folios in a learned
language.   True it is, that his Latinity savours
of barbarism; but it is equally true, that professional men, who could have written in this language **with** purity and elegance, have yet affected an obscure and even barbarous stile, merely
to give their works a more mysterious and sci-
entific air : and Paracelsus, possibly, may have
done so too [221].

[221] M. de la Monnoie is persuaded, that Francis Aretin
industriously affected barbarous expressions in his works
upon law ; lest, being deemed a polite writer, he should not
be thought a profound lawyer. The same barbarous humour prevailed at the same time among physicians and divines : those among them, who first attempted to introduce
politeness, were reckoned neither physicians, nor divines,
but grammarians only. They **were** scarce cured of this prejudice in **the** days of Lud. Vives, whose words upon the
subject **are really** curious : *Quæ Lyranus et Hugo scribunt,
Theologia est ; quæ Erasmus, Grammatica. Idem de Hieronymo,
Ambrosio, Augustino, Hilario dicturi, nisi nomina obstarent ;
tametsi hic etiam nescio quid mussant. Quod si Joannes Picus
apologiam suam corrupto illo non scripsisset sermone, haudquaquam
haberetur Theologus, sed Grammaticus.* De Causis Corrupt.
Eloquent. l. i.

Mean

Mean while, whether he was, or was not, *illiterate*, so far as relates to languages, is of no import in the question between us ; because it does not at all affect his abilities as a physician, or the judgment of Erasmus in consulting him. A critical knowledge, or (as some will have it) any knowledge at all, in the Greek and Latin tongues, though " an ornamental " acquisition, and such as no physician, who " has had a regular education, is found with- " out, is not yet absolutely necessary to the " successful practice of medicine [223] :" and I have a piece now before me, written in 1724, and entitled " *Pharmacopolæ Justificati*, or, Apo- " thecaries vindicated from the imputation of " ignorance ; wherein is shewn, that an acade- " mical education is no way necessary to qua- " lify a man for the practice of physic." The truth is, that, whatever forms and distances may be outwardly kept up, for the sake of do- ing things decently and in order [224], the apothecary

[223] On *the Duties and Offices of a Physician*, p. 5. 1770. 8vo.

[224] Nimia familiaritas cum Pharmacopœo parit contemp- tum, says Fr. Hoffman, in *Medic. Politic.* Pars ii. c. 1. reg. 8.—Yet some, even physicians, have contended, that the partitions, which have kept physician, surgeon, and apo- thecary asunder, should be removed ; and that the three pro- fessions, as it were three departments, should be thrown to- gether. Hear one, who attended the plague at London in 1665,

thecary will ever suppose in secret, that he *understands the administration of medicines in the cure of diseases, as well as the physician;* and in 1704, when the contest ran high between the Dispensary-physicians (as they were then called) and the apothecaries, reasons were openly given to prove it [225]. And it must be confessed, that physicians themselves have countenanced this idea; since, from Galen downwards, they have almost unanimously agreed, that the knowledge of physic cannot be acquired from books. When Sir Richard Blackmore asked Sydenham, what books he should read to qualify him for

1665, and who speaks the sentiments of many of his brethren: "My judgment is," says he, "that it is no such "preposterous thing, as some account it, for a physician, "who intends to acquire excellency in his science, to begin "with *Pharmacopœa* and *Chyrurgia.*—I have acted many "years formerly, but especially now of late when there was "most need, the part of a physitian, chyrurgion, and apo- "thecary, as becomes every honest able man, lawfully "called to this noble faculty. Take it for an infallible "verity, that it is impossible, without miraculous inspira- "tion, for a physitian to discharge his duty in this honour- "able profession, unless he bring to *unity* that, which of "late hath been made a *trinity*." ΛΟΙΜΟΤΟΜΙΑ: *The Pest Anatomized*. By George Thompson, M. D. 1666, 12mo. Pref. to Reader.

[225] The title of the piece alluded to runs thus: "Rea- "sons, why the Apothecary may be supposed to understand "the administration," &c. as above; and the motto from Ovid is, *Et herbarum est subjecta potentia nobis.*

practice?

practice? " Read Don Quixote," says Sydenham: " 'tis a very good book; I read it ftill."
This Blackmore relates himself, in the preface
to his *Treatife on the Small Pox*; and mentions
there alfo another " celebrated phyfician,"
meaning Ratcliff, as declaring on his death-
bed, that he " would leave behind him the
" whole myftery of phyfic upon half a fheet of
" paper."

But furely thefe famous practitioners could
not ftrictly mean, what they have been ufually
underftood to mean. Galen fays exprefsly,
that phyfic cannot be learned from books:
but, as he adds, neither can any other art be
learned from books [226]. So Cicero had faid,
that " neither *phyficians*, nor generals, nor ora-
" tors, although they may have drawn the pre-
" cepts of their art from books, can ever attain
" to any thing great without ufe and practice [227]."
But, did any man in his wits ever deny this?
Take, not arts and fciences but, human nature
in general: by ftudying it in books only, you
will know it no more, than you would know a
man's perfon, from having feen only his picture.
It is rare, that a picture would enable you to
know the original, if it occurred: I think that

---

[226] Εκ βιβλίων μητι κυβερνήτης τινὰ γιγνόμενος γίνεϑαι, μότε
ἄλλης τίχνης ἐργάτης. De Aliment. faciend. cap. i.

[227] De Offic. I. 18.

books,

books, without obfervation and experience, would ftill lefs enable you to know mankind and the world. But, becaufe attention and practice are neceffary, does it follow that books are altogether ufelefs?

" A thoufand writers perhaps for a thoufand " years," fays Freind, " have been improving " the art and profeffion of phyfic : and he, that " induftrioufly ftudies thofe authors, will, in " the fhort period of life, find out as much, " as if he had lived a thoufand years him- " felf, or employed thofe thoufand years in " the ftudy of phyfic²¹⁸." But this afcribes too much to books, and too little to obfervation and experience : fuffice it to fay, that books muft unavoidably fuggeft variety of ufeful hints and edifying matter, direct practitioners often what to look for, and thus ferve in fome mea-fure as guides in their refearches. Yet when I allow thus much to books, I do not mean by books thofe hypothetical productions, fpun from the brains of *doctores umbratici*, without any re-gard to the phænomena ;—for thefe, inftead of pointing out what is, may lead men to look for, aye, and (as paradoxical as it may found) often to find, what is not²¹⁹—but I mean thofe

narrationes

²¹⁸ Hift. of Phyfic. II. 63.

²¹⁹ Men, who have theories to fupport, as they will often *find what is not*, fo they will as often *overlook what is*. Pre-

judiced

narrationes medicinales, Lord Bacon mentions: thofe hiftorical narrations of medical cafes, on which alone, fo far as books are concerned, a folid foundation for practice can be raifed ; and to the *intermiffion* of which *Hippocratic diligence* he afcribes the very flow progrefs that phyfic has made [230].

Will it be faid, that books and methods of practice, even formed upon obfervations thus accurately made, will neverthelefs fix a biafs upon the underftanding, give it infenfibly a confined and fyftematic habit, and previoufly indifpofe it for enlarged and impartial contemplation? But this, were it really an objection, would bear againft all other, as well as medical, inftitution : for, while any fort of education fhall be thought expedient, men muft be cultivated and fafhioned according to fome fyftem, fome digefted and eftablifhed form, of doctrine. If there be any original power of intellect, this doctrine will afterwards be brought to the teft of reafon and nature ; and men will then

judiced and predetermined, they will fee no facts, but what they come prepared to fee : as, on the other hand, they will greedily catch at any thing, however obfcure and doubtful, which may feem to favour a private fyftem. This is the true fpirit of hypothetical procedures, and the grand fource of error among men.

[230] De Augm. Scient. iv. 2.

P

embrace

embrace or reject upon conviction, what they had aforetime learned by rote. If there be no such power of intellect,—if the practitioner be not of a sort to examine things himself, but deems it safer as well as easier to rely upon others, and to practise what his tutors and the schools have taught him—why, all which can be said is, that they, who cannot lead, must be content to follow. And this, indeed, must be the case with mankind in general; who, as Thucydides observed long ago of historical knowledge, and it will equally apply to all other knowledge, *find the search after truth so very grievous and distressing, that they easily acquiesce in what is ready prepared to their hands* [231].

And, now, enough of *wild* and *illiterate*; especially, as many may be conceived most impatient to ask, whether I am in earnest, and seriously mean to *vindicate* so strange a character, as that of *Paracelsus?* Why, no, not absolutely, as I have said; but, surely, from any thing this writer has advanced against him. For what is it, after all, that he has advanced? He has pronounced him *wild* and *illiterate:* he has condemned him for assuming that *bold, self-important*, and *confident* air, which was necessary

---

[231] Ὄυτως ἀταλαίπωρος τοῖς πολλοῖς ἡ ζήτησις τῆς ἀληθείας ἀληθείας, καὶ ἐπὶ τὰ ἕτοιμα μᾶλλον τρέπονται. Lib. i.

to *recommend him to the world :* and he has ob-
liquely cenfured in him the want of that *diffidence, doubt,* and *hefitation;* which, though effential to a *philofopher,* would have *ruined* him
as a *phyfician.* But are not thefe ftri&ures of a
moft peculiar complexion, and can they be confidered without fome degree of wonder? If a
bold, felf-important, and *confident* air be necefiary
to recommend a man to the world, why is Paracelfus to be blamed for affuming it? What!
is Paracelfus to be blamed for accommodating
himfelf to mankind, by affuming fuch qualities,
as their infirmities require?—On the other
hand, if *diffidence, doubt,* and *hefitation,* be accompanied with attitudes and modes of behaviour, which would reprobate him with mankind; if they would not only put him out of
all condition to ferve others, but be alfo a fure
and certain means of ruin to himfelf; would
it not be madnefs in him to appear *diffident,
doubtful,* and *hefitating?*

As angry as this writer feems at a bold dogmatical behaviour in phyficians, there is no
order of men, in my humble opinion, to whom
it is more allowable, and even necefiary; none,
whom it more concerns *nihil tam vereri,* as
Tully fays, *quam ne dubitare aliqua de re vide-
rentur:* and there ftands upon record an honeft
apothecary, whofe wifdom in this refpe& I

P 2   greatly

greatly reverence. He knew the mischievous
consequences of seeming at a loss, or of being
deficient, in any thing. When his boy therefore sent away unserved a customer, who
enquired for plantane-water, with an excuse
that they had none, " Sirrah," said he, though
" you could find no *aqua plantaginis* in the
" shop, you might have found *aqua pumpa-*
" *ginis* enough in the yard: and that would
" have done just as well." Without this firm
and persevering assurance, what would many a
celebrated practitioner have been ? What raised
Ratcliff to the heights he attained, and enabled
him to tyrannize, in the manner he did, over
his brethren as well as his patients ? Was it his
transcendent superlative skill in physic ? Consult the files : read his prescriptions. You will
soon perceive, that it was no such thing. No :
it was an assuming, encroaching, confident
spirit ; it was a dogmatical, overbearing, insolent manner [232]. And what else is it, that causes
so many to succeed and flourish, in these blessed
days of ours,—for *sunt hodiè, qui forsan olim
nominabuntur*—but the self-same qualities ; accompanied, as his were, with a knowledge of
mankind, and with temper and address to make
the most of it ? And as these qualities are allowable to recommend the physician, so they are

[232] See *A Panegyric upon Impudence*, below.

alfo

alfo neceffary to revive and confirm the patient: juft as the contrary qualities, the *doubt*, the *diffidence*, the *hefitation*, which would *ruin* the phyfician, would ruin alfo the patient, by deftroying his hopes, and plunging him into defpair.

Mean while, let it not be imagined, that I would explode all *diffidence, doubt*, and *hefitation*: very far from it. I not only allow, that they *help to conftitute the character of a true philofopher*; but I am of opinion with Defcartes, that they are the foundation of all true philofophy. I object, not fo much to them, as to the fituation in which this writer places them; and only contend, that they muft never be the *oftenfible* qualities (for that is the matter between us) in a phyfician, who means to do bufinefs. The truth is, he hath inadvertently confounded the characters of philofopher and phyfician, the man and the profeffor, efoteric and exoteric: ideas, which muft ever be kept diftinct, if we would act with any juftnefs amongft men and manners.

I formerly knew a pleafant philofopher (he muft, if alive, be fuperannuated now) who caufed to be infcribed over the door of his mufeum, " Let none but *men* enter here." He did not mean *men*, in oppofition to *women*;—for I fuppofe, that the members of the *Blue Stocking Club*,

P 3   fome

fome of them at leaft, might have found ad-
mittance here—but he meant *men*, as diftinguifhed from *profeffional* men; from divines,
lawyers, phyficians, &c. Thus, it was ufual
with him, when any familiar was approaching,
to admonifh him aloud, with a *gaieté de cœur*,
" to lay afide his cloke before he entered [233];"
that is, to diveft himfelf of every thing profeffional, of all exoteric trappings whatever [234]:
nor do I remember to have feen him more dif-
concerted, than upon the entrance of counfellor
Tanturian. This folemn mortal, far removed
from eafe and nature, fagely ftalked in with all
his pontificalia, juft as he arrived from Weft-
minfter Hall. Nor did his behaviour mend
the matter in the leaft: for, inftead of entering
heartily into the fpirit of fuch a meeting, and
converfing with that open, candid, chearful air,
which muft ever be the life and foul of it, he
was ftiff, referved, and even faturnine. He
looked with a caft of jealoufy and diftruft upon

[233] And it was as ufual with him, at their departure, to
imitate the Spartans in their affemblies: where the eldeft
among them, pointing at the door, was wont to cry aloud,
Let nothing that has been faid pafs thofe doors: διὰ τέτων θύρων
ὀδεὶς ἰξέρχεται λόγος. Plutarch. Inftitut. Lacon.

[234] Burleigh, Lord Treafurer, ufed to put off his cares,
when he put off his cloaths; and, when he laid down his
gown, would fay, *Lie there, Lord Treafurer.* Camden's *Reign
of* Queen Eliz.

all

all about him; and was as guarded in his move-ments, as if he feared to be kidnapped. He brought to my imagination the ridiculous pic-ture of Hobbes, whom Eachard makes so very circumspect and wary, that he refused to sit down to a conference with Timothy, till sure that Timothy would not *get behind him, and bite him by the legs*[215].

But to proceed. In such a society as the above, the *diffidence, doubt,* and *hesitation,* are exactly in their place. Men are here assembled, as men: they endeavour to put off every pecu-liarity, whether arising from temperament or profession: they are, for the time being, with-out complexion and private humour, without prejudice and passion, without even opinions and habits of thinking; that, by being thus enabled to contemplate pure nature through the medium of pure reason, they may the more surely arrive at real knowledge. Here, if any where, must be found that *feast of reason,* of which the Poet speaks; and on which a very great philosopher, **as well as** most excellent man, delivered himself **thus in** raptures to a friend: *O felicia tempora, quandò nobis sic ridere histrioniam licuit, quam seu veram seu affectatam totus exercet mundus! quandò inter philosophandum*

---

[215] Dr. Eachard's Works, 1705, 8vo.

tam

tam fæpè licuit dicere, SOLI SUMUS [236] *: licet nobis verum difquirere fine invidia* [237]. Here, I fay, the qualities are in their place : here, it not only becomes, but it is neceffary for, men to be *diffident*, to *doubt*, to *hefitate :* while all affeCtation of appearing wifer than others, all vain defire of fhining in difputation, all ftriving after victory inftead of truth, in a word, all *felf-importance, confidence, boldnefs*, and whatever partaketh of this kind of fpirit, fhould be totally excluded from fuch a fociety, as utterly fubverting its intent and meaning, and folely configned to exoteric purpofes.

But, it may be faid, are qualities like thefe to be configned to any purpofes whatever ? to be encouraged, or even borne with, in any fituation ? and can you poffibly mean to recommend them ? I will declare explicitly what I do

---

[236] Thefe are affemblies, where men confort with, becaufe they love one another, and where honeft focial affeCtion is not adulterated with motives of avarice or ambition.

[237] Gaffendi **Præfat.** in *Exerc. Parad. contra Ariftot.*—Balzac feems to have had a ftrong relifh for this faid eafe and freedom in converfing. He had a party one evening at his houfe ; when each endeavoured to difplay what he knew, and to exprefs himfelf with a guarded accuracy and precifion. After all were withdrawn but Menage, " Come," fays Balzac, taking him by the hand, " let us now we are " alone fpeak freely, and without the fear of commiting " folecifms :" *a préfent que nous fommes feuls, parlons librement, & fans crainte de faire des folécifmes.* Menagiana, tom. i.

mean,

mean, and what I do not mean. I do not mean,
then, to recommend any thing odious and bad :
but I mean to deal with mankind, as they only
can be, and ought to be, dealt with, if I am to
deal with them at all. Is medicine, or the practice of phyfic, neceffary to men, or is it not ?
If not, let the prefent generation of practitioners
retire upon penfions, and be there a ftop henceforward to this branch of education. If it be
neceffary, then let phyficians ufe fuch means, as
fhall recommend them to thofe who may want
them. But *confidence, felf-importance, boldnefs,*
are the means to recommend them ; while
diffidence, doubt, and *hefitation,* are fure to ob-
ftruct their progrefs. So you fay, and fo I
believe : for a man, who walks grave, erect,
and folemn, has a confirmed yet fpirited air,
and pronounces with a tone of decifion and authority, will certainly be thought to know more,
and be fooner employed, than a far abler
man [238], who, with a peaking pitiful afpect, appears

---

[238] A French writer, fpeaking of perfons of a certain caft,
fays, *s'ils reftent dans l'inaction, & fe bornent prudament au
aroit de juger décifivement, ils ufurpent dans l'opinion une
efpèce de fupériorité fur les talens mêmes. On les croit capables
de faire tout ce qu'ils n'ont pas fait & uniquement parce qu'ils
n'ont rien fait :* that is, " if they remain inactive, and
" wifely confine themfelves to the privilege of judging de-
" cifively," and with dictatorial authority upon every thing
that occurs, " they gain in the eftimation of men a kind of
" fuperiority **even** over real abilities and genius. They will
" be

pears to fhrink and droop, and does nothing apparently but with fear and trembling.

This perverfe judgment our author imputes
to the *weaknefs* and *credulity*, which, he fays,
*even the moft fenfible have ever fhewn in medical
matters :* and this he moft piteoufly *laments.*
But nothing can be more piteous than this his
piteous *lamentation.* Why does he lament, that
men and things are fo and fo formed and con-
ftituted ? or, that he is to ufe means neceffary
to ends, if thefe ends are neceffary to be ac-
complifhed ? All things animate, as well as ina-
nimate, muft be treated according to their feveral natures : a lion requires one mode of treatment, a horfe another, and fo on. Yes, but man
is a very fuperiour being, and ought to be
governed by reafon : but, fuppofe man will not;
why muft he, like a poor dejected poltroon, be
carried blubbering along the ftreets, and pour-
ing forth *lamentations,* becaufe man will not be
what he is not formed to be ?—Let me refrefh

" be thought capable of doing every thing which they have
" not done, and *folely becaufe they have not done it."* Du Clofs,
Confid. fur les Mœurs, ch. xii. Yes, " if they remain inac-
" tive :" but, when once they become writers or actors, the
illufion vanifhes; their admirers are difmayed and hang down
their heads ; and you may juftly apply to them, what Tacitus
fays of Galba, *viz.* that " by the confent of all, he would
" have been thought capable of reigning, if he had *not*
" reigned"—*major privato vifus, dum privatus fuit ; & omnium confenfu capax imperii, nifi imperaffet.* Hift. I.

him;

him, upon this sorrowful occasion, with a little scrap of Greek; which I know will speak comfort to him, if only as calling up the idea of old Eton: Τὰ τοιαῦτα λῆρον ἡγησάμενος, τῆτο μόνον ἐξ ἅπαντος θηράσῃ, ὅπως, τὸ παρὸν ἶυ θέμενος, παραδράμῃς γελῶν τὰ πολλὰ, **καὶ** περὶ μηδὲν ἐσπυδάκως [239]: which, for the benefit of the English reader, I thus translate, as literally as I can:
" Don't jumble discordant qualities blindly to-
" gether, but keep each distinct, and in its
" proper department: your *diffidence*, *doubt*,
" and *hesitation*, for the philosopher; your
" *boldness*, *self-importance*, and *confidence*, for
" the physician."

I persuade myself, that I have now vindicated Paracelsus, so far as he can want a vindication from the strictures of this writer: let us add a word or two upon other traits of his character, and upon other of his qualities, which by some perhaps may be thought to want apology, more than those already noted. His attachment to *alchymy*, his pretence to the **philosopher's** *stone*, and his **elixir** *proprietatis*, may be ranked (I presume) among those weaknesses, which have been common to him and other great men. I suppose also, that he will not be censured for consulting indiscriminately all sorts of people, as well as physicians, because this is no more than what the father of physic himself has

[239] Luciani Νεκυομαντεία.

prescribed:

prescribed [240] : and, if he may seem to have acted a little fanatically in burning with form the works of Galen, his good sense and candor must be acknowledged in the value he set upon Hippocrates. Come we then to what may seem the most plausible charge against him; I mean, his " pretending to *magic*, affecting to " carry a *demon* about with him, and *coining* " *new and barbarous terms*, to which nobody " could affix any ideas;" for these, it will be said, are not barely foolish and absurd, but favour strongly of knavery and imposture.

Gentlemen may allow themselves liberties, and use what language they please; but of this I am very sure, that if all are knaves and impostors, who affect to pass for what they are not, the greater part of mankind must submit to be deemed such. One man affects more knowledge, another more property, than he has: why? because ignorance and poverty are attended with contempt, and would hinder from emerging. Dealers and all who traffic represent their commodities *bigger than the life*, and secretly applaud themselves, when they have disposed of them as such. Physicians assume *ostensible* qualities, to procure themselves patients; and when they have procured them, scruple not to deceive them for the good of their bodies, as divines often do for the good

240 Hippocrat. *de Præcept.*

of

of their souls. Now all these are, strictly speaking, arts of imposture; yet necessary, as should seem, in the commerce of life, because justified by the universal consent and practice of mankind.

I will not deny that Paracelsus might carry this grimace somewhat too far; but, if he ran a little into one extreme, the present medical gentry have certainly run into the other, by laying aside elaborate wigs, gold-headed canes, and other pompous paraphernalia. It has been said, that this grand revolution in physic was actually brought about by a female, *nam fuit ante Helenam, &c*; but, let who would bring it about, it was highly impolitic. There is no effectual way of arresting the attention of men in general, and of acquiring reputation enough even to serve them, without affecting things uncommon and extraordinary. Common sense and common things make no impression. Descartes was wild in philosophy, as Paracelsus was in physic, and doubtless admired on this very account; for I take Voltaire to be indisputably right, when he says, that " Gassendus would have been thought the greater " man, if he had not been the more reasonable, " of the two [241]." The ridiculous *Bayes* in the *Rehearsal*, as gross a fool as he was, had

[241] *Gassendi eut moins de réputation que Descartes, parce qu'il étoit plus raisonnable——*

wit

wit enough to difcern, that common fenfe is a poor low creeping thing, which would never produce any effect; and, as his object was to *elevate* and *furprife,* fo he fought things ftrange, and altogether remote from it. He defpifes Beaumont and Jonfon, for copying fervilely after nature ; and foars himfelf above it, " for " fome perfons of quality and friends of his, " who underftand what *flame and power in wri-* " *ting is.*"

The flighteft and moft curfory glance over human life will evince, that the principle here adopted is the fureft groundwork of admiration among men; that the moft diftinguifhed perfonages, in the feveral departments of it, have been real *Bayefes* ; and that the fyftem of *Bayefifm,* if I may fo call it, muft be carefully purfued and cultivated by every man, who means to *fhine,* and *make a figure* in the world.— *Defunt cætera* [242].

[242] Though this *Vindication of Paracelfus* be apparently ironical, and more for the fake of pleafantry than ferious argument, yet it contains fome edifying reflections, and this above all, *viz.* that *mankind are to be dealt with as they are, and not according to vain and fantaftic ideas of a perfection, of which they are not capable.* See Nos XIV. and LV.

LXV.

LXV.

A PANEGYRIC UPON IMPUDENCE.

ORATORS and men of wit have frequently amused themselves with maintaining paradoxes. Thus, Erasmus has written a panegyric upon *folly:* Montaigne has said fine things upon *ignorance,* which he somewhere calls " the softest pillow a man can lay his " head upon:" and Cardan, in his *Encomium Neronis,* has, I suppose, defended every vice and every folly. It is astonishing to me, that no one has yet done justice to *impudence;* which has so many advantages, and for which so much may be said. Did it never strike you, what simple, naked, uncompounded *impudence* will do? what strange and astonishing effects it will produce? Aye, and without birth, without property, without principle, without even artifice and address, without indeed any single quality, but the *æs frontis triplex,* " the front of threefold " brass."—Object not folly, vice, or villainy however black: these are puny things: from a visage truly bronzed and seared, from features muscularly fixed and hardened, issues forth a broad overpowering glare, by which all these

are

are as totally hid, as the fpots of the fun by
the luftre of his beams.   Were this not fo, how
is it, that impudence fhall make impreffions to
advantage ; fhall procure admiffion to the
higheft perfonages, *and no queftions afked* ; fhall
fuffice (in fhort) to make a man's fortune,
where no modeft merit could even render itfelf
vifible [241] ? I afk no more to infure fuccefs,
than that there be but enough of it [243] : without fuccefs a man is ruined and undone, there
being no mean.   Should one ravage half the
globe, and deftroy a million of his fellow-
creatures, yet, if at length he arrive at empire,
as Cæfar did, he fhall be admired while living
as an hero, and adored perhaps as a god when
dead : though, were the very fame perfon, like

[241] "Impudence," fays *Ofborn*, " is no virtue, yet able to
" beggar them all ; being for the moft part in good plight,
" when the reft ftarve, and capable of carrying her followers
" up to the higheft preferments : as ufeful in a court, as
" armour in a camp. Scotchmen have ever made good
" the truth of this, who will go farther with a fhilling, than
" an Englifhman can ordinarily pafs for a crown." *Advice
to a Son.*—But this to my thinking is rather a mark of fuperiour wifdom, than of fuperiour impudence : I fufpect an
error of the prefs, and that inftead of *Scotchmen* it fhould
have been *Irifhmen.* Not that I approve of *national* ftrictures :
there is no occafion to apply either to *Scotland* or *Ireland* for
impudence of the very firft metal.

[242] *Qui femel verecundiæ fines tranfierit, oportet effe gnaviter
impudentem.* Cicero.

Cataline,

Catiline, to fail in the attempt, he would be
hanged as a little fcoundrel robber, and his
name devoted to infamy or oblivion [244].

Pray, what do you think the elder Pliny
fuggefts, when he affirms it to be " the preroga-
" tive of the Art of Healing, that any man,
" who profeffes himfelf a phyfician, is inftantly
" received as fuch [245]?" He certainly fuggefts,

[244] This comparifon of a hero with a robber hath been
often made. " Father Mafcaron told us from the pulpit to-
" day," fays Madam de Maintenon, " that the *hero was a*
" *robber, who did at the head of an army, what a highwayman*
" *did alone.* Our mafter," fhe adds, " was not pleafed
" with the comparifon :" *notre maitre n' a pas été content de
la comparaifon.* Lettres, 9 Fev. 1675.—Boileau's language
is equally forcible, in Sat. xi. v. 75.

> *Un injufte guerrier, terreur de l' univers,*
> *N'eft qu'un plus grand voleur, que du Tefte, &c.*

" I am a pirate," faid one of that order to Alexander,
" becaufe I have only a fingle veffel : had I a great fleet,
" I fhould be a conqueror."—Seneca calls conquerors *magnos
et furiofos latrones*; and juftly : *quid enim*, as St. Auguftin
fays, *funt regna, remotâ juftitiâ, nifi magna latrocinia?*

[245] *In hâc artium folâ evenit, ut cuicunque medicum fe pro-
feffo ftatim credatur.* Nat. Hift. xxix.—I cannot, however,
confine this to phyfic : it is true, more or lefs, of *all* the
profeffions :

> For he that has but impudence
> To *all* things has a fair pretence.

and, certainly, it is moft true of divinity. Let any peafant
or village mechanic ftart forth as a preacher, without any
preparation or qualification of any kind, will he not inftantly
be followed, and liftened to as a divine?

Q.   that

that such sort of professors in his days, like the
itinerant and advertising doctors of ours, had
a more than ordinary portion of that bold,
self-important, and confident look and manner,
which, with a very little heightening, may justly
be called impudence. And what but this could
enable a little paltry physician, of no name or
character, to gain so mighty an ascendency over
such a spirit, as that of Lewis XI. of France?
Read the account in Philip de Commines; and
then blame me, if you can, for thinking so
highly of this accomplishment.—True it is,
that Lewis was afraid of death even to horror,
and so as not to bear the sound of the word; and
I grant, that **on** this same fear the empire of
physic, as well as the empire of divinity, is
chiefly founded: but I insist, that neither the
one nor the other will ever be raised effectually,
without the aid and co-operation of this great
and sovereign quality.

Pope Gregory VII. who governed the church
from 1073 to 1085, is celebrated for having
carried ecclesiastical dominion to the height:
for he was the first who maintained and established, that popes, by excommunication, may
depose kings from their states, and loose subjects
from their allegiance. And how did he effect
this? Not by genius or eloquence; not by a
knowledge of canon law, and the constitutions
of the holy see; no, nor by the arts of policy

and grimaces of his religion (with all which he was amply endowed) but by a moſt inſolent, daring, uſurping ſpirit. He ſeized the papal chair by force, as it were; threw the church into confuſion to gratify his ambition; made kings his ſlaves, and biſhops his creatures; and eſtabliſhed in his own perſon a tyranny over things both ſpiritual and temporal.—But my admiration of impudence tranſports me too far: I will ſay no more upon it.

LXVI.

OF COURTS.

COURTS have always been eſteemed places of iniquity and corruption. - According to ſome, the moment a man ſteps into the precincts of a court, he ſhould ſeem forcibly carried away with his brother-courtiers, to commit all manner of ſin and wickedneſs; as if by a vortex, rolling round the center of royalty, which involves them all in one common guilt.—Indeed, an ancient poet has made a courtier ſay, that the palaces of kings and virtue are incompatible [246]: and our unfortunate Ra-

[246] ——————————exeat aulâ
Qui volet eſſe pius: virtus et ſumma poteſtas
Non coeunt.—————   Lucan.

leigh

leigh feems to have entertained an idea of this
fort, as if iniquity was not accidental merely,
but abfolutely effential, to the profeffion of a
courtier: I have lived, fays he, in his fpeech
from the fcaffold, " I have lived a finful life,
" in all finful callings, having been a foldier,
" a captain, a fea-captain, and *a courtier* [247],
" which are all places of wickednefs and
" vice."

If I could believe this opinion to be well-
grounded, it would greatly lower my notions of
the divine inftitution of government; of mo-
narchical government, more particularly. While
I have been meditating in the drawing-room
upon a birth-day, a reverential awe, almoft
bordering upon devotion, has gradually over-
fpread and arrefted all my powers: and this
cannot feem ftrange, while I confider myfelf as
it were on holy ground, and in the prefence of
him, who reprefents the King of Kings. But,
according to Raleigh, inftead of the palace of
a righteous monarch, I am to fancy myfelf
rather in a kind of Pandæmonium; or upon
that particular fpot, where fome of the moft
wicked fpirits in the land are frequently affembled to work unrighteoufnefs: and where a

[247] " Father la Chaife is an honeft man," fays Mad. de
Maintenon; " but the air of the court taints the pureft
" virtue." Lettr. 78.

man

man can no more preserve his innocence and integrity, than he could his person from infection in a pest-house. It was certainly this idea, which made the famous *Richard Baxter*, in the *Account* of his own *Life*, so feelingly represent it as " one of the greatest blessings, " that in his youth he very narrowly escaped " getting a place at court."

And, as courts are confessedly not places of *virtue*, so it seems equally certain, that they are not places to seek *happiness* in. There is no occasion for any near approach, to know the caballing among the great officers of state, and their unwearied attempts to undermine and supplant one another: the miserable effects of these are felt sufficiently at the remotest distances. And for those mechanical toy-shop things, the little gentry of the palace, who are only so much furniture, nor more concerned in the administration of affairs than the chairs and tables—even these are not without their suspicions, jealousies, whisperings, backbitings, and all the little arts of envy and malevolence; from the same principle and with the same view, but only upon a smaller scale, and for objects less important.—But, for a more particular and nearer view of the happiness of court-life, see some striking traits in the following Number.

Q 3 LXVII.

LXVII.

OF MADAM DE MAINTENON,

A MOST extraordinary perſon, who, from a low condition and many misfortunes, became the wife of Lewis XIV. She was of an ancient family [248], her name Frances Daubigné; and Mezeray ſpeaks of M. Daubigné, her grandfather, who was a leader among the Proteſtants in France, as a man of " great courage " and boldneſs, of a ready wit, and of a fine " taſte in polite learning, as well as of good " experience in matters of war." She is ſaid to have been born in a priſon at Niort, where her father was then confined, 1635; and carried to America, when four years old.

Returning to France, upon the death of her father in 1647, and her livelyhood being precarious, ſhe became the wife of the famous Scarron in 1651. She was then ſixteen, and Scarron forty: Scarron too was very deformed, infirm, impotent, and (after all) in no advantageous circumſtances to her; for he ſubſiſted only by a penſion from the court. She lived with him many years: and Voltaire has not ſcrupled to ſay, that " this part of her life was un-

[248] *Siecle de Louis XIV.*

" doubtedly

"doubtedly the happieſt." She had indeed
ſenſe and wit ; but ſhe had another quality too
which might help to ſupport her, and that
was devotion. Obſerve the language ſhe held
to a female friend in trouble, when ſhe was not
more than nineteen : " Addreſs yourſelf to ſome
" good man, who may conduct you in the ways
" of the Lord. All is vanity, all is vexation
" of ſpirit. Throw yourſelf into the arms of
" God. There is none but God alone on whom
" to depend, and who never faileth them that
" love him [249]."

Mean while, though Scarron was not formed
to inſpire any tranſcendent happineſs, yet, in
anſwer to thoſe who wanted her to engage in
a ſecond match, ſhe runs a compariſon between the new gentleman and Scarron, and gives
the preference to Scarron altogether : ſhe gives,
indeed, a very excellent character of him. But
the truth ſeems to be, that ſhe had no great
notion of the married ſtate : " I have too
" much experienced, ſays ſhe, that there can
" be nothing very delightful in marriage ; but
" I know that there is in liberty :" *Je l'ai trop
éprouvé, que le marriage ne ſçauroit être delicieux ;*

[249] *Adreſſez-vous à quelque homme de bien, qui vous conduiſe
dans les voies du Seigneur. Tout eſt vanité, tout eſt affliction
d'eſprit. Jettez-vous dans les bras de Dieu. Il n'y a que lui
dont on ne ſe laſſe point, & qui ne ſe laſſe jamais de ceux qui
l'aiment.* Lettres de M. de Maintenon, 1758, 9 tom. 12mo.

& je

& je trouve que la liberté l'est. Thus she writes, March 1666, in a letter to Ninon de L'Enclos, who was sure to agree with her.

Scarron dying in 1660, she became as indigent as she was before she had him. Her friends did all they could to have his pension continued to her, and petitions were frequently given in, beginning always with " The widow " Scarron most humbly prays your Majesty, " &c. ;" but these petitions signified nothing, and the King grew so weary of them, that he has been heard to say, " Must I be always " pestered with the widow Scarron ?" At length, however, a larger pension was settled on her, and the King at the same time said to her, " Madam, I have made you wait a long time ; " but you have so many friends, that I was re- " solved to have this merit with you on my " own account."

In 1671, she was entrusted with the care of the Duke of Maine, a son of the King's by Madam de Montespan ; and thus was introduced to court. She had occasion to write sometimes to the King : her letters charmed him, and this was the origin of her fortune : her own personal merit effected all the rest. The King bought her the lands of Maintenon in 1674, with a magnificent castle; and, seeing her extremely pleased with her estate, called her publicly Madam de Maintenon. This change of name was perhaps of great and important use to her ;

for

for she could hardly have been raised to the rank she afterwards obtained, with the name of the widow Scarron.

Meanwhile her elevation was to her only a retreat. Shut up in a room, which was on the same floor with the King's, she confined herself to the society of two or three ladies; and even these she saw but seldom. The King came every day to her apartment, and there did business with his ministers; while she employed herself in needle work, never shewing the least inclination to meddle, often seeming wholly inattentive, and always avoiding whatever had the least appearance of cabal or intrigue. This was her stile and manner of living; but from this stile and manner of living, as is easy to be supposed, she gradually grew unhappy. Besides, her situation with M. de Montespan must have been extremely difficult. This mistress would naturally be jealous of her; and, accordingly, was constantly "hurting her with the King, " while the little Duke of Maine as constantly " reconciled her to him:" *la mère me brouille avec le Roi, son fils me reconcilie avec lui.* Lettres. Once, when these two ladies were quarrelling, the King came suddenly in, and after some time made them embrace one another; saying with a smile, that it was " easier for him to " give peace to Europe, than to two women :" *qu'il lui étoit plus aisé de donner la paix a l'Europe, que de la donner a deux femmes.* Ib.

About

About the end of 1685, Lewis XIV. married M. de Maintenon; by the advice, as was said, of Father la Chaife. He was then in his 48th, fhe in her 50th year. How this ftrange event was brought about, has been matter of wonder to all: devotion was certainly one great, if not the fole, inftrument. For Lewis, notwithftanding a moft pompous magnificent exterior, had a very minute fpirit within; and efpecially in matters of religious concern. He was wont to tremble before his confeffor, and carried about him reliques, as fhe herfelf relates. But obferve the following extracts from her letters, which, furely, are edifying in an high degree; and for the fake of which I have prefixed this fhort account of her.

" The King has fpent two hours in my
" clofet: I difcourfed with him about his falva-
" tion, and he gave me an attentive hearing.
" He has good fentiments, and frequently
" turns his thoughts towards God. It would
" be great pity, if God did not enlighten a foul
" that is made for him.—The King abounds
" with good fentiments: I endeavour to bring
" him back to God: he fometimes reads the
" Bible, and thinks it the fineft of all books.
" He confeffes his weakneffes, and acknow-
" ledges his faults, to me. We muft wait for
" the workings of grace." All this, and abundantly more of the kind, was in 1679.

Voltaire, fpeaking of the Edict of Nantes, which was revoked in 1685, fays, that M. de
Maintenon

Maintenon " did not urge this meafure, but
" that fhe did not oppofe it ;" *qu'elle ne la
preffa point, mais qu'elle ne s'oppofa point* [250]:
but, I think, the following paffages from her
Letters will not fuffer us to believe her altogether paffive. " The King thinks ferioufly
" about the converfion of heretics, and in a
" little time it will be profecuted warmly."
This Letter is dated 28 Oct. 1679, fix years
before the event.—" The King thinks ferioufly
" of his falvation, and that of his fubjects : if
" God preferves him, there will be but one
" religion in the kingdom. I fancy no Hugo-
" nots will be left in Poitou, except our rela-
" tions : methinks, nothing is wanting to my
" felicity, but the converfion of my family.
" —The King intends to fet about a total con-
" verfion of the heretics : he has frequent
" conferences on this fubject with Le Tellier
" and Chateauneuf, *where I am not one too*
" *many.* The King is ready to do every thing,
" which may beft promote the caufe of reli-
" gion : this undertaking will render him glo-
" rious in the fight of God and man, as it will
" bring all his fubjects into the pale of the
" church, and prove the deftruction of he-
" refy."

Nothing, fhe fays, *is wanting to my felicity,
but the converfion of my family.* Yes, but there
was a great deal wanting ; for fhe had fcarcely

[250] Siecle de Louis, &c.

been

been the wife of Lewis three years, when she
began to write in the following strain to her
friends. "I experience more than ever, that
"nothing can make amends for the loss of
"freedom. Philosophy sets us above grandeur,
"but nothing sets above heaviness of heart.
"I envy your solitude and tranquillity; and
"am no longer surprised, that Queen Christina
"descended from a throne, to live with more
"freedom. Hope not for perfect felicity:
"there is none upon earth; and, if there was,
"it would not be at court"[251]. Except those
"who fill the highest stations, I know none so
"unhappy as those who envy them. Why
"cannot I," says she to Madam de la Maison-
fort, "why cannot I give you my experience?
"why cannot I make you sensible of that unea-
"siness which wears out the great, and of the
"difficulties they labour under to employ their
"time? Do not you see that I am dying with

[251] Philip de Commines seems to have thought otherwise:
*Je l'ay cogneu, & ay esté son serviteur, à la fleur de son age, & en
ses grandes prosperitez; mais je le ne vey onques sans peine & sans
souci. Peu d'esperance doivent avoir les pauvres & menuës gens
au fait de ce monde; puis que si grand Roy, &c.:* that is to say,
"If happiness could not be found in the court of so great
"a monarch as Lewis XI., how must the villager hope for it
"in a cot?" Very feasibly, Monsieur Commines: his enjoy-
ments will be more sincere and pure, and he will have no
unnatural fantastic miseries to interrupt and disturb them.
Memoires, liv. vi. ch. 13.

"melancholy,

" melancholy, in a height of fortune, which
" once my imagination could scarcely have
" conceived? I have been young and beauti-
" ful, have had a relish for pleasures, and have
" been the universal object of love. In a more
" advanced age I have spent my time in intel-
" lectual amusements. I have at last risen to
" favour; but I protest to you, my dear girl,
" that every one of these conditions leaves in
" the mind a dismal vacuity." If any thing,
says Voltaire, could shew the vanity of ambition, it would be this Letter. She could
have no uneasiness, but only the uniformity of
her life at court; and this made her say once to
the count Daubigné, her brother, *I can hold it
no longer; I wish I were dead.*

The court grew now every day less gay and
more serious, after the King began to live retired with M. de Maintenon. Her relations
complained, that she was not sufficiently attentive to their interest; and she says, " they
" will not be sensible of what she has done for
" them, till they meet together in the valley of
" Jehosaphat. Some imagine I govern the
" state: they perceive not, I am persuaded, that
" God has heaped so many blessings upon me,
" only that I might attend to the King's salva-
" tion." The convent of St. Cyr was built at
the end of the park at Versailles, in 1686; in the
regulation of which establishment she employed
many of her hours. At the death of the
King,

King, in 1715, fhe retired wholly to it; fpent the remainder of her days in devotion; and died there in 1719, aged 84 [252].

Though courts are certainly not places of happinefs, yet this lady (as fhould feem) would not have been completely happy in any fituation whatever. There was fomething difcontented, querulous, and pettifh about her : when the girls at St. Cyr had deviated a little from her orders, *I have always repented*, fays fhe, *of my endeavours to direct women; men are infinitely more tractable and docile.* She was, however, a woman of many virtues, and of piety more than enough : fhe was indeed *righteous overmuch*.

---

[252] June 11, 1717, the Czar Peter made her a vifit, as fhe writes to Madam de Caylus; and fhe received him on her bed. " At feven in the evening he arrived, and fat " down by my bed-fide. He afked, if I was fick ? I faid I was. " He afked my ailment ? I anfwered, great age and no " ftrong conftitution. His vifit was very fhort : he caufed " the curtain to be opened at the bed's-feet, in order to " have a peep at me ; and you'll allow, that it muft have " given him a mighty fatisfaction." *Lettres.*

LXVIII.

LXVIII.

AMBITION NO MARK OF MAGNANIMITY.

I HAVE often wondered, how ambition came to be thought the mark of a *great* foul. Montaigne and Montesquieu join it to a *little* one; and they have certainly this in their favour, that it is as common to the lowest and meanest, as to the most exalted compositions [253]. Yet Dryden calls ambition " the glorious fault " of angels and of gods:" and even Clarendon has not fcrupled to fay, that, if ambition " be a " vice, it loves to grow in a rich foil." If by *growing in a rich foil,* he means growing out of a *great* foul, we may be the more furprifed, becaufe he afcribes the exorbitant ambition of Cardinal Wolfey to the *poverty and lownefs of his birth,* and makes it *moft natural to men of the meaneft extraction* [254]. It is, I believe, a matter of fact, that men of mean birth, who are bred in low fentiments, and accuftomed to ftare at parade and fhew (falfely, very falfely, called *magnificence*) with a kind of adoration, are always the moft inordinate in their purfuits after them, and of all others the hardeft to be fatisfied:

[253] *Gloriam, honorem, bonus ignavus æquè fibi exoptant.* Sal.
[254] Tracts, in folio.

while

while others of ingenuous and liberal parentage, being familiarized to them from the firſt opening of their eyes, are more often content with the ſphere they are born in, and with a ſupply for thoſe habits to which they are trained.

But to proceed.—Pray, did Lord Melcombe's ambition to *make a figure* originate from greatneſs of ſoul?—George Bubb was the ſon of an apothecary in Dorſetſhire, and nephew of George Dodington Eſq. who left him an eſtate and his name. This ambitious man was not without abilities; but the meanneſs of his ſpirit ſurpaſſes all conception. Tranſcripts from his *Diary* would be endleſs : we will only give one farther [255] trait of it. After many ſervilities, cringing attentions, and various little tricks, which low-born perſons uſually practiſe to crawl up to preferment, this ſon of an apothecary was received into the family of Frederic Prince of Wales; who " promiſed him, when he ſhould " come to the crown, a peerage and the ſeals " of the Southern Province, together with the " management of the Houſe of Lords." *Diary,* p. 4. This was in March 1749. Some time after he was informed, that the Prince's family had an averſion to him ; and, in a fit of pious deſpondency, exclaims, " God forgive them : " I have not deſerved it of them." *Ib.* p. 81. At length, in 1750-51, when death deprived the

[255] See above, N° VII.

world

world of the Prince, and all were precipitated into the blackness of despair, this devout person again ejaculates, " Father of mercy ! thy hand " that wounds alone can save." *Ib.* p. 100. —Reader, behold the *greatness* of soul from which *ambition* springs [256] !

LXIX.

TWO LETTERS OF SARAH DUCHESS OF MARL-BOROUGH.

THIS old Sarah, as she was then called, published, in 1742, an *Account of her Conduct* under Queen Anne : which *account*, by the way, gives an excellent insight into the manœuvres of a court. She was assisted herein by Mr. Hooke the historian ; to whom, though oppressed with the infirmities of age, and almost bedrid, she would continue speaking for six hours together. She delivered to him, without any notes, her account in the most lively as well as the most connected manner : and, though the correction of the language was left to Hooke,

---

[256] The same may be estimated of the *Love of Fame*, which Milton somewhere calls " the last infirmity of noble minds;" and which *Hume* has pronounced to be " justly so called." *Hist. of England,* ch. viii.

R

yet

yet the whole is plainly animated with her
fpirit; and, as fome philofophers have faid of
foul with regard to body, fhe was *tota in toto, et
tota in qualibet parte*. She was of a ftrong underftanding and uncommon fagacity, which I
premife to juftify my wonder at the ftrange neglect of education among the females; for her
woman would have written as well, and perhaps
better.   Here follow, merely as curiofities, two
letters from her own hand-writing, directed
" for Doctor Clarke att his hous near Sᵗ James'
" Church," without alteration of either grammar or orthography; that is, *verbatim et lite-
ratim*, as *Mrs. Bellamy* expreffes it.

Saterday

I give you many thanks for the favour of your
leter to me, and am glad I ded not hear of the
poor Bifhop of Bangors illnefs tell the danger is
over, I have never feen Lᵈ sun : fence I came out
of Town, but I expect him here to day at din-
ner, I wifh I may have any thing to fay from
him that is worth troubling either of you with,
but you will be gon before my leter can come to
you, and therefore I will write to the Bifhop,
the furgeons affure me that they fee no danger
in the Duke of Marlborough's fhoulder however they will not yet confent that hee fhall
goe to Woodftock, I fufpect that caution may
proceed from their knowing that one of them
                                            muft

muſt bee always with us when we are at ſuch a
diſtance from London, and therefore they will
defer our going as long as they can to attend
their other buſineſs, I do and have told them
that I will buy them at their own rates, and I
have known but very few miniſters or faverits
that were not to bee bought, which muſt be
done in this caſe, for when they ſhall come and
tell me that his ſhoulder may be dreſſed by
any body, I can't ſleep fifty mile from London, if one of the beſt ſurgeons does not lye in
the hous, by this account I am apt to think at
your return upon the 22d of Auguſt you will
find us here, but where ever I ſhall happen to
bee you are ſure of being always wellcome to
your moſt faithfull,

               humble ſervant and friend
my humble ſerviſs   S. Marlborough.
  to Mrs Clarke.

---

having this opertunity of writing to you by the
Surgeon which will come to you before you
leave London, I have a mind to tell you that
my Lord Sunderland was here as I expected, I
had a great deal of diſcourſe with him upon the
B. of Bangor and your affaires, tis impoſſible
for me to write all the particulars, but hee pro-
feſſes all the value and eſteem imaginable for
you both, he aſſures me that the B. of Bangor
is to be B. of Bath and Wells when it falls,

            but

but he only fix's him there becaufe it is the
moft probable to bee vacant firft, but if any
other fhould fall before that, except fome of
the very great ones hee will bee for the B.
of Bangors having it, what he continues to
think of for you is a very good thing which
Doctor Younger has at St Paul's, which is confiftent with what you have, and when I fpoake
of what you wifhed for your brother hee expreffed as much pleafure in doing that for him,
as you could have in it yourfelf, and faid hee
knew him and ownd that he was a very good
man and had a grete deal of merrit, hee added
that he defign to get a thoufand pound in the
winter of the King for the B. of Bangor to help
him tell fomthing happend that was better than
what he has, hee appeared to me to bee very de-
firous of ferving you both in any thing that
fhould happen to bee in his power, and I do
really believe that hee thinks himfelf that men
of your abillitys, would be of fo much ufe to
him, that he fencerely wifh's that you would
help him to eafe fom things which makes it
more difficult to compafs what I defire then
perhaps you will beleive, tho I hope you
will never doubt of my being with all the
truth imaginable your moft faithful friend
and humble fervant

                                S : Marlborough.

Sunday the 26 of July
    windfor lodge

                                    I hope

I hope you will give the B. of Bangor an account of the substance of this leter.

LXX.

OF WIT AND WITTICISMS.

SOMEBODY speaking of Lord Chesterfield as a wit, " Aye," says Sam. Johnson, " he is a wit among lords, and a lord among " wits." *Tuumne, obsecro ?* I should have replied to Johnson : *vetus credidi.* And so it is ; for Proclus said long ago of Critias, that he was " a novice among philosophers, and a philo-" sopher among novices : ἰδιώτης μὲν ἐν φιλοσό-" φοις, φιλόσοφος δὲ ἐν ἰδιώταις [257].

Johnson's application of this, if Johnson did apply it, was not amiss. Lord Chesterfield was a witling, rather than a man of genuine wit : his wit, as it has been called, was chiefly premeditated, and mechanical as I may say. Bishop Newton relates, in the *Account* of his own *Life*, that Lord Chesterfield used to lay *baits* and *traps* for the introduction of witty stories and witticisms, which he brought ready

---

[257] Proclus, in Timæum Platonis, apud vocem ΚΡΙΤΙΑΣ.

prepared

prepared to let off in company; and so I have often heard. But how nauseous, how mean, how disgusting, the idea! Such management shews a littleness of soul, as well as a littleness of understanding; and a man of spirit would disdain it. Wit should be a sudden instantaneous production, by a stroke of imagination upon the object or occasion, as fire from the collision of flint and steel: but witticisms ready made—Oh, heavens! Bayes's *good things* beat 'em hollow.

LXXI.

OF LOGIC, OR THE ART OF REASONING.

L OGIC, or (as it may truly be called) the art of disputing sophistically, makes a considerable part of our academical education: yet Gassendus, who was a very great *reasoner*, has attempted to prove, that it is, in truth, neither necessary nor useful. He thinks, that reason, or innate force and energy of understanding, is sufficient of itself [258]; that its

[258] Dialectica *naturalis* est ipsamet ratio, vel ingenita illa intellectûs vis et energia, quâ ratiocinamur, et discurrimus: —et tantam videmus esse naturæ solertiam, ut quisque facilè, per se, et sine observatione, præstet quicquid necessarium est. *Adversus Aristotel.* lib. ii. exercit. 1. *Quod nulla sit necessitas utilitasque Dialecticæ.*

own

own *natural* movements, without any discipline from *art*, are equal to the investigation and settling of truth; that it no more wants the assistance of Logic to conduct to this, than the eye wants a lanthorn to enable it to see the sun: and, however he might admit as curious, he would doubtless have rejected as useless, all such productions, as Quillet's *Callipædia*, Thevenot on the *Art of Swimming*, or Borelli *de Motu Animalium*; upon the firmest persuasion, that the innate force and energy of nature, when instinct honestly does her best, is sure to attain those several objects, without any didactic rules or precepts.

If Logic therefore be not necessary, it is probably of no great use: and indeed it has been deemed not only an impertinent but a pernicious science. " Logic," says Lord Bacon, " is " usually taught too early in life. That minds, " raw and unfurnished with matter, should be- " gin their cultivation from such a science, is " just like learning to weigh or measure the " wind. Hence, what in young men should " be manly reasoning, often degenerates into " ridiculous affectations and childish sophis- " try [259]." Certainly, where materials are wanting, the dispute must turn altogether upon words; and the whole will be con-

----

[259] De Augm. Scient. l. 2.

ducted

ducted with the sleight and legerdemain of so-
phistry. We have a pleasant instance upon
record of this school-errantry, this trick of
seeming to prove something, when in reality
you prove nothing. A countryman, for the
entertainment of his son, when returned from
the University, ordered six eggs to be boiled;
two for him, two for his mother, and two for
himself: but the son, itching to give a speci-
men of his newly acquired science, boiled only
three. To the father, asking the reason of this,
" *Why*," says the son, " *there are six.*" " How
" so?" says the father, " I can make but three."
" *No!*" **replies** the young sophister, " *is not*
" *here one?* (counting them out) *is not there*
" *two? and is not there three? and do not one, two,*
" *and three, make six?*" " Well then," says the
father, " I'll take two, your mother shall have
" one, and you shall have the other three."

Many appearances may tempt one to suspect, that the understanding, disciplined with
Logic, is not so competent for the investigation of truth, as if left to its natural operations.
" A man of wit," says Bayle, " who applies
" himself long and closely to Logic, seldom
" fails of becoming a caviller [260]; and by his
" sophistical

---

[260] These *syllogistici* are terrible company to men in general, and fit only for one another. With them you cannot be
said

" sophistical subtleties perplexes and embroils
" the very theses he hath defended. He chuses
" to destroy his own work, rather than forbear
" disputing ; and he starts such objections
" against his own opinions, that his whole art
" cannot solve them. Such is the fate of those,
" who apply themselves too much to the sub-
" tleties of dialectics [261]." This is the opinion
of Bayle, who probably knew from feeling and
experience the truth of what he said ; for he
was a very great Logician, as well as a very
great Sceptic.

Our memorable Chillingworth is another instance to prove, that Logic, instead of assist-
ing, may possibly obstruct and hurt the understanding. Chillingworth, says Lord Clarendon,
who knew him well, " was a man of great
" subtlety of understanding, and had spent all
" his younger time in disputation ; of which
" he arrived to so great a mastery, as not to
" be inferior to any man in those skirmishes :

said to have conversation, but altercation rather : for there
is something so captious and litigious in their spirit, that
they draw every the most trifling thing that can be started
into a dispute. Before such, you must not expect to talk at
ease ; that ease and indolence, which make a man careless
about both ideas and language : no, you must be wary and
correct ; you must be always upon the defensive ; you must
keep a perpetual guard, as you would over your purse, were
a pickpocket in the room.

[261] Dict. CHRYSIPPUS.

but

" but he had, with his notable perfection in
" this exercise, contracted such an irresolution
" and habit of doubting, that by degrees he
" grew confident in nothing, and a sceptic at
" least in the greatest mysteries of faith. All
" his doubts grew out of himself, when he
" assisted his scruples with the strength of his
" own reason, and was then too hard for him-
" self [262]."

To conclude.—What was the meaning of
that stricture upon Seneca, *Verborum minutiis
rerum frangit pondera*, which, according to Lord
Bacon, may thus be applied to the schoolmen,
*Quæstionum minutiis scientiarum frangunt solidita-
tem?* Why, that by their *litigiosa subtilitas*, as
he calls it, by their *logical* refinements and dis-
tinctions, they had *chopped* truth so down into
mincemeat, as to leave it not only without
proportion or form, but almost without substance.

[262] Life by himself, i. 56. 8vo.

LXXII.

LXXII.

THE LOVE OF MONEY THE RUIN OF STATES.

"NOTHING is great," fays Longinus, "a contempt of which is great [263];" as riches, honours, and fo forth. Yet, how rarely do we meet with fo much greatnefs (and a little, methinks, fhould fuffice) as will enable a man to defpife riches! Every reptile can moralize upon them in as heroic terms as Seneca himfelf, but will at the fame time fubmit to the meaneft tricks for the meaneft profits.

Salluft, in his Second **Oration** to Cæfar about regulating the Roman **Commonwealth,** advifes him, above all things, " **either to** abolifh, or " (**as** far as he can) to diminifh, the love of " money :" for that, otherwife, not only no reformation of manners could be made, **but** even government itfelf could not be **fupported** [264].

To

---

[263] Περὶ Ὕψους, fect. 7.

[264] *Multò maxumum bonum patriæ, civibus, tibi, liberis, poftremò humanæ genti, pepereris, fi ftudium pecuniæ aut fuftuleris, aut, quod res ferret, minueris : aliter neque privata res, neque publica, neque domi, neque militiæ, regi poteft.*—Salluft is an author very *à propos* to our prefent times and manners; both his Hiftories, with his two Orations to Cæfar, inculcat-

ing

To abolish the love of money, were it possible, would doubtless be excellent: but then, it might be said, we must forego the admiration of the far greater part of mankind, who value people only for the *figure* they make. I grant it readily, and that this may, perhaps, at first occasion some small struggle in the breast [265]; but a single reflection, methinks, might serve to quiet the tumult. For, if you must needs have this popular esteem, which surely a wise man might well do without, you must be content to share it with your dentist, your hair-dresser, *Madame Mara* [266], and Mrs. E——, who sells paint and paste to *mend God's works* with.

Meanwhile, this *studium pecuniæ*, this love of money, the gaining of which seems to be thought the great object of living, is (as it has most truly been called) the *root of all evil*. Look into the several departments of law, politics, trade; into the other departments of life: nay, examine this greediness of spirit, even in private families, and especially when accompanied (as it often is) with vanity and a passion for *figuring*;—examine all this carefully and

ing in almost every page, that this *appetentia alieni* and *profusio sui*, as he expresses it, was the corruption of Roman manners, and would be the ruin of the Roman state.

[265] *Ubi bonus deteriorem divitiis magis clarum magisque acceptum videt, primò æstuat, multaque in pectore volvit.* Ibid.

[266] An insolent, saucy, singing wench.

well,

well, and you will eafily perceive it to be the true
and genuine fource of nine tenths of the folly,
meannefs, vice, and mifery, which prevail
among mankind—that it is not only the corruption of all manners, but muft fooner or later
be the ruin of all ftates.

LXXIII.

OF ADVERTISEMENTS.

I HAVE often thought, that the manners of
our *better* fort of people (as by curtefy they
are called) might be well traced from the public advertifements; and could wifh, that fome
little *virtù*-man, juft equal to the work, would
exert himfelf to make a collection of thofe
which are the moft characteriftical. Fielding
has preferved, in his T. J. xiii. 5, an advertife-
ment of Broughton's for Lectures upon Box-
ing, dated 1 Feb. 1747; doubtlefs, with a view
of letting pofterity fee, 6000 years hence, what
civilized, humane, and polifhed perfons the
Chriftians of thefe primitive ages were. Other
advertifements might equally ferve this curious
purpofe. The fame Fielding mentions a " Mrs.
" Huffey, a celebrated mantua-maker in the
" Strand, famous for fetting off the fhapes of
" women," and fo forth; but does not fay that
fhe advertifed.—" *Foreign Perfumery*, by Abry
" perfumer

8

" perfumer to the Countefs of Artois," who offers at the fame time *(dog-cheap)* a vaft number of things, wherewith to mend the *human form divine,* and among others, the *Creme de Beauté* : my comfort, however, is, that in the very fame Paper, 19 May 1785, was advertifed Dr. Watts's *Improvement of the Mind.*— " Harrifon begs to inform the ladies, that he " has invented a fummer-cuſhion, entirely dif " ferent from any thing yet thought of. Some " very fine eſſence of roſe, orange, and jeſſa " min pomades, only a few days from Paris. " His fummer-rouge at 1 s. 6 d. per pot. 30 " May 1785." This hair-dreſſer, who was lately a journeyman only, has now (as I am told) befides a fplendid town-houfe, a villa and a carriage.

The ftile of thefe advertifements alfo is often as fingular as the matter of them. Monf. Veftris, in a Morning Chronicle, May 1784, addreſſes himfelf, upon the fubject of his movements, to a *judicious* and *generous* public. *Generous* perhaps may be borne with, becaufe the epithet is given to every fool who fquanders his money ; but it is a downright abufe and proftitution of the term *judicious,* when it refpects fuch objects, as make the amufement (I had almoft faid the bufinefs) of our *better* fort. *The Dancing Dogs! The Learned Pig! The Learned Fox! General Jackoo! &c.*
&c.

&c. &c. [268] I one day aſked a delicate *thing
of the ton*, whether he would not ſee this famous
monkey carried to the maſquerade? " *Lah!*"
ſays he mincingly, ánd affecting horror, " *the
" brute comes too near us:*" as if this *human*
ninny cóuld poſſibly be degraded by the reſem-
blance. " *Near* us!" replied I ; " why, he
" is *ſuperior* to at leaſt half of his admirers."
But to proceed.

" April 1785, Mr. Lepicq, after ſo many
" proofs of the public's partiality to him, finds
" his *feelings* truly *overpowered* by their pa-
" tronage," &c. I wiſh, with all my heart,
that the public would be more compaſſionate
and tender to the *feelings* of Mr. Lepicq.
Even Mr. Lunardi has not eſcaped this affectation in the ſtile of his advertiſements. " Mr.
" Lunardi is peculiarly happy in experiencing,
" that the attachment of the public to him is
" *in uniſon with his feelings* ;" and, March
1785, we are told, that " certain ladies mean
" to *try the nature of their ſenſations*, by aſcend-
" ing a few yards in Mr. Lunardi's balloon."

[268] Thus Trinculo in Shakeſpeare, taking Caliban for a
fiſh, exclaims : " Were I *in England* now, and had but this
" fiſh painted, not an holiday fool *there*, but would give a
" piece of ſilver. *There* would this monſter make a man ;
" any ſtrange beaſt *there* makes a man," &c.: and, which is
very remarkable, the claſs of people, who 'moſt waſte their
money upon rarities of this kind, are uſually the loudeſt in
their clamours againſt taxations.

6   By

By the way, this curiosity among the ladies to *try the nature of their sensations* need not be encouraged by Mr. Lunardi; it being likely to lead them into perils enough, without risking their necks in his balloon.

The following advertisement is of a more serious cast, and from which (I am sorry to say) too strong a trait of our manners may be drawn. " Morn. Post, April 1785. Ladies " or gentlemen possessed of estates or incomes " for life, desirous of raising money by grant " of annuities either for their own or the lives " of others—clergymen on their livings—offi- " cers on their pay—or persons of any descrip- " tion—may be accommodated on the most " *liberal* terms, by applying to —." I very sincerely wish, that the author of this advertisement may come to be hanged; and shall conclude with another, which will open a more pleasing prospect to many of my readers,—to all (I presume) within the bills of mortality. " Wood's Coffee-house, Covent Garden, " *TURTLE.* Three fine turtles dressed " this day in the highest perfection. Families " may be supplied with any quantity, to any " part of town or country. Will continue " dressing every day during the season. N. B. " Some very fine lively turtle to be disposed " of."

LXXIV.

LXXIV.

THE VICES OF YOUTH AND OLD AGE, AND THE
DIFFERENCE BETWEEN THE ONE AND THE
OTHER.

MEN are Stoics in their early years, Epicureans in their later; social in youth, selfish in old age. In early life they believe all men honest, till they know them to be knaves; in late life they believe all men knaves, till they know them to be honest. Young men not only take virtue for a solid good, but affect it often with enthusiastic ardor; old men usually treat it as an empty name, or (to use the words of Lord Rochester) " if they do talk of " it as a fine thing, yet this is only because " they think it a decent way of speaking, and " necessary for their credit and affairs [269]." Thus, some how or other, men pass, in the course of living, from one of these extremes to the other; and, from having thought too well of human nature at first, think at last, perhaps, too ill of it.

It has usually been observed, and I believe justly, that youth is the season of virtue: but, says a certain preacher, " it might have been " observed with equal truth, that *youth is the* " *season of vice*; since every age of human life " has vices as well as virtues, which are almost

[269] Burnet's Life and Death of Rochester, p. 23.

S " *peculiar*

" *peculiar* to itfelf [270]." True : but the vices, peculiar to youth, may, with fome indulgence at leaft, be deemed fins againft prudence, rather than againft virtue: they are fins of the body, rather than fins of the foul, if the diftinction may be allowed; that is, they do not fo much proceed from iniquity or depravity of *heart*, as from heat in the blood and ftrength of paffion.

Jones was of a gay and vigorous conftitution, and occafionally indulged with women and wine, beyond what ftrict chaftity and temperance permit; but *Jones* had franknefs, honefty of heart, warm affections, focial and fympathetic feelings. *Blifil*, on the other hand, kept up in all its rigour the form of morals, and affumed upon occafion the garb of fainthood; but *Blifil* was without fenfibility, referved, felfifh, cunning, a villain. Such feems to have been the difference between the armies of the Parliament and Charles I.; the foldiers of Charles being rather profligate in morals, while thofe of the Parliament were in faith and obfervances very faints. *Yes*, fays a Cavalier to a Roundhead who was boafting of this, *thou fayeft true : for in our army we have drinking and wenching, the fins of men ; but in yours you have thofe of devils, fpiritual pride and rebellion* [271].

270 Balguy's Sermons, 1785.

271 Sir Philip Warwick's Memoirs of Charles I. p. 253.

9   LXXV.

LXXV.

OF THE ABUSE OF MEDALS, AND OF LEWIS XIV.

MEDALS should record glorious deeds, and be subsidiary vouchers to good history; but they have been stamped for actions as inhuman and oppressive, as ambition and cruelty could devise. Of these the reign of Lewis XIV., called Lewis *The Great* by those, who (as Evelyn says) *blaspheme for bread,* will furnish sufficient instances, without going farther. Evelyn very properly uses the term *blaspheme* [272]; for, while some of their inscriptions are arrogant and vain-glorious, others are profane and even impious. To produce an instance or two out of a thousand. One medal represents Lewis standing between the cities of Genoa and Luxemburg, holding the world on the point of his sword — *victori perpetuo, ob expugnatas urbes ducentas;* not *ob servatos cives,* for preserving citizens and promoting human happiness, but for laying whole cities and countries in desolation and ashes. Another, upon the revocation of the Edict of Nantes in 1685 — *vicies centena millia Calvinianæ Ecclesiæ revocata, &c.* that is, for hav-

[272] Evelyn's *Discourse of Medals,* p. 82.

ing

ing converted two millions of proteſtants by dragonading and deſtruction. Others are as remarkable for their modeſty, as theſe for their piety :—*quod libet licet*, " what I liſt is law"— *ſtat pro ratione voluntas*, " the cauſe is in my " will, I will"—*nuſquam meta mihi*, " I have " no boundary."

These are the effects of arbitrary power: theſe things are ſeen only under abſolute monarchs (as Voltaire ſaid upon another occaſion [273]) and might, one would think, ſerve as a leſſon to mankind ; but they will not. Other medals are profane and impious : they radiate the king with the beams of the ſun (they do no more, ſays Evelyn, in their pictures of God the Father [274]), as if alone ſufficient to govern the univerſe :

Non alio cerni majeſtas ſe velit ore,
Non aliud mundus poſcat habere caput :

comparing him to that luminary in no fewer than ſeventy-five devices and inſcriptions. All this, and a thouſand times as much, for *Louis le Grand*, for *le Roi tres Chriſtienne*. And who was this Lewis *the Great*, this *moſt Chriſ-*

---

[273] Peliſſon was confined four years and a half in the Baſtile, purely for having been faithful to his friend and maſter Fouquet ; and then ſpent the remainder of his life in writing eloges upon the King. *C'eſt une choſe qu'on ne voit que dans les monarchies.*

[274] Evelyn, p. 79.

tian King? A moſt vain, oſtentatious, parading
bully, whoſe glory conſiſted of devaſtations
abroad, and oppreſſions at home; which glory
however, infamous as it was, he could never
have attained, but for the pitiful part our
Charles II. acted. And for greatneſs, that of
Lewis was to real greatneſs, what the *ſimulacra*
of Epicurus were to real bodies: it reſembled
the ſacrifice, with which Prometheus formerly
attempted to impoſe upon Jupiter, *viz.* "not
" a real ox, but only an ox's hide, ſtuffed with
" ſtraw, and leaves, and twigs [275]:" it was, in
ſhort, all appearance, devoid of ſubſtance [276].

No language however was too magnificent
for this enormous idol or image of greatneſs.
The Jeſuit Meneſtrier, in a pompous folio,
1691, thus beſpeaks him in his dedication:
" **To Lewis** the Great, the invincible, the
" wiſe, the conqueror, the wonder of his age,
" terror of his enemies, lover of his people,
" arbiter of peace and war, *adminiſtrator of the*
" *univerſe,* and *worthy to be its maſter,* are of-
" fered with profound ſubmiſſion the *medals* of
" an accompliſhed hero; preſenting him the
" hiſtory of a reign worthy of immortality, and

[275] Adduxit Prometheus, loco bovis veri, pellem bovis
ſtramine, & foliis, et viminibus ſuffarcinatam. *Bacon.*

[276] For traits of this hero's interior littleneſs and meanneſs, ſee No LXVII. *Of Madam de Maintenon.*

S 3

" the

"the veneration of all ages." So that, as appears, this excess of flattery, this profaneness and impiety, was not confined to wits and poets, or such as *blaspheme for bread*, but had infected all orders, even the most sacred.

Of this slavish adulation to princes, numerous instances may be seen in Casaubon's *Animadvers. in Athenæum*, lib. vi. cap. 14, 15, *&c.*

LXXVI.

THOU SHALT NOT DO EVIL, THAT GOOD MAY COME OF IT.

ALL christians will readily subscribe to this; but the whole history of christianity shews, that few will allow any thing to be *evil*, which, according to their conceptions, leads to *good*. That all fraud is evil, must (one would think) be universally allowed; but the man of religion dissents, and distinguishes. "Fraud," says he, "is not always a pernicious thing, but is "good or bad according to the intention of "him who uses it. A fraud in season, and "practised with judgment, is attended with "great

" great good : it ought not indeed to be
" deemed so much a fraud, as a certain wise
" and politic way of managing [177]." This he
urges : and he urges it in the language of
Chrysostom, who contends for the **utility of**
fraud in military, civil, and even domestic
concerns ; and, particularly, makes it as necessary in physicians to deceive for the good of
bodies, as he would infer it to be in divines for
the good of souls.

Jerom, another writer in the times of primitive christianity, in like manner adopted this
principle of deceiving ; and plainly believed
no deviation from rectitude to be unlawful,
which flowed from piety and zeal for christianity : *non condemnamus errorem*, says he, *qui
de odio Judæorum et fidei pietate descendit*. And,
speaking in another place of controversial writings against the Pagans, he holds it allowable
to urge all arguments false as well as true; to
use tricks in disputation ; in short, to employ any artifice whatever, which may best
serve to refute and conquer an adversary : and
he justifies this practice by the examples of

[177] Ἡ ἀπάτη ὀκ ἀεὶ πρᾶγμα ἐπιβλαβὲς, ἀλλὰ παρὰ τὴν τῶν
χρωμένων προαίρεσιν γίνεται φαῦλον ἢ καλόν—ἔχει κέρδ Ꝍ εὐκαιρ Ꝍ
ἀπάτη, καὶ μετὰ τῆς ὀρθῆς γινομένη διανοίας — μᾶλλον δὲ ὀδὲ
ἀπάτην τὸ τοιοῦτο δι᾽ καλῖν, ἀλλ᾽ οἰκονομίαν τινὰ καὶ σοφίαν.
                         De Sacerdot. lib. i. sub fin.

Origen and Eusebius against Celsus and Porphyry [278].

The real truth is, and it is in vain to dissem-
ble it, that christians in all ages have never
scrupled at any *means*, to bring about what
they deemed a good and pious *end* [279] : else
whence those, not only frauds and tricks, but
persecutions, inquisitions, and the various terrible modes of conversion, which have been
practised in the church, from its earliest establishment down to the present hour? whence
the infatuation to be persuaded, that men
might actually *do God service*, while they made
havock and destruction of his creatures?

But there are no lengths to which men may
not be carried, when influenced by zeal and
bigotry, without any controul from reason and
common sense. The very devout and over-
righteous have ever been *above ordinances,* as the
cant of fanaticism expresses it. The Antino-
mians of all ages have insisted, that " the obli-
" gations of morality and natural law are sus-
" pended; that the elect, guided by an inter-
" nal principle, more perfect and divine, are

---

[278] Opera, tom. iv. p. 113. 236. *edit. Benedict.*

[279] From the allowance and practice of *pious frauds* it
comes to pass, by an easy transition, that many vastly good
people, who would not *swear* for the world, or commit any
sin of *eclát*, yet will not scruple occasionally to *lye*—the
meanest of all sins.

" superior

" superior to the *beggarly elements* of justice
" and humanity;" and that, in short, every
thing is lawful to the saints. To what purpose
shall it be said to such, *ye shall not do evil, that
good may come of it?*

Mean while it is certain, that this principle
of *doing* (or, which is the same thing, of suf-
fering) *evil, that good may come of it,* has by
no means been confined to the pale of the
church: it has indeed been countenanced by
the universal practice of mankind, as well in
civil as religious concerns. Ancient and modern
writers have been quoted to justify the expedient
of deceiving the people[280]: and a man, who
should detect and expose any received and established system in either government or religion,
however false or futile its foundation[281], would
be

[280] *Hæc Pontifex Scævola nosse populos non vult—expedire
igitur existimat falli in religione civitates, quod dicere etiam
in libris rerum divinarum ipse Varro non dubitat.* Aug. de
Civ. iv. 27.

[281] *A very indifferent religion, well believed, will go a
great way,* says Jeremy Collier, *the famous non-juror; an
honest heathen is none of the worst men.* View of the Im-
morality and Profaneness of the English Stage, p. 28.—Jeremy Collier must have liked the following passage from
Curtius—*nulla res efficaciùs multitudinem regit, quam super-
stitio; alioqui impotens, sæva, mutabilis: ubi vana religione
capta est, meliùs vatibus quam ducibus suis paret.* But the latter part of it, so much to the relish of Jeremy, may probably
have

be perfecuted by his compatriots as a bad
member of fociety. And why? becaufe thefe
fyftems are deemed ufeful and even neceffary to
keep the people in order[281].

And if from bodies and eftablifhments we
defcend to individuals or fingle inftances, we
fhall find the worft and bafeft *means* employed
to bring about (what have been deemed) juft
and lawful *ends*. When the Earl of Suffolk
fled into Flanders, to promote an infurrection
againft Henry the VIIth, Henry doubtlefs
thought himfelf warranted to countermine and
fubdue him. For this purpofe, he caufed Sir
Robert Curfon, captain of the caftle at Ham-
mes, to fly from his charge, and to feign himfelf the Earl's fervant. Curfon did fo; and,
having infinuated himfelf into the fecrets of
the Earl, and become his confident, communi-
cated every thing to Henry. Mean while Henry, to confirm the credit of Curfon, caufed to

have made the whole unpalatable to the ftatefman: who, it is
obfervable, hath never been forward to employ the prieft in
any of his manœuvres, when he could poffibly do without
him. Q. Curt. iv. 39.

[282] But do not men, who thus contend for the utility of
all religions to the fupport of government, appear to put
all religions upon a level, confounding the true with the
falfe? and, if government can as well be fupported by
fraud and impofture, as by a genuine and pure religion,
muft not the God of *truth* and the God of *order* feem two
diftinct beings?

be publifhed at Paul's Crofs the Pope's Bull of excommunication and curfe againft the Earl of Suffolk and Sir Robert Curfon : " wherein " it muft be confeffed," fays Lord Bacon very gently, " that *heaven was made too much to bow* " *to earth,* and religion to policy [283]."

In the time of Cromwell, a thoufand tricks were played to find out and convict the difaffected ; and an accurfed order of villains, who were called *Duckoys* and *Trapans,* were employed to worm out their fecrets under hypocritical pretences, and then betray them. Thus overreached, Colonel Andrews loft his head ; nor, fays my author, " was the Prefident *Brad-* " *fhaw* afhamed openly to declare in court, " that by counterfeit letters he had correfpond- " ed with him in the name of the *King* [284]."— Even in the cafe of petty traitors, thefe arts have not been judged too mean to be practifed ; and, unlefs my memory deceives me, John the Painter's conviction could not be made full and complete, till fome pretended

[283] Hift. of Henry VII.—Zopyrus acted precifely the fame part for Darius againft the Affyrians, whom he betrayed ; only, to gain their confidence more effectually, he caufed his nofe, ears, and lips to be cut off, and then feigned to have been treated thus cruelly by Darius. Juftin. Hift. i. 10.

[284] Bates's *Elenchus Motuum, &c.* Part II.

friends

friends had cajoled and drawn him to convict himfelf.

All fuch arts, however, are not only mean, but bafe and wicked. A man, who would pre-ferve his integrity untainted, fhould not put himfelf into the attitude of a villain, no, not for a moment. The inward feelings foon ac-commodate themfelves to the outward fituation and garb; the artificial character foon becomes natural: and therefore I fhould diflike, as a player, to act a bad man; but I would not, as an advocate, defend a bad caufe.

LXXVII.

THE BIBLE SHOULD NOT BE USED IN TEACH-ING TO READ.

HENRY KNYGHTON, a canon of Lei-cefter, complained heavily of Wickliff, his neighbour and contemporary [285], " for having " tranflated out of Latin into Englifh the gof-" pel, which Chrift had entrufted with the " clergy and doctors of the church, that *they* " might minifter it to the laity and weaker

---

[285] Wickliff was rector of Lutterworth in Leicefterfhire, and died in 1384.

" fort,

" fort, according to the exigency of times and
" their several occasions : so that by this means
" the gospel jewel, or evangelical pearl, was
" made *vulgar*, was thrown about, and trod-
" den under foot of swine [286]." The Moham-
medans have been very careful to preserve their
Koran from the prophanation here complained
of : it is, says Mr. Sale, the translator, " in
" the greatest reverence among them. They
" dare not so much as touch it, without be-
" ing first washed or legally purified : which,
" lest they should do inadvertently, they write
" these words on the cover, *Let none touch it*
" *but who are clean*. They read it with a su-
" perstitious reverence, never holding it be-
" low their girdles : they adorn it with gold
" and precious stones, &c. [287]" Henry Knyghton would have approved and commended all
this, as just, *decent, and in order :* but what
would Henry Knyghton have said, if he had
seen the Bible thumbed and dirtied in our
schools, thrown by the boys at one another's
heads, and consigned perhaps at length to the
most humiliating offices ?

[286] Lewis's *Hist. of Translations of the Bible,* p. 20. 1729.
8vo.

[287] Sale's Preliminary Discourse to the *Koran*, 4to.—The
Jews had the same veneration for their law ; not daring to
touch it with unwashen hands, nor then neither without a
cover. *Vide Millium de Mohammedismo ante Mohammed.*
p. 366.

It

It should seem from Lord Bacon, that this familiarity with the Bible might lead by degrees to an actual privation of all religion, yea, even a sense of God's existence: for, reckoning up the sorts of atheists, he lays little stress upon the contemplative, sophistical, philosophical atheists, as they are called. Among these, says he, " atheism is rather in the *lip*, than in the " *heart:* these will ever be talking of their " opinion, as if they were wavering about it, " and would gladly be strengthened by the " consent of others. These seem to be more " than they are: but the great atheists indeed " are hypocrites, who are ever handling holy " things, without the least sense or feeling of " their being so: so that these must needs be " *cauterized* in the end [288]." Now, according to these ideas, may not the constant official handling of holy things make men atheists, by making them gradually lose a sense of their holiness? Look at sextons, parish-clerks, singing boys, choir-men (I need go no higher) and see what sense or feeling they have of the holiness of the things about them.—Boys are taught to read in the Bible, because the Bible is a good book [289]: the school-house is often a

part

[288] Essays, xvi.

[289] The benefit or utility, arising from these unions, is altogether imaginary. " Wanting an English book for my " scholars

part of the church, becaufe the church is an holy place [292]. Surely our pious anceftors did not know, that familiarity breeds contempt; for more effectual means could not be contrived to extinguifh or prevent all fenfe of holinefs.

There is yet another reafon, why boys fhould not be taught to read by the ufe of the Bible, if there be any fuch thing as affociation of ideas. The Bible, diftinct from its religious importance, is certainly a very curious as well as ufeful book : but the Bible is ufually the laft book men take up, either for inftruction or amufement. Why? becaufe they have formerly been teazed, and buffeted, and flogged about it; and becaufe they hate the fcenery,

"fcholars to tranflate," fays a learned fchool-mafter, "which might improve them in fenfe and Latin at once "(two things which fhould never be divided in teaching) " I thought nothing more proper for that purpofe, than Ba- "con's Effays." As if a fchool-boy would attend to or (if he would) could comprehend, the ftrong deep fenfe of Bacon : juft as well might it be faid, that boys fhould be taught in the Bible and at the church, becaufe religion and learning fhould never be divided. Pref. to Bacon's Effays, tranflated by Willymot, 1720. 2 vols. 8vo.

292 By this means the church-yard, which is alfo confecrated, and muft certainly have fome degree of holinefs, as well as the church, becomes as it were a licenfed playground for the fchool-boys, and at the fame time a beargarden for the parifh.

which

which it naturally revives. 'Tis pity but a little knowledge of human nature had been cultivated by thefe good people, together with their piety and learning.

LXXVIII.

THE ECCENTRICITIES AND CAPRICES OF IMAGINATION.

A CERTAIN writer, apologizing for the irregularities of great genii, delivers himfelf thus. " The gifts of imagination bring " the heavieft tafk upon the vigilance of rea- " fon; and to bear thofe faculties with uner- " ring rectitude or invariable propriety, re- " quires a degree of firmnefs and of cool at- " tention, which doth not always attend the " higher gifts of the mind. Yet, difficult as " nature herfelf feems to have reduced the tafk " of regularity to genius, it is the fupreme " confolation of dullnefs to feize upon thofe " exceffes, which are the overflowings of fa- " culties they never enjoyed [291]."—Are not the *gifts of imagination* here miftaken for the ftrength of paffions? Doubtlefs, where ftrong

---

[291] Langhorne's Life of Wm Collins.

paffions accompany great parts, as perhaps
they often do, there imagination may increafe
their force and activity : but, where paffions
are calm and gentle, imagination of itfelf
fhould feem to have no conflict but *fpecula-
tively* with reafon. There indeed it wages an
eternal war ; and, if not controuled and ftrictly
regulated, will carry the patient into endlefs
extravagancies. I ufe with propriety the term
patient : becaufe men, under the influence of
imagination, are moft truly diftempered. The
degree of this diftemper will be in proportion
to the prevalence of imagination over reafon,
and, according to this proportion, amount to
more or lefs of the whimfical; but, when reafon fhall become as it were extinct, and imagination govern alone, then the diftemper will be
madnefs under the wildeft and moft fantaftic
modes. Thus one of thefe invalids, perhaps,
fhall be all forrow for having been moft unjuftly
deprived of the crown ; though his vocation,
poor man ! be that of a fchoolmafter. Another
is all joy, like Horace's madman ; and it may
feem even cruelty to cure him. A third all
fear ; and dares not make water, left he fhould
caufe a deluge [292].

The operations and caprices of imagination
are various and endlefs ; and, as they cannot be
reduced to regularity or fyftem, fo it is highly
improbable that any certain method of cure

[292] Riverij *Praxis Medica*, p. 188.

T   fhould

should ever be found out for them. It hath generally been thought, that matter of fact might most succefsfully be opposed to the delusions of imagination, as being proof to the senfes, and carrying conviction unavoidably to the understanding: but I suspect, that the understanding, or reasoning faculty, hath little to do in all these cafes: at least so it should seem from the two following, which are very remarkable, and well attested.

Fienus, in his curious little book *de viribus imaginationis*, records from Donatus the cafe of a man, who fancied his body increased to such a fize, that he durst not attempt to pafs through the door of his chamber. The physician, believing that nothing could more effectually cure this error of imagination, than to shew that the thing could actually be done, caused the patient to be thrust forcibly through it: who, struck with horror, and falling suddenly into agonies, complained of being crushed to pieces, and expired soon after [293].—Reason, certainly, was not concerned here.

The other cafe, as related by Van Swieten in his Commentaries upon Boerhaave [294], is that of a learned man, who had studied, till he fancied his legs to be of glafs; in confequence of which, he durst not attempt to stir, but was constantly under anxiety about them. His maid, bringing one day some wood to the fire,

[293] P. 131. L. Bat. 1635.   [294] *Aphorism.* 1113.

threw

threw it carelessly down; and was severely re-
primanded by her master, who was terrified not
a little for his legs of glass. The surly wench,
out of all patience with his megrims, as she
called them, gave him a blow with a log upon
the parts affected: which so enraged him, that
he instantly rose up, and from that moment re-
covered the use of his legs.—Was reason concerned any more here? or, was it not rather
one blind impulse acting against another?

LXXIX.

A TRAIT OF QUEEN ELIZABETH.

THE following copy of an original letter
from this Queen to Heaton, Bishop of Ely,
is taken from the Register of Ely:

" Proud Prelate,
" I understand you are backward in com-
" plying with your agreement: but I would
" have you to know, that I, who made you
" what you are, can unmake you; and, if you
" do not forthwith fulfil your engagement,
" by —— I will immediately unfrock you.
" Your's, as you demean yourself,
" ELIZABETH."

Heaton, it feems, had promifed the Queen to exchange fome part of the land belonging to the fee for an equivalent, and did fo; but it was in confequence of the above letter.

LXXX.

ONE TRAIT OF OLIVER CROMWELL.

TO his Highnefs the Lord Protector of the commonwealth of England, Scotland, and Ireland.

The humble petition of Marjery, the wife of William Beacham, mariner, fheweth, That your petitioner's hufband hath been active and faith-full in the wars of this commonwealth, both by fea and land; and hath undergone many hazards by imprifonment and fights, to the endangering of his life; and at laft loft the ufe of his right arm, and is utterly difabled from future fervice, as doth appear by the certificate annexed; and yet hath no more than forty fhillings penfion from Chatham by the year; that your petitioner, having one only fonne, who is tractable to learn, and not having wherewith to bring him up, by reafon of their prefent low eftate, occafioned by the publique

fervice

service aforesaid, humbly prayeth, that your highness would vouchsafe to present her said sonne Randolph Beacham, to be scholler in Sutton's-hospital, called the Charter-House.

> " OLIVER, P. We referre this petition and
> " certificate to the commissioners of Sut-
> " ton's-hospital.
> " July 28th, 1655."

A Letter sent by Oliver to his secretary on the above petition.

> " You receive from me, this 28th instant, a
> " petition of Marjery Beacham, desiring the
> " admission of her son into the Charter-House.
> " I know the man; who was employed one
> " day in a very important secret service, which
> " he did effectually, to our great benefit and
> " the commonwealth's. The petition is a
> " brief relation of a fact, without any flattery.
> " I have wrote under it a common reference
> " to the commissioners, but I *mean* a great
> " deal more; that it *shall* be done, without
> " their debate, or consideration of the matter:
> " and so do you privately hint to ———.
> " I have not the particular shining bauble or
> " feather in my cap, for crouds to gaze at or
> " kneel to; but I have power and resolution
> " for foes to tremble at. To be short, I know
> " how to deny petitions; and whatever I think
> " proper, for outward form, to referre to any

" officer

" officer or office, I expect that such my com-
" pliance with custom shall be also looked
" upon as an indication of my will and plea-
" sure to have the thing done.   See therefore,
" that the boy is admitted.

" July 28, 1655.   " Thy true friend,

              " OLIVER, P."

Thus it is always, when tyranny gains the
ascendant : the forms are preserved, the substance is gone.   And thus it was in ancient
Rome : consuls, prætors, tribunes, and other
officers, were elected duly and in form, long
after the empire had lost its liberty, and all
were subjected to the will of one. It is curious
to observe, with what apparently conscientious
respect Tiberius, for instance, abstained from
interfering with these personages, either at
their elections, or with their deliberations in
the senate; while the dissembling tyrant was
the capricious and arbitrary director of the
puppets, and the sole spring of every movement.   Perhaps other nations might be found,
who have fancied themselves free, because in
possession of ancient and known forms, though
the substance or vital spirit of liberty was really
departed, and some secret influence has governed the whole : and perhaps the *progression
of manners*, as it has been called, and the necessary course of human things, will always
have it so.

                              LXXXI.

ANOTHER TRAIT OF OLIVER CROMWELL.

THERE never was an impoſtor, who wanted to lead and govern, but enjoined, in
the firſt place, that men ſhould quit reaſon,
and ſtifle common-ſenſe. This has always
been the corner-ſtone, when religion has been
either the means to be employed, or the end to
be brought about. There is extant a curious
letter from Oliver Cromwell to Colonel Hammond, which illuſtrates this poſition in an
high degree. Hammond was governor of the
Iſle of Wight, during the confinement of
Charles I. in Cariſbrook Caſtle; and had conceived ſome ſcruples concerning his royal
charge, which made him deſirous to quit the
army and retire. Cromwell, in a letter of
Nov. 25, 1648, about two months before the
beheading of Charles, endeavours to remove
theſe ſcruples; but how? not by topics drawn
from reaſon or policy, but by canting and
whining about faith and grace.

" Dear Robin, our *fleſhly reaſonings* enſnare
" us: theſe make us ſay, *heavy, ſad, pleaſant,*
" *eaſy.* Was there not a little of this, when
" Robert Hammond, through diſſatisfaction,

T 4 " deſired

" defired retirement from the army, and
" thought of quiet in the Ifle of Wight?—
" Dear Robin, thou and I were never worthy
" to be door-keepers in this fervice. If thou
" *wilt* feek, feek to know the mind of God in
" all that chain of providence, whereby God
" brought thee thither, and that perfon to
" thee; how before and fince God has ordered
" him, and affairs concerning him : and then
" tell me, whether there be not fome glorious
" and high meaning in all this, above what
" thou haft yet attained ; and, laying afide thy
" *flefhly reafon*, feek of the Lord to teach
" thee what that is."—In the following paffage
he reafons, and fhews that he could talk fenfe
if he would: " Authorities and Powers are
" the ordinance of God; this or that fpecies
" of human inftitution and limited, fome
" with larger, others with ftricter bonds, each
" according to its conftitution. I do not
" therefore think, authorities may do any
" thing, and yet obedience be due; **but** all
" agree there are cafes, in which it is lawful to
" refift."—Reafoning, however, would not do
with Hammond; and therefore Cromwell de-
fifts from it, as totally to be diftrufted. " But
" truly thefe kind of *reafonings* may be but
" *flefhly*, either with or againft; **and let us** be-
" ware, left *flefhly reafonings*, &c.—**Dear** Ro-
" bin, tempting of God ordinarily is either by
" acting

" acting prefumptuoufly in *carnal* confidence,
" or in unbelief through diffidence : both
" thefe ways Ifrael tempted God in the wil-
" dernefs, and he was grieved with them.
" The encountering difficulties therefore makes
" us not to tempt God, but acting before and
" without *faith*. If the Lord hath in any
" meafure perfuaded his people, as generally
" he hath, of the lawfulnefs, nay of the duty,
" this perfuafion prevailing upon the heart is
" *faith*; and acting thereupon is acting in
" *faith*; and the more the difficulties are, the
" more *faith*.—Dear Robin, beware of men,
" look up to the Lord. Let him be free to
" fpeak, and command in thy heart. Take
" heed of the things, I fear, thou haft *reafoned*
" thyfelf into; and thou fhalt be able through
" him, without confulting flefh and blood, to
" do *valiantly* for him and for his people."

Thus ftrengthened, Hammond perfevered
pioufly in his duty, and the king was brought
valiantly to the block about two months after;
and thus knavery hath practifed upon folly and
madnefs, in all ages of the world, and among
all ranks of men.

LXXXII.

EXTRACTS FROM LETTERS OF MR. LOCKE TO
DR. MAPLETOFT, UPON LOVE AND MATRI-
MONY.

DR. John Mapletoft, born about 1631, was
professor of physic in Gresham College,
when these letters were written; and continued
so till 1679. Then he married, and in 1682
became a divine. It appears from the following extracts, that Locke had a strong desire to
succeed Mapletoft at Gresham: for though, as
Le Clerc says [295], he never would practise re-
gularly, and for the sake of profit, yet he was
very knowing in the science, and highly esteem-
ed by all the professors of it. The collection,
from whence these extracts are made, furnish a
striking proof of the high opinion that was
entertained of his skill in medicine: for in one
of the letters, dated Paris, 4 Dec. 1677, he tells
you, that he " was sent for to the lady ambassa-
" drice, after having met with so little success
" from the French physicians, that she was re-
" solved to try them no more."—Locke however did not succeed to Gresham.

[295] Biblioth. Choif. vi. 349.

Paris,

Paris, 22 June 1677.

—— " If either abfence (which fometimes increafes our defires) or love (which we fee every day produces ftrange effects in the world) have foftened you, or difpofed you to a liking of any of our fine new things, 'tis but faying fo, and I am ready to furnifh you, and fhould be forry not to be employed. I mention love, for you know I have a particular intereft of my own in it. When you look that way, no body will be readier (as you may guefs) to throw an old fhoe after you; much for your own fake, and a little for a friend of yours. But were I to advife, perhaps I fhould fay to you, that your lodgings at Grefham College were a very quiet and comfortable habitation."——

Paris, 9 Aug. 1677.

—— " Though your letter hath fatisfied me that you are very well, yet it hath put new doubts into me; and, methinks, I fee you going to lofe yourfelf. I will fay no worfe of it, not knowing how far the matter is gone; elfe I would afk you, whether fhe were young, old, or middle-aged; each of which is fure to meet you with the horns of a dilemma. I fee you are, whatever you think, hot upon the fcent: if you have nothing elfe to defend you, but

but thofe maxims you build on, I fear the chafe will lead you where you yourfelf will be caught. For be as grave and fteady as you pleafe, refolve as much as you will, never to go out of your way or pace for any an *hey-trony-nony* whatever, you are not a jot the fafer for all this fturdinefs. For, believe it, Sir, this fort of game, having a defign to be caught, will hunt juft at the purfuer's rate, and will go no fafter before, than will juft ferve to make you follow : and let me affure you, upon as good authority as honeft Tom Bagnall's, that *vivus videnfque pereo* is the lamentable ditty of many an honeft gentleman. But if you or the fates have determined, (for the poor fates are ftill to be accufed in the cafe) if your mettle be up, and, bold as Sir Francis Drake, you will fhoot the defperate gulph ; yet confider, that though the riches of Peru lie that way, how well you can endure the warm navigation of the Mare de Zur, which all travellers affure us is nick-named *Pacificum*.

" But hold, I go too far : all this perhaps, notwithftanding your ancient good principles, will be herefy to you by the time it comes to England; and therefore I conjure you by our friendfhip to burn this as foon as you have read it, that it never may rife up in judgment againft me. I fee one is never fure of one's
self ;

self; and the time may come when I may re-
sign myself to the empire of the soft sex, and
abominate myself for these miserable errors.
However as the matter now stands, I have dis-
charged my conscience, and pray do not let me
suffer for it: for I know you lovers are a sort
of people, that are bound to sacrifice all to
your mistresses. But, to be serious with you,
if your heart does hang that way, I wish you
good luck: may Hymen be as kind to you, as
ever he was to any body; and then I am sure
you will be much happier than any forlorn
batchelor can be. If it be like to be, I beg
you to continue the care of my interest in the
case; and remember it is for one, who knows
how to value the quiet and retirement you are
going to quit. You have no more to do for
me, than what lovers use to do upon their own
account, *viz.* keep the matter as secret and private as you can; and then, when it is ripe and
resolved, give me but notice, and I shall quick-
ly be with you: for 'tis by your directions I
shall better govern my motions, than by the
flight of thrushes and fieldfares. Some remains of my cough will probably keep me
longer here than the time you mention; but,
not knowing whether the air of France will
ever quite remove my old companion or no,

I shall

I shall neglect that uncertainty, upon the consideration of so comfortable an importance [296]."—

———————

LXXXIII.

A LETTER OF ALGERNOON SYDNEY TO DR. MAPLETOFT.

THE following letter is dated from Geneva, July the 6th; but the year is not mentioned. It must, however, have been written in 1662; for, early in 1663, Dr. Mapletoft returned to England, after having lived near a year at Rome in the house of Algernoon Sydney. The letter, though upon a very light occasion, yet breathes the same severe and acrimonious spirit, for which that republican was always remarkable : he was then in a state of voluntary exile, because he would not personally accept at the Restoration of the oblivion and indemnity, granted generally to the whole nation.

[296] —*Comfortable importance.* It is remarkable, that Andrew Marvel made himself very merry with this expression, which had been used by Parker, in the *Rehearsal Transprosed*, 1672, 12mo.

" Sir,

" SIR,

" Coming to Venice five or fix days after your departure from Padua, I received a letter of your's, giving me notice of your taking the way of France in the company of Sir John Vaughan ; concluding that I did not intend to remove from Rome, nor make the journey into Germany of which I had fpoken, becaufe the feafon was not fit for it. I am fo much your fervant, that I was glad to hear you had joined yourfelf unto better company, than that which I had offered unto you ; but, by your favour, if you had remembred how little I do ufe to difguife my intentions, and how far I was from having any intereft, that in this particular fhould fway me beyond my inclinations and cuftoms, you would never have judged that I would ftay at Rome, when I did publifh my refolution of removing. The truth is, my head is not fo hot, as thofe of the youths, who ordinarily run from place to place, without knowing why or confidering when ; but I did obferve the feafon, and when I found it fit for travelling with convenience, I did execute the defign which I had formerly refolved, and have advanced as far as this place with more convenience, than ever I did make any other in my life. When I came hither, I was informed by feveral perfons that thofe foolifh boys, who were with you at the Ville de Vien-

na, when they were here, pretended to be very
well acquainted with me, as I think to gain the
more credit to the report which they spread,
that I was turned Roman Catholick. I am not
naturally very follicitous of such matters ; but,
hearing that you intend to feek the fame company, I think it worth the pains of writing a
few lines, to defire you to tell them from me,
that it would become them in good manners
not to talk at that rate of men, that they ought
to ufe with a little more refpect ; and that the
framing of foolifh and malicious untruths is
moft unworthy of any, who do fo much as pretend to the name of honeft men. After I have
paffed fome few days in this place, I intend to
purfue my formerly refolved journey ; but that
is fo little important to you, that I will not
trouble you with an account of it. When I
come to fix, it is probable you will by fome
way or other know where I am; and then, if
you have any thing to command me, you may
eafily know how to addrefs your letters unto
your very humble and affectionate fervant,

AL. SYDNEY."

LXXXIII.

LXXXIV.

FROM MR. NELSON'S LETTERS TO DR. MAPLE-
TOFT.

London, 2 Jan. 1679.

" YOUR friend and fchoolfellow, Mr.
Dryden, has been feverely beaten for
being the fuppofed author of a late very abu-
five lampoon. There has been a good fum of
money offered to find who fet them on work:
'tis faid they received their orders from the
Duchefs of Portfmouth, who is concerned in
the lampoon."—

London, 12 Dec. 1679.

— " Tis the petitioning of Parliament, that
has enraged him; (Charles II.) and he fwears
by God, they may knock out his brains, but
fhall never cut off his head."—This relates to
a difpute the King had with the Commons,
about the impeachment of Lord Danby.

Cranéford, 17 July, 1708.

He mentions, in this letter, a defign of
" immediately fetting up fifty-two parochial
libraries, which, fays he, at 16 *l.* a library, will
amount to 832 *l.*;" and there paffed the fame
year, an act for the better prefervation of paro-

U   chial

chial libraries. *Parochial* libraries imply a greater defign, as fhould feem, than can ever be executed : but might not a *County* library, under wife regulations, and with a catalogue for proper perfons who fhould chufe to purchafe it, be an object worthy of attention ?

————————

LXXXV.

OF GREAT MEN; AND OF DR. SAMUEL JOHNSON.

GREAT man ? fays Voltaire, *we muft by no means be lavifh of this title* [297]. We can indeed hardly ever apply it at all, if by *great* be meant univerfally fo ; that is, *omnibus numeris abfolutus.* Lord Bacon was a great man, a very great man ; yet only partially fo. He had a great and comprehenfive underftanding, perhaps the greateft that hath yet fhone forth among the fons of men : but it does not appear, that he would have been great in either field or cabinet ; and for greatnefs of foul, as it is called, the poet, who ftiles him the *wifeft* and the *brighteft*, brands him at the fame time for the *meaneft of mankind.*

[297] *Grand homme ? il ne faut pas prodiguer ce titre.* Siecle de Louis, in Cat. DOUIAT.

Churchill,

Churchill, Duke of Marlborough, was a very great man : even Bolingbroke, who certainly was not prejudiced in his favour, allows him to have been " the greateſt general as well as the " greateſt miniſter, that our country or per- " haps any other has produced [298]." Yet Churchill, **Duke** of Marlborough, was illiterate to an extreme; of an underſtanding totally un- cultivated; and in which, if you could have crept under the glare of his exterior, **you** would pro- bably have diſcerned weakneſſes; equal to thoſe of the weakeſt men.—Julius Cæſar was a very great general, and a very great ſtateſman; but he was more. Julius Cæſar was a man of let- ters, and a fine writer; had a moſt compre- henſive as well as cultivated underſtanding; and, withal, a moſt uncommon greatneſs of ſoul. Julius Cæſar is, in my humble opinion, the *greateſt* man upon record.—Lewis XIV, like many other tyrants ſurrounded by pimps and flatterers, had the title of Great conferred upon him : but Lewis's greatneſs was to real greatneſs, what the bombaſt is to the ſublime, or the *ſimulacra* of Epicurus to real bodies.

The late Dr. Samuel Johnſon was a man of great parts, and was indiſputably a great man, if great parts ſimply can make one [299]: but Dr. Samuel

[298] *Upon Hiſtory.* Letter viii.

[299] He was probably learned; but I do not reckon learn- ing among the **attributes** of great men. Learning may be

attained

Samuel Johnſon was the meaneſt of bigots, a
dupe and ſlave to the moſt contemptible prejudices [300]; and, upon ſubjects the moſt important, is known to have held opinions, which
are abſolutely a diſgrace to human underſtanding.

The Preſident Montesquieu has ſaid, that
" the **rank or** place, which poſterity beſtows,
" is ſubject like all others to the whim and
" caprice of fortune [301] :" and our Wollaſton
was ſo diſguſted with the fooliſh and iniquitous
judgments of men, that he betook himſelf
early in life to retirement,—*propter iniqua hominum judicia,* as he left to be inſcribed upon
his tomb-ſtone.   If any thing could cure a
man's anxiety, and render him indifferent, about
what is ſaid or thought of him, now or here-

---

attained by little men, who will apply : but learning without parts, or a capacity to uſe it, is merely dead unweildy
matter, *caput mortuum,* devoid of life or ſpirit.   Like wealth
or titles, it often ſerves only to make a blockhead conſpi-
cuous.

[300] One would think, from a paſſage in the *Rambler,* that
he himſelf did a little ſuſpect this : " the pride of wit and
" knowledge," ſays he, " is often mortified by finding,
" that they can confer no ſecurity againſt the common er-
" rors, which miſlead the weakeſt and meaneſt of man-
" kind." N° 6.

[301] *Les places que la poſterité donne ſont ſujettes, comme les
autres, aux caprices de la fortune.* Grand. des Rom. c. 1.

after,

after, it would be these blind, absurd, iniquitous judgments of men; who break riotously
forth into praise or censure, without regard to
truth or justice, but just as passion and prejudice impell.

Dr. Johnson " seems, together with the
" ablest head, possessed of the very best heart
" at present existing ;" says one writer. " Ne-
" ver on earth did one mortal body encom-
" pass such true greatness and such true good-
" ness," says another [302]; who observes also,
that his *Lives of the Poets* " would alone have
" been sufficient to immortalize his name."
How *able* his *head*, or (as a third expresses it)
what *stupendous strength of understanding* he
might have, cannot be precisely defined; but it
is certain, that this *stupendous understanding* was
not *strong* enough to force its way through the
meanest prejudices, with which it was once en-
tangled. And for the *very best heart, and such
true goodness as one mortal body did never before
encompass,*—this is the language of journalists
and periodical writers: let us hear the testimony of those, who have always known him
personally, and intimately.

Bishop Newton, speaking of the above *Lives
of the Poets,* says, that " malevolence predomi-
" nates in every part; and that, though some

[302] Gent's Magazine, for Dec. 1784.

" passages

" paſſages are judicious and well written, yet
" they make not ſufficient compenſation for ſo
" much ſpleen and ill humour [303]." An *impartial* account (ſo it is called) of *Dr. Johnſon* in
the *European Magazine* [304], ſaid to be written
by the ingenious *Miſs Seward*, ſets forth, that
he was indeed a man of very great parts, and of
many good qualities, which it is far from our
intent to deny or detract from; but that his
character was a very mixed, and (ſhe might have
added) a very imperfect, *one*. His writings
are repreſented as excellent and fine, where
not " diſgraced, as in his criticiſms, with the
" faults of his diſpoſition. He had ſtrong af-
" fections," it is ſaid, " where literary envy
" did not interfere; but that envy was of ſuch
" deadly potency, as to load his converſation,
" as it has loaded his biographic works, with
" the rancour of party-violence, with national
" averſion, bitter ſarcaſm, and unchriſtian-like
" invective. He turned from the compoſi-
" tions of riſing genius with a viſible horror,
" which proved too plainly, that envy was the
" boſom-ſerpent of this literary deſpot. His
" pride was infinite; yet, amidſt all the over-
" bearing arrogance it produced, his heart
" melted at the ſight, or at the repreſentation,
" of diſeaſe and poverty; and, in the hours of

---

[303] *Life* by himſelf.　　　　[304] For May, 1785.

" affluence,

" affluence, his purſe was ever open to relieve
" them. He was a furious Jacobite, while
" one hope for the Stuart line remained; and
" his politics, always leaning towards deſpo-
" tiſm, were inimical to liberty, **and** the na-
" tural rights of mankind. He was punctual
" in his devotions; but his religious faith had
" much more of bigot-fierceneſs, than of that
" gentleneſs which the goſpel inculcates," *&c.*

If this repreſentation be in any degree juſt,
and I have never heard of its being either diſ-
owned or contradicted, what are we to think
of panegyriſts, who aſcribe to him *ſuch true
greatneſs and ſuch true goodneſs, as were never
before encompaſſed by one mortal body* [305] *?*

LXXXVI.

UPON DAVID HUME'S MORAL CHARACTER.

DR. Adam Smith, in his Appendix to the
Life of Mr. Hume, after repreſenting him
(and juſtly) as a man " of the moſt extenſive
" learning, the greateſt depth of thought, and
" a capacity in every reſpect the moſt com-

[305] See the next Nº, particularly the cloſe of it.

U 4   " prehenſive,"

"prehenfive," fuppofes him to have *approach-ed as nearly to the idea of a perfectly wife and vir-tuous man, as perhaps the nature of human frailty will permit.*

A French writer hath obferved of his **coun-**trymen, that they never fpeak with moderation upon any thing—*nous aimons à tout prodiguer*— but, whether they praife or cenfure, are always extravagant and *outrées.* The fame may be faid of the Englifh, who are equally lavifh of titles and pompous epithets [306]; and give them (I will not fay with the above writer, *to all ex-cepting thofe who deferve them* [307], but certainly) to many who do not deferve them.

Mr. Hume was undoubtedly a very virtuous and very excellent man : he was honeft, hu-mane, benevolent, good-natured : he was free from what **are** called the vices of *eclât* ; **at** leaft I have never heard, that he allowed him-felf any profane liberties with either women or wine. Neverthelefs, was he fo fupremely ex-cellent, as Dr. Smith defcribes him? was there

---

[306] Our laft N° hath furnifhed an illuftrious inftance of this.

[307] Speaking of certain foreign Journalifts, *Journaliftes étrangers,* (I doubt, he means the Englifh) he fays, that *dans leurs mémoires periodiques, qu' on peut appeller comme M. de Vol-taire appelle l' hiftoire, d'immenfes archives de menfonge & d' un peu de vérité, prefque tout eft loué, excepté ce qui mérite de l'être.* Melanges de Literature, &c, tom. i. p. 392. 143.

not something little, contracted, (I had almost
said) worldly, in his make? did not his soul
want much of that dignity and greatness, which
is necessary to make virtue of the *first* and *purest*
metal?

We have already presented Mr. Hume under
a very unphilosophic attitude, sporting about
Charon at the close of his life[308]. But there
are other *traits* of his conduct, no less unphilosophic and degrading[309]. It has been said,
but we know not how truly, that he was *paulo
attentior ad rem*, a little too closely attached to
the pelf: but he was obliged by his circumstances to practise a severe œconomy in his
younger days, as he relates in his *Life*; and the
apology he makes for Monk, Duke of Albe-
marle, may be thought to serve well enough

---

[308] Nº xxx.—The Bravado is always a character to be
suspected: for, as we have above observed, *realities are seldom
solicitous about appearances.* Nº LXI.

[309] We have heard, that he had a passion to be *admired by
the French*; and what does the ingenious author of the *Letters
on Infidelity* mean, **when he** alludes to *somebody* " running
" round a counter with his drawn sword after a *Reviewer*,
" and quitting a room on the entrance of his antagonist?"
p. 28.—We know these are but weaknesses; but they certainly detract somewhat from the lustre of that *perfect wisdom and virtue*, that supremely *philosophical government of the
passions*, for which Mr. Hume's apologists have so loudly celebrated him. *Apology for the Life and Writings of David
Hume, Esq.* p. 12.

for

for himself. "Burnet," says he, "charges this "nobleman with avarice : but, as he appears "not to have been in the least tainted with "rapacity, his frugal conduct may more can- "didly be imputed to the habits, acquired in "early life, while he was possessed of a very "narrow fortune [310]."

We would gladly acquiesce under this apo- logy; but we cannot account for his attendance upon the embassies to Paris, first in 1763, and then in 1767, from any other motive than that of interest or profit. At the earliest of these dates, Mr. Hume was "turned of fifty; a passion "for literature had been the ruling passion of "his life, and the great source of his enjoy- "ments ;" he had a quick and lively sense of independency, and values himself as it were upon "having never preferred a request to one "great man, or even making advances of "friendship to any of them;" he was "become "not only independent, but opulent ; and had "retired to his native country, determined "never more to set his foot out of it, but to "be buried henceforward in a philosophical "retreat." All this being so, and so he repre- sents it, how could he possibly be seduced from the shades of contemplation and retirement, into scenes so new and remote from his former

[310] Hist. of Great Britain, *anno* 1670.

habits

habits and tenor of life—how submit to walk
in a great man's train, to mix with the *petit
maîtres* of Paris, and probably to talk bad
French in a Scotch brogue—how, unless im-
pelled by some little passion from within? and
what can this little passion have been?

Monf. d'Alembert, the author of the *Melanges, &c.* quoted above, could by no means
think well of Hume's attendance upon these
embassies; as plainly appears from his strictures
upon Lucian. " Lucian hath left us a strong
" and highly coloured piece upon such *literati,*
" as devote themselves to the service of *the
" great.* It grieves me," says he, " that this
" same Lucian, after having justly observed
" that friendship with *the great* is no better
" than slavery, did at length accept a place
" in the service of the emperor. He had be-
" gun by being a philosopher; the reputation
" of his works made him sought after; to pur-
" sue more effectually what he had begun, he
" should have made his retirement sure; but
" he became insensibly a man of the world,
" and ended by being a courtier. *This last is
" the lowest part a man of letters can act* [311]."

Mean while, and notwithstanding appearances, we shall not decide upon Mr. Hume's

[311] *Ce dernier rôle est le plus bas que puisse jouer un homme de
lettres,* ib. tom. i. p. 372.

motives.

motives. We are far from meaning to depreciate Mr. Hume, or to impute to him any thing falsely: yea, the time was, when we defended him from false imputations[312]. Our aim in this, as well as the foregoing N°, is only to discountenance those extravagant eloges, so frequently and so blindly given to an imagined perfection, which human nature, when cultivated in the best and happiest manner, never was, nor ever will be, able to attain.

LXXXVII.

CONCERNING THE DISPUTE BETWEEN MR. HUME AND MR. ROUSSEAU[313].

THE simple Enthusiast is a quiet and harmless creature. He sees visions, and he dreams dreams; but he keeps these visions and dreams to himself, and enjoys the comfort of them in silent meditation. The Fanatic is ever restless and turbulent; and, though a dreamer as well as the Enthusiast, is not however content, like him, with what passes within himself,

---

[312] See the following N°.

[313] This N° is part of a *Letter to the Hon. Mr. Horace Walpole*, published at the end of 1766, 12mo.

but

but is impatient to rage and riot abroad : ἐ μόνον, ἐνθεσιᾷν, ἀλλὰ βακχίνειν. Society muſt intereſt itſelf in favour of his reveries; nor is it too much for their ſake, even to diſturb the public peace.

Enthuſiaſm and Fanaticiſm are, both of them, a mixture of Folly and Madneſs; and for the latter, if diſhoneſty and rancour be not of its eſſence, they are at leaſt conſiſtent with it, and almoſt always found to tincture it very ſtrongly.

The term *Fanatic* has uſually been applied to the Religioniſt, when diſordered, and not in his right mind : may it not, under the ſame circumſtances, ſuit as well the Philoſopher? The Religioniſt, I know, is ſuppoſed to do all for the glory of God; the Philoſopher, to act only for the glory of himſelf. But the difference is trifling; apparent ſurely, not real. Self at the bottom is the principle of action ; and however the one may clamour for Religion, and the other for Virtue [314], yet the glory of *himſelf* is the great object of both. But I will not contend : let the Religioniſt, if you pleaſe, walk firſt. It would grieve one, that two members of So-

---

[314] " *Mr. Rouſſeau* is ſo paſſionate an admirer of *Virtue*, " that his eyes always ſparkle at the bare mention of that " word." So at leaſt he relates of himſelf. *Account of the Diſpute between* Mr. Hume *and* Mr. Rouſſeau, *by* Mr. Hume, p. 63.

ciety,

ciety, fo ufeful and fo amiable, fhould quarrel about precedency.

These reflections owe their birth to the mif-underftanding, which hath arifen between *Mr. Hume* and *Mr. Rouffeau* ; and they are addreffed to you, Sir, becaufe you are fuppofed to have occafioned it by the flippancy of your wit. I do not believe, that you were even the inno-cent occafion of this *fracas*. Dark fufpicions and tormenting jealoufies had plainly occupied the imagination of *Mr. Rouffeau, before* your Letter was written ; and a quarrel muft have happened, if it had *never* been written.

The firft intimation of thefe fufpicions from *Mr. Rouffeau* himfelf appears in his letter to *Mr. Hume* of March 22, 1766 ; wherein we read, as follows. " The affair of the carriage " is not yet adjufted, becaufe I know I was im-" pofed on : it is a trifling fault however, " which may be only the effect of an *obliging* " *vanity*, unlefs it fhould happen to be repeat-" ed. If you were concerned in it, I would " advife you to give up, once for all, thefe " little impofitions, which cannot proceed from " any good motive, when converted into fnares " for fimplicity [315]. Simplicity indeed ? If *Mr. Rouffeau*'s be fimplicity, it is of a new and very peculiar kind.—Well : but what were thefe *fnares* for *fimplicity* ? Why truly,

[315] Difpute, p. 14.

Mr.

Mr. Rousseau being mean enough to affect poverty, and yet too proud to be relieved, expedients were sought to serve, without disgusting him; and, among the rest, this of advertising a chaise at an under-price, contrived by *Mr. Davenport*, and assented to by *Mr. Hume*.

But was not *Mr. Hume*, however well-meaning, too officious? Was there not something indelicate in these sort of services? and was it not natural for *Mr. Rousseau*, to suspect these *obliging* acts, as resulting from *vanity?*—they, who ask such questions, do not consider, how extremely distressed *Mr. Rousseau* appeared to *Mr. Hume*. In his letter to *Mr. Clairaut*, of March the 3d, 1765, he implores that gentleman to correct a work, which he is " obliged, " he says, to republish for subsistence, *pour* " *avoir du pain*; declares himself overwhelmed " with a torrent of misfortunes; and assures " him, that this would be doing a very great " charity to the most unhappy of men [115]."

Is not this to call out, in effect, for the contributions of charitable and well-disposed persons, to preserve a poor wretch from perishing through want? It is true, this was not the real state of *Mr. Rousseau*; for we find him speaking afterwards of his sufficiency in a strain of triumph: " I did not come over, says he, to beg

[115] Dispute, p. 7.

" my

" my bread in England; I brought the means
" of subsistence with me [317]." But *Mr. Hume*
at that time knew nothing of this; and had
therefore just reason to say, that " this affecta-
" tion of extreme poverty and distress was a
" mere pretence, a petty kind of imposture,
" which *Mr. Rousseau* successfully employed to
" excite the compassion of the public," and by
that means if he could to engross its attention.

    Soon after, Sir, your letter came forth; in
which you exhibited this fantastic mortal more
clearly to view, by giving the outlines of his
character with much good sense and wit. That
you should do this with sense and wit, I do not
wonder; but I wonder extremely, that any man
of sense and wit should disapprove of your doing this. *Mr. D'Alembert* says, that " we
" ought not to ridicule the unfortunate, espe-
" cially when they have done us no harm [318]."
But, was *Mr. Rousseau* really *unfortunate?* Has
he not exaggerated matters? With regard to
his poverty most certainly he has; and, perhaps, with regard to his persecutions. You
seem to have known this; for, if I understand
you, it is chiefly against this, that your ridicule
is directed. You believed, that these exaggera-
tions were the tricks of a *Charlatan*, who wanted the public to talk of nothing but him; and

[317] Dispute, p. 41.   [318] Dispute, p. 94.

you

you juſtly thought, that the gentleſt puniſhment he deſerved was to be laughed at a little.
It may be that *Mr. Rouſſeau* had never injured
or offended you, *perſonally* or *privately:* but
an author aſſumes a kind of *public* character; and every man has a right to correct his
notions and his manners too, ſo far as theſe
manners regard the *public,* if either the one or
the other ſhall ſtand in need of correction.
Mr. D'Alembert is a very reſpectable perſon,
but ſurely has not decided here with his uſual
accuracy.

But to what purpoſe dwell on your innocent
letter? The grounds of diſcontent were laid in
Mr. Rouſſeau, and the impulſe to quarrel with
Mr. Hume had doubtleſs begun to operate, before your letter came to his hands. He ſeems to
have imagined, that, as ſoon as he arrived at
Dover, the Engliſh ſhould have been affected,
as they were at the *Reſtoration,* or upon the
landing of the *Prince of Orange.* " Before I
" arrived in England," ſays he, " there was
" not a nation in Europe, in which I had a
" greater reputation—The public papers were
" full of encomiums on me—my arrival was
" publiſhed with triumph—England prided
" itſelf in affording me refuge [319]."

" You ſee, Sir, that the arrival of *Mr. John*

---

[319] Diſpute, p. 43.

James

James Rousseau was, in his own estimation, a national concern; so that it was natural for him to expect, and he plainly did expect, that the eyes, the ears, the thoughts of every individual, should be taken at once from their several occupations and pursuits, and fixed entirely upon him alone. The manner of his reception did by no means answer to these fine ideas, conceived beforehand; so far from it, that all of a sudden, as he himself relates, " without the " least assignable cause, the tone was changed ; " and that so speedily and totally, that of all " the caprices of the public never was known " any thing more surprising [120]." However, while he was in London or near it, some visited him out of curiosity, as others did out of vanity; and thus, though greatly disappointed, he was not as yet in any high degree miserable.

But, alas ! things grew daily from bad to worse; till at length, he says, " not one of those, " who had so much praised me in my absence, " appeared, now I was present, to think even " of my existence [121]." He flies into the country; still presuming, and most certainly desiring, that the attention of the Town might fly thither after him :

Et fugit ad salices, et se cupit ante videri.

[120] Dispute, p. 43.   [121] Dispute, p. 45.

It

It is true, were a judgment to be formed from *Mr. Rouffeau*'s declarations, we fhould of courfe conclude, that to be buried in folitude was the very thing he wifhed: for he fpeaks of " rural " walks, as the only pleafures of his life [122]." " You live and converfe with the world," fays he to *Mr. Hume*; " I with myfelf in folitude.— " I live retired from the world, I am ignorant " of what paffes in it.—I am told nothing, and " I know only what I feel [123]." The picture, you fee, Sir, of a poor abject animal, who fcarcely perceives by reflection, but only knows what he feels by fenfation.

Now nothing can be more unfit to reprefent the original truly and as it is, than this fort of colouring. So far is *Mr. Rouffeau* from defiring *not to know* what is doing in the world, that his own letters fhew him to have been conftant-ly fearching the public papers and magazines for intelligence of himfelf; or, to fpeak more properly, for puffs to feed his vanity. So far is *Mr. Rouffeau* from wifhing to live *unknown* and unregarded, that a greater caufe of mifery to him, I am perfuaded, does not exift.

" Arriving at this folitary, convenient, and " agreeable habitation," fays he, " I became " tranquil, independent: and this feemed to " be the wifhed-for moment, when all my mif-

[122] Difpute, p. 60. [123] Difpute, p. 29. 34.

" fortunes

" fortunes fhould have an end. On the con-
" trary, it was now they began; misfortunes
" more cruel than any I had yet experi-
" enced [324]." I verily believe, becaufe I fo
eafily conceive, it. He was never perhaps in
a fituation before, where he was fo little liable
to be molefted; where he was fo unnoticed, fo
altogether left to his own will and humour.
For the good people of England, after the firft
ftare was over, had (as their way is) entirely
done with him. Far from continuing to admire, they had ceafed to mention him; and, if
they had not totally forgot, they cared no more
about him, than if he had been in Swifferland.
His mifery increafed: your letter appeared [325]:
it became extreme. He fell into a paroxyfm:
he raged: and, in fhort, as fometimes happen-
eth among wild beafts, he fell upon his *keep-*

[324] Difpute, p. 40.

[325] " In this letter," fays *Mr. Rouffeau,* " I knew the
" pen of *Mr. D'Alembert* as certainly, as if I had feen him
" write it. In a moment a ray of light difcovered to me
" the fecret caufe of that touching and fudden change,
" which I had obferved in the public refpecting me; and
" I faw that the plot, which was put in execution at Lon-
" don, had been laid at Paris." Difpute, p. 58, 59.
Alas! this *ray of light,* darting upon the brain, has occa-
-fioned many an unhappy mortal, before Mr. *Rouffeau,* to
fee, and *hear,* and *feel* too, what never exifted out of his
own difordered cranium.

er.

er [116]. To speak without a figure, he quar-
relled with his greatest friend and benefactor
Mr. Hume, by all accounts a very quiet person; and who in the present case seems only
faulty, in having condescended to humour a
man, whom it **is** not possible to oblige: and
nothing doubtless but the exceeding humanity
of Mr. *Hume,* and his prejudices for *Mr. Rouffeau,* could hinder one of his penetration from
discerning **somewhat** earlier, than he seems to
have done, that *Rouffeau* was a savage, whom no
offices of kindness could civilize and tame.

The dispute between these gentlemen is now
before the public; which seems reasonably well
convinced, that *Mr. Hume* is the first man,
who was ever obliged to defend himself in
form against such a train of ridiculous and
groundless imputations. *Mr. Rouffeau* really
brings them in such a manner, as if he meant
to betray his own cause, and to acquit *Mr.
Hume,* while he affects to accuse him. In his
letter of June 23, he says, " I thank you for
" the good offices in matters of interest, which
" you have used as a mask [117] "—for what? truly
to do him ill ones. He abounds with such paf-

[116] *Je tiens J. J. R.*—*Mr. Rouffeau* affirms, that he " heard
" *Mr. Hume* pronounce, with an extreme vehemence, the
" above words, *I keep John James Rouffeau,* several times
" in his sleep." Dispute, pag. 76.
[117] Dispute, p. 30.

sages

fages as thefe. In his letter of July 10, after
having urged all he could invent againſt *Mr.
Hume,* he ſays, that " every circumſtance of the
" affair is equally incomprehenſible. A con-
" duct ſuch as yours is not in nature : it is a
" contradiction ; and yet it is demonſtrable to
" me [328]." Thus the *credo quia impoſſibile,*
which even the religioniſt is now grown
aſhamed of, is at length adopted by the philoſopher.

No man however but *Mr. Rouſſeau* will be
able to perceive the leaſt contradiction. The
marks of friendſhip from *Mr. Hume* to him
were, as the French editor obſerves, the leaſt
equivocal, *les moins equivoques* [329]: they did not
conſiſt of *verbiage* and profeſſions, but of true
and real ſervices. A *Chriſtian's* faith is generally allowed to be beſt determined by his
works : and what better teſt can be contrived
for the ſincerity of a friend ? Indeed the Me-
thodiſts in religion are wont to reaſon otherwiſe ; eſteeming all, who contend for works, as
looſe and ſceptical in the faith : and *Mr. Rouſſeau,* who is certainly a Methodiſt in philoſophy, ſeems to have reaſoned thus of *Mr.
Hume* ; elſe he would never have oppoſed a ſeries of ſuppoſitions, or rather ſuſpicions, of his
own againſt *Mr. Hume,* to a ſeries of facts in
that gentleman's favour.

[328] Diſpute, p. 82.　[329] Advertiſement to Diſpute, &c.

But

But *Mr. Rousseau*, as I have been given to understand, must not be confined altogether to philosophy. An advocate of his declared, in my hearing, that he was indeed a very good Christian; at least a better than *Mr. Hume*, who, it was feared, is only a philosopher. Concerning these important points I can neither affirm, nor deny any thing. *Mr. Rousseau* is evidently an heap of inconsistencies and contradictions, so that he may, or he may not, be a Christian; for, where there is nothing systematical or regular in the conduct of the understanding, there is no criterion or test, by which a judgment about principles can be formed with any certainty. In the mean time I meddle with no man's faith. That affair lies wholly between God and himself, and can be no concern of mine. Yet, were we to judge of Christianity, as exemplified in the conduct of this believer, I should make no scruple to say, with *Averroes*, *Sit anima mea cum philosophis:* for I had rather be such a philosopher as *Mr. Hume*, than such a Christian as *Mr. Rousseau*.

The French editor seems afraid, Sir, lest this quarrel between philosophers should *bring a scandal upon philosophy*. Not much, I should think, if any at all: sects and professions of every kind, religious as well as civil, have long been too wise to be responsible for individuals. But whatever disgrace it may bring

upon

upon the philosophers, he supposes, that the *dunces* will reap from it no small comfort: which, if the numbers of each be rightly estimated, is supposing it to produce more physical good than evil by far. Let us not **envy** them this consolation: it seems indeed necessary, that they should sometimes have it: for who can say, what might otherwise happen? Genii of a superior order might gain **too** great an ascendency: they might in time pass for more than Genii: they might be reputed Gods, as *Paul* and *Barnabas* were at *Lystra*, if they did not discover by things of this kind, that they are *men of like passions* with the meanest of their species.

Other reflections more solid may be made, and lessons more useful drawn, from the dispute between these celebrated personages. We may learn from the character of *Mr. Rousseau*, and from his very strange treatment of *Mr. Hume*, to what extravagancies the human mind is capable of being carried, when the humour *atrabilaire* has once thoroughly infected it. A person thus distempered, or rather thus *possessed*, (for is he not a Demoniac?) is able to conceive any thing. The power of imagination in such a one is creative beyond measure. Existence or non-existence are precisely to him the same: for he makes no difference at all between facts, on which alone depends the certainty

tainty

tainty of all human information; I fay, between the plaineft and moft notorious facts,
and fuppofitions the moft wild, the moft improbable, the moft vifionary. He overlooks
or contemns the former, as non-entities: he
builds demonftrations upon the latter. In fhort,
he cannot fee what actually is, while he fees in-
tuitively what is not; and things do or do not
exift with him, as they happen to fuit with his
prejudices and paffions.

We learn from the fame object, that fuperior
abilities, and even fhining force of genius, are
confiftent with great mifery in him who pof-
feffes them, if his temperament be thoroughly
bad. Rigid philofophy, I know, will not allow this temperament to be within the reach
of even alteratives; but Chriftianity teaches,
that it may be greatly corrected and amended,
if not cured. And it is furprifing that *Mr.
Rouffeau*, who is fo good a Chriftian, fhould not
have laboured this point more abundantly; as
his whole happinefs feems to have depended
upon it.

From the ftrange and unexpected fituation
of *Mr. Hume* it appears, that an active benevolence may fometimes expofe a man to inconveni-
encies and troubles; as it almoft always does to
ingratitude. I have often wondered, why men,
as they grow old, fhould grow lefs benevolent (for I take the fact to be inconteftable);

5   but

but this and similar instances have helped me to account for it. And sorry am I to say it; but, alas! human nature, thy pride cannot bear to be too much obliged[330]. It is danger-ous, I have been told, with regard to the Great; and if there be not an equal danger in obliging the smaller gentry, it is not from want of will, but want of power, to hurt their bene-factors.

It appears again, that the utmost prudence and kindness are no security against the basest and most injurious usage, when a man's ill stars shall have connected him with folly or kna-very; or, which is commonly the case, with these two substances united in one person. People of this make see every thing in a wrong light. They misinterpret from folly, they mis-represent from malice, every well-meant word and deed. They treat their truest friends as their most inveterate enemies; and load the best men with imputations, which can belong to none but the worst. No wonder then, that the *Stoical*, not to say the Christian, principle of *doing good* should wax weak and cold with increasing years: no wonder that so many should, like *Epicurus*, contract their sphere of action, and suffer their happiness to depend on

---

[330] *Quidam, quo plus debent, magis oderint. Leve æs alie-num debitorem facit, grave inimicum.* Senec. Epist. 19.

none but themfelves. Doubtlefs the great bufinefs of a wife man's life is to keep himfelf, as
much as may be, from being teazed by fools,
and over-reached by knaves : and neither can
be done to any purpofe, but by avoiding both
the one and the other. "Live freely and un-
"known," fays a philofopher. "Solitude will
"procure you the true and only pleafure of
"being always fatisfied with yourfelf. Fools
"and knaves, feen at a diftance, will only
"move your compaffion ; but will force you,
"when near, to either hate or defpife them [131]."

---

[131] *Vivez librement & ignoré. La folitude vous procurera
le vrai & unique plaifir d'etre toujours content de foi. Les fots
& les mechans n' exciteront que votre compaffion vûs de loin ;
mais vûs de près il faudrait les haïr ou les meprifer.*

TANTUM.